FLAME-JEWEL OF THE ANCIENTS

By
EDWIN L. GRABER

I0541593

ARMCHAIR FICTION
PO Box 4369, Medford, Oregon 97504

*For more information about Armchair Books and products, visit our
website at…*

www.armchairfiction.com

Or email us at…

armchairfiction@yahoo.com

IT WAS THE SOURCE OF ULTIMATE POWER

The Tane Jewel was thought to be only a legend—a tiny golden sphere, no bigger than a Terran grapefruit, containing limitless power. Its origins were unknown, but according to the legends, it was thought to have been possessed by the incredible Tane—the strange race of creatures who had ruled the Galaxy long before the advent of the human race.

However, when two massive Terran Galactic battleships were obliterated by a small Delban battle cruiser, the legend suddenly became a horrifying reality. The Tane Jewel had been discovered in deep space and was now the prize possession of the Delban Empire and its ruthless dictator, Gort Bro-Doral, whose scientists had tapped its terrifying energy. Now this madman had the galaxy's most powerful weapon in his arsenal. The future of civilized planets everywhere were greatly in doubt…

FOR A COMPLETE SECOND NOVEL, TURN TO PAGE 91

CAST OF CHARACTERS

CAPTAIN GLAYNE

This seasoned commander in the Stellar Guardians was given the task of finding a way to stop the galaxy's most powerful weapon.

NIALA CHODRED

She was a gorgeous Terran spy, and she had a big shot space captain right where she wanted him—in the palm of her hand.

GORT BRO-DORAL

This madman possessed the Tane Jewel— and there was no planet big enough to hide from its terrifying power.

HOTEH GANSER

His dried, withered appearance was most deceptive—inside his skull was one of the most sinister brains in the galaxy.

GRAYSEN

Glayne's grizzled old Executive Officer—loyal to the core, and willing to sacrifice his life if necessary.

DEL THORDER

As chairman of the Lorle planetary council, he faced the decision of how to fight an impending battle his planet was sure to lose.

HARBIN

His task was simple, land on the roof of a palace, attack the guards, then kidnap the two most dangerous men in the galaxy.

CHAPTER ONE

THE TWO TERRAN SUPER Galactics glided side by side in the immensity of the interstellar void. Secure in the knowledge that they were the mightiest battleships ever built in the known galaxy, they didn't bother to raise their anti-energy shields. They knew, absolutely, that no other war craft in the universe could equal their strength...

Jukes, the third pilot, lounged carelessly in his gimbal-slung shock seat, idly watching the screen before him. Aside from his sister ship, there was nothing to be seen but the harsh points of starlight. Cautiously he looked over his shoulder to see if the executive officer was nearby. Then, apparently satisfied, lit a cigarette and blew an expansive plume of smoke at the serried banks of instruments that were terraced about him.

Suddenly the intermittent glowing of a red blinker aroused him. Throwing the butt to the deck, he bent forward, squinting into the screen. Far down in one corner he detected an irregularly sparkling mote moving slowly across the blazing points of the distant stars. With a single motion of his arm he swept the Call to Quarters alarm studs and began to speak rapidly into his throat transmitter. As the muffled vibrating thunder of his ship's drivers rose, he could make out his sister ship gradually swinging into an approach orbit.

A double tap on his shoulder informed him that the first pilot was there to take over. Smoothly he slipped from the shock seat and took up his station with the other two pilots near the auxiliary control boards. Everywhere about him was excited, orderly confusion as the huge warship stripped for possible action. The orbit calculators at his left took up the excited jabbering chorus and somewhere above the third pilot was aware of the massive charge accumulators for the Kellander miatron blasters whining up the scale.

"It's a Delban," he muttered to his fellow pilots. "Just a pipsqueak, too, blast his miserable, trespassing soul. A light cruiser, from what I saw of him."

The younger one looked at him eagerly. "Do you think he'll fight?"

The third pilot snorted. "One Stellar class cruiser against two Terran Galactics? He'd be out of his mind."

Just then the battle screen lit up and a babbling group of gunnery officers crowded about, feeding firing data to waiting miatron crews. Over their shoulders the third pilot could make out the Delban cruiser as it lay there, slim and deadly against the vast, star-studded vault of space.

"What I'd like to know is why the devil he doesn't run for it," the older pilot said to no one in particular. "Something's up, I'm sure. Delbans just don't act like this."

The third pilot grunted absently, his eyes fixed on the battle screen. The two Galactics now lay on either side of the Delban. His sister ship began to communicate with the new arrival, her yellow beam glowing with baleful intensity. But the pilot wasn't watching. He had noticed something odd about that cruiser. It seemed to bulge in the wrong places. It was completely enclosed by a peculiar mesh antenna that glinted ominously in the faint light.

Then the Delban fired.

For a moment there was stunned amazement in the huge plotting room. It was the very absurdity of the situation rather than mere surprise. To make the blasphemy worse, the Delban had licked out with the beam of a secondary Kellander projector rather than with her main miatron batteries. The damage was slight, the communicator bulb of the other Galactic having been reduced to twisted slag. But this was the grossest of all insults in space warfare and demanded immediate retaliation. The third pilot held his breath in anticipation.

Then it came. The plotting room exploded into frantic activity. Generators screamed into ear-splitting crescendos as the main driver engines were coupled into them to raise the anti-energy shield. The Kellander miatron blasters hurled ravening bolts of energy at the audacious Delban, reducing accumulator loads to zero in instants. The remainder of the driver atomics was coupled into the Kellander accumulators sending up loads that were fed through the continuously thundering miatrons at the Delban cruiser. Literally *trillions* of megawatts lapped at the Delban shield, making it glow up the spectral scale in a brilliant spider web of absorbing power foci. But it held.

THE Delban shield held! The third pilot was unbelievably shocked as he stared at the battle screen. It was simply not conceivable that the two mightiest warships in space could not penetrate the shield of a pipsqueak Stellar cruiser.

Where were they getting the power? The question blazed up in the third pilot's consciousness as he stared at the slim, deadly Delban. Abruptly he recalled where he had seen the Delban's peculiar external mesh antenna.

"Broadcast power!" he blurted to his comrades. "Those devils are receiving broadcast power!"

The other two pilots looked at him incredulously. "Hell!" snorted the older one. "You can't transmit the stuff across interstellar distances."

The third pilot didn't reply. As he watched the screen he suddenly knew they were in trouble. By rights this should have been the greatest shock of all but his mind was so dulled with amazement that he could only shake his head.

The Delban's firing had gradually increased in strength until now both the Terran battleship's mighty shields were themselves glowing up the spectral scale in its spidery force web. Despite the older pilot's doubts, he realized that only broadcast power in huge quantities could account for those overloaded shields. Where were they getting it to broadcast, though? Only an infinite source of supply could do the job.

Paralyzed, he watched the screen. He was aware of the miatron blasters falling silent as the straining driver atomics were diverted to hold the shield. Their sister Galactic's blasters had all fallen silent as all the power of her own huge drivers was shunted into the shield generators. Their own shield was trembling and shuddering under the inconceivable impact of the energies that surged at it from the Delban.

Suddenly the pilot saw their sister ship's shield coruscate in a multi-hued spider web of shorting power foci. Then it buckled. The third pilot instinctively averted his face from the indescribably brilliant, eye-searing nova that followed.

His own ship screamed. The drivers, the generators, the converters and accumulators—all of them screamed in ultrasonic crescendos in an effort to maintain the crumbling shield. The force webs shorted one after another in brilliant red fire. The third pilot saw it rupture out he never felt it...

For days the twin novae burned in the endless night, then slowly faded to blackened cinders.

CHAPTER TWO

THE TRI-DI FILM CAME TO AN end and the Council Chamber's soft fluorescents picked up in strength. For a moment the members of Lorle Sector's High Council were stunned and bewildered at what they had seen.

Captain Glayne waited patiently for the explosion which he knew would come. For about the tenth time that morning he fervently cursed all civilians. Not even the valiant efforts of Chairman Dell Thorder could keep them in check. A vast wave of irritation filled him as he listened to the piercing squeak of a fat Councilor named Trask.

"It will mean war, I say—and we haven't had a war involving Terra for seventy years. Lorle Sector must remain neutral—especially if Delb Sector has weapons that can crush super Galactic battleships. Now I say," he squeaked, oblivious of the fact that no one was paying any attention, "that we must request Captain Glayne to leave immediately because his presence might be deemed an overt act by our friends, the Delbans. True, the Stellar Guardians—"

He was suddenly cut off by the staccato thunder of Dell Thorder's gavel. The chairman's thin, ascetic face wore a worried expression as his eyes swept the now silent Council. Of them all, he was the only man Glayne admired. For thirty years he had maneuvered the nine-planet Lorle Sector through the treacherous shoals of Combine politics and never once had the cry of "boss" or "dictator" seriously been raised against him.

"I must confess," he began quietly, "that I do not myself understand fully the implications of this situation. I do know that the fact that Imperial Terra has lost two large battleships is inconsequential. The real point is that the Terran Combine is facing imminent destruction at the hands of Gort Bro-Doral and his Delban Empire. Because we are Delb Sector's nearest neighbor, we may expect the first blow to fall on us. Since it is a known fact that the Intelligence Service of the Stellar Guardians is the finest in the galaxy. I have sent for Captain Glayne to explain certain of the technical aspects of the new Delban weapon in order that we may determine what action to take."

Thorder silently gestured to Glayne who arose and faced the hostile stares of the councilors. Their unexpressed antipathy was amusing rather than irritating. The meager little navy that Lorle Sector did possess drained away funds that could otherwise be used in their pork barrel. However, they all had something to worry about, which Thorder hadn't mentioned. The Revolution, which had smashed the Delb-Lorle Axis thirty years before, had made Gort Bro-Doral a ruthless enemy who would not rest until his ships had utterly destroyed the Lorle cities in retaliation. So far they had depended upon Imperial Terra to support them against the Bro's passionate desire for power. But now the Terran navy was helpless and Lorle was in a desperate plight.

"What Dell Thorder told you is true," he began in a firm, clear voice. "Unfortunately it is an understatement because it implies that there is a possibility of discovering a counter-weapon to offset that of the Delbans. Such is not the case.

"For a long time we have been prone to think in terms of optimum sizes for warships. We were accustomed to believe that we had reached the pinnacle of development in destructive weapons. The fatal radiations of atomic generators and converters make it necessary to divert a part of the power into shields. These shields are limited in size by the ship size, and the ship size in turn is limited by the size of its power plant. But there is a point of diminishing returns—that is, we cannot build ships larger than the Galactic class battleships without losing efficiency. So for a long time we have believed that there was a limit to the amount of power available in any given class of warship.

"Unfortunately this no longer applies for the Delbans. As you have just seen on the tri-di film obtained by Stellar Guardian Intelligence, a single Stellar cruiser engaged and destroyed two Terran Galactics. This means, as Chairman Thorder has suggested, that the entire fleet strength of the nine hundred Sectors of the Terran Combine is now quite helpless against the Delban Grand Fleet."

Glayne paused for a moment. In spite of the room's air conditioning, many of the Councilors were mopping their faces anxiously. The one called Trask was chewing his lower lip nervously, not liking a bit what the tall Guardian officer had to say. Glayne felt a twinge of sympathy for his three hundred and fifty million constituents.

"The crux of the whole problem is the source of this new Delban power. Experts in our organization are absolutely certain that they are using broadcast power, but this information is based on the tri-di film you have seen which our agents have stolen from the Terran Admiralty Office at Lunaport. It may be a fake, but that is hardly likely. The implications of broadcast power are so tremendous as to defy reason. Even under the best laboratory conditions the power lost in transmission makes it impractical. Consequently any source that produces energies capable of smashing two Terran Galactic battleships at perhaps stellar distances is vast beyond conjecture. As incredible as this sounds, we believe that the Delbans have it. As to its precise nature, we are still in the dark. However, the Stellar Guardians, at least, are in a position to investigate."

Dell Thorder cleared his throat at this point and Glayne stopped.

"You see our position," said the weary Chairman. "Almost any countermeasure we attempt can be interpreted as an overt act by Bro-Doral. Hence any action on our part will make our ruin sooner instead of later. However, there is one thin possibility and that is Captain Glayne. It is true that he is a mercenary belonging to the Stellar Guardians. But Kairn's Intelligence vouches for him absolutely and I am informed that he is as competent as any man in the Lorle Fleet.

"Because of the peculiar nature of the Stellar Guardian organization, he can carry out investigations where any such move on our part would be suicidal. In my opinion, our only possible chance is to employ him in this capacity to locate the Delban power transmitter—if one exists. It is possible that an all-out attack with all the units we can muster will succeed in destroying it."

As Thorder finished, Glayne took a deep breath. He stood motionless by the immense circular table. He knew that the Councilors, like all small planet men, were impressed with his great shoulders and their suggestion of tremendous physical strength. But if they knew what torment he had to endure under high driver thrust as a result of his great size, they wouldn't be so impressed.

Dell Thorder coughed. "Captain Glayne, would you mind stepping into the outer room while we take a vote? We will inform you directly."

GLAYNE nodded silently and left the Chamber. Disregarding the anteroom's soft chairs, he stood against the wall, waiting. His space-tanned face hardened as he looked thoughtfully from the glassene window at the jewel-like city of Lorle Capital, a dazzling white under the noon sun. Mentally he pictured the sleek Delban cruisers flashing overhead in fast orbits, pouring phenomenal torrents of energy into the pathetic shield the city would attempt to set up. The Lorle High Council would trust him. In the end, even Trask would. They were all rabbits looking around desperately for someone to defend them. They would hire him; they would pat him on the back and shake his hand; they would make him solemnly swear the Guardian Oath to struggle against all their enemies. And Glayne would promise to do all of these things.

But he would lie.

He would do none of these things. Instead he would do all in his power to bring war to Lorle. He would commit an overt act against the Delbans and they would cry for Lorle blood. Their fast, sleek ships would deal out death and destruction to the very cities that he would swear ever so solemnly to defend to his last breath. With a coldly objective part of his mind he marveled at the consummate treachery he would perform.

But another part of his mind was aghast.

He was unable to suppress the bitter waves of remorse that filled him. Again he remembered the serious, heavy-jowled face of Garstow, Grand Admiral of the Stellar Guardians. In the Dorleb Headquarters, only forty hours before, Garstow had said,

"Glayne, we need time. Some Sector must be thrown to the wolves. While the Delbans are occupied with that unfortunate Sector, we will have time to unravel their broadcast scramblers, build antennae of our own, and perhaps even locate their power transmitter. The Policy Organ has decided upon Lorle Sector. And it has decided that you, Glayne, are the man for the job."

Glayne had listened in stunned silence to Garstow. A protest rose automatically to his lips but he had crushed it back with a click of his booted heels. And now here he was in Lorle Capital with his Stellar class cruiser *Algol* ready for action. When the fat men with rabbit eyes emerged from the Council Chamber and empowered him to work for them, he would be ready to move. A sudden raid on Delban space commerce, an energy bomb hurtling into a Delban city from a stolen Lorle warship—anyone of a dozen expedients would have the ruthless Gort Bro-Doral screaming down on the helpless cities of Lorle.

As he stared at the afternoon brilliance of Lorle Capital he realized that his treachery was an ironic manifestation of a greater loyalty. People forgot that the Stellar Guardians were dedicated to the ideal of human progress. The great mercenary organization recognized the inevitability of war and determined that wars should be fought according to rules. But the Delbans were now in a position to flout all rules and destroy all human progress. Hence all rules were forgotten and ruthless treachery was the order of the day as every resource was exploited to crush Gort Bro-Doral and his Delban Empire.

Then the door of the Council Chamber opened and Dell Thorder stepped into the anteroom. He faced Glayne silently for a moment, lines of weariness etched in his tired, old face.

Then he thrust out his hand and said simply, "We wish you the best of luck, Glayne."

The Guardian Captain took the outstretched hand and almost winced at the trust he saw in Thorder's eyes. The weight of the crushing responsibility bowed down the Chairman's frail shoulders, but he seemed to burn with an indomitable determination to defend his people. He was not a rabbit but a warrior. And Glayne was going to betray him.

"I'll do my best," he said in quick, husky tones.

He felt like a swine as he closed the door behind him.

CHAPTER THREE

IT WAS A SECOND-CLASS NIGHT spot called The Varga. Glayne would meet the Stellar Guardian espionage chief for the Lorle Sector here. As he stood at the entrance bar absorbing the customary drink prior to entering the first stage, he swept the place with cold grey eyes. Evidently the city commission of Lorle Capital was going through a phase of Puritanism because the deadly Kesla lights were absent and the swirling strains of the reportedly *jawth*-fed orchestra were considerably toned down. Nevertheless, the general impression was quite sufficiently exotic to suit Glayne as he entered the dimly-lit first stage.

Vaguely he was aware of the less restrained laughter of patrons who had already reached the second stage, having passed through the vibrator screen that simulated a soothing color movement. The function of the vibrator was to give jaded sensibilities the physical fillip necessary to convince reluctant laggards that they really were ready for the second stage. Glayne was also aware of his table's slight movement toward the vibrator screen and he felt a wave of irritation at the prospect of chasing through nine stages in this outlandish place looking for his contact.

Suddenly the annunciator light in the center of his table began to glow an intermittent red-orange. Glayne looked at it, eyes narrowed. Experimentally be stabbed its speaker stud and a voice seemed to emerge from the empty air before his face.

"Captain, you look so lonely and disconsolate sitting by yourself. Won't you join me?" It was a woman's voice, low and casual. Glayne was briefly startled—he had expected that his contact would be a man. Then it occurred to him that she was not his contact, but that doubt vanished when be remembered that he had discarded his uniform for the light grey business jumper of a young business executive. How could she know him for a Captain in the Stellar Guardians unless she was his contact?

On the other hand, she had not made herself known with the code, which had been selected beforehand. Puzzled and suspicious, he flicked the transmitter stud and said cautiously, "Where are you?"

"You can't miss me, darling," she replied. "Just stand up."

Glayne hesitated, hefting the heavy, comforting weight of the Cardy blaster under his arm pit. With a shrug he tossed off the remnants of the blue-green *borse* that stirred lambently in the exquisite goblet. Then he stood up.

She was perfectly correct. He couldn't miss her from ten light years, much less thirty feet. She was tan and graceful in a tailored green jumper which half suggested, half concealed the long, smooth curves of her young body. She had coppery blondish-red hair and wide-set green eyes that smiled boldly at him. She rested a hand on her hip in mock impatience.

"Well, don't just stand there, fat-head!" she cried across the tables. "What do you usually do when you haven't seen someone for years and years?"

With an effort Glayne collected himself, assayed a weak smile, and maneuvered around the tables to her side.

"Oh, you look perfectly gorgeous," she said, oblivious to the amused people around her. "Dance with me—you always were a divine dancer. You know, I was telling Jani just today how I wished you'd come for a visit—we haven't seen you for such a long time…

She prattled gaily on, somewhat dazed. Glayne led her to the resilient dance floor, an absurdity that had suddenly become the very latest rage overnight. The girl slipped smoothly into his arms, her fragrant, perfumed hair under his chin.

He wasn't at all prepared for the hard tones of her voice when she said, "I regret to inform you, Captain Glayne, that the agent you were supposed to meet here is dead. He had an unfortunate accident with a Cardy gun."

Glayne stiffened perceptibly. "Who did it?"

"Probably Delban espionage. They know that something is in the fire and they're not wearing kid gloves to find out what it is."

"Did they discover the identity of the person he was supposed to meet?"

"No," she replied. "But they're looking. Fortunately the organization was not in the dark as to whom he would meet. Otherwise I could never have found you."

Glayne's eyes narrowed. Too many people knew what was going on. That made it very dangerous. But what made it even more dangerous was the fact that he himself did not know what was going on. Agents of three organizations were involved in the search for information and the tangled maze of plots would be deadly for anyone caught in the middle. He was silent for a moment, battle-trained senses sifting his surroundings instinctively. Something…somewhere…was odd.

"If you will notice their eyes," the girl remarked dryly, "you will find that a good proportion of the Varga's clientele are high on Soames drug."

GLAYNE started and looked more closely at the couples entering the stage. Then he saw what she meant. Here and there he saw eyes—burning eyes—eyes that glittered with a brilliant fire that emanated from huge, dilated pupils. They were using the marvelous Soames energizing drug; it fairly blazed from their slitted lids. Its purpose was to accelerate physical reaction speeds—but why use it on a small planet like Lorle IV? With the question came the answer. Their quarry had the .95 reaction index of a big planet man. That was Glayne's index. And that meant that they were right on top of him.

"I think," he intoned softly to the girl, "it would be wise for us to move on to the next stage."

In reply she slipped smoothly from his arms, seized him by the sleeve of his loose fitting jumper, and propelled him to the tingle screen. When he balked she grinned at him and stood in the field of the screen herself and laughed at him. It was a bubbly, elated laugh. Glayne liked it. And he liked the way the soothing color movements of the tingle screen caressed the long curves of her figure. But he didn't like the nervous manner in which the glittering, dilated pupils flickered at them and held them curiously, then flickered casually away.

The girl was clever, he realized. The keyed-up Delban agents would be far less likely to suspect an intoxicated couple of dark designs. Suddenly the blondish red-headed girl stumbled, accidentally pushed from the other side of the screen. Instinctively Glayne reached out to steady her— reached out with a long, liquid motion of his powerful arm. In one instant every Soames-dilated eye in the room was upon him. In another, Cardy guns were magically appearing in a dozen hands.

But, fast as they were, Glayne was faster. He drew his own weapon with blurred speed, fired, and flung himself and the girl through the screen into the second stage. The Delban agents hesitated to fire blindly through the screen and rushed after them. The big Guardian hurtled through the exotic darkness of the second-stage with the girl in his left arm. He scattered and smashed tables right and left, littering the floor with bewildered and drunken patrons.

The exit toward which he was heading was suddenly no longer an exit. It was filled with a crowd of huge, glittering eyes and wicked looking Cardy guns. In a single movement, Glayne dropped to the floor and fired.

The second stage was in an uproar. Now agents were pouring through the tingle screen in pursuit. Desperately Glayne sought for a means of escape. Then he saw the portal that evidently led to the kitchen or the bar. He grabbed the dazed red-head and rushed through the portal, swept down a short corridor, turned, and straight-armed two tray-bearing waiters as he dashed through a second portal. And suddenly he was behind the entrance bar where he had taken his first drink. He tensed for a fraction of a second, then vaulted the low bar.

A bartender and two customers stared at them with blank amazement but there was not a Delban agent in sight. Swiftly Glayne set the girl upon her feet and together they fled from the building. He noted approvingly the capable-looking Cardy she held in her small fist.

"My flier is outside," he said. "They've probably surrounded the place, but in the confusion the ones outside won't know us. We'll try to bluff through."

She nodded and put her gun away. As they approached the flier parking area she clutched his arm with intoxicated possessiveness. Glayne was right; here and there a Delban agent glanced at them suspiciously—then looked contemptuously away. The object of their search would be alone. Controlling his heavy breathing with difficulty, Glayne approached an attendant, digging out his microwave key jewel.

"Here! Get my air-jet," he panted.

But instead of the expected response, the man stiffened for a measureless instant, then whirled with blurred speed. A Cardy blaster magically materialized in his hand and his eyes burned with Soames-induced ferocity. But Glayne was a shade faster. His left streaked with dazzling speed into the agent's stomach and the Delban folded up, his motor nerves paralyzed from the blow in the solar plexus.

Crouching, they ran toward Glayne's air-jet. A Cardy bolt splashed into the side of a flier just above Glayne's head, battering the tough beralloy and sending a shower of white-hot droplets in all directions. As they reached his air-jet, Glayne whirled and fired rapidly and with murderous accuracy at the pursuing Delban agents. As they scuttled for cover, Glayne turned and waved the talisman through the microwave field and the door swung open.

Instantly he shoved the girt into the cabin, then climbed in behind her. He let the tiny atomic engine thunder beyond audibility, then fed power to the jets in huge gulps. With a tremendous surge the little craft leaped into the air and roared over the roof of the Yarga. A couple of Delban energy bolts slapped viciously into the air-jet, but soon Glayne outdistanced them, flying low over the dark countryside.

The girl sighed beside him. "This has been a very warm evening. Do you think they'll catch us?"

"I don't think they're organized that well," Glayne grunted, busy with the course-computer. "Their whole assault was hasty and ill-timed. I doubt if they even had time to set up an air net."

"But, now that they're out in the open, they'll move quickly. Do you have a specific plan in mind, Captain Glayne?"

The Guardian frowned and cast a quick glance at her. He was puzzled by her insistence. "My Flagship, the *Algol*, is maneuvered into a fast orbit behind inert detector screens. About ninety miles out. I've just set course to intercept her before we hit dayside."

In reply the girl bent past his shoulder toward the luminous figures that floated in the dial of the computer, announcing the course. The delicate lines of her face were hard in the faint light. Again Glayne felt a twinge of uneasiness and it was not dispelled by the soft touch of her body against his.

"What is your name?" he asked belatedly, trying to make out the features of her face in the dim light from the instrument panel.

She chuckled in the darkness and he fancied he heard a note of triumph. "Lieutenant Niala Chodred," she said. "Espionage Bureau of Imperial Terra. At your service, Captain."

Of Imperial Terra! The words fairly blazed in Glayne's consciousness. His hand shot like lightning for the Cardy in his arm-pit holster, then stopped in mid-motion as he became aware of a hard, cylindrical object thrust into his ribs. It was her tiny Cardy blaster.

Through the waves of chagrin and impotent fury that surged up within him, Glayne heard her say mockingly, "Guardian warriors are supposed to function like machines when on missions, aren't they, Captain? Since when are machines rattled by pretty girls?"

The lines on Glayne's face deepened but he said nothing. Her taunting rebuke was well-deserved. He had certainly lacked the emotionless precision that was the Guardian ideal. But the mere fact that he had been caught napping was inconsequential beside the implications of her presence as a Terran agent. How much did Terra know? The question hammered urgently in Glayne's mind.

Even as it flashed through his head, he heard her amused voice say, "In time of crisis, Captain Glayne, the Stellar Guardians invariably throw allies and friends to the dogs in order to gain time. This is common knowledge. So all we had to do was determine the direction of the Guardian move. We immediately thought of Lorle. And we even thought that you might be the man the Guardians would send, Glayne, because we have a complete file on your activities for the past ten years. We know that you have been on good terms with Delban brass since that successful exploring job you performed at Jorger Sun, five years ago."

With growing horror, Glayne listened to her unfold the deepest Guardian secrets—derived by Terran Espionage through simple induction. What a fool he had been for trusting her even for a minute! Unless he could stop her, she could utterly destroy all Guardian hopes to overcome the Delbans. His great body tensed as he stared at her from the corner of his eye, watching for the slightest sign of inattention.

"Glayne," she continued, in a hard, objective voice with no trace of amusement, "Imperial Terra is not itself adverse to a policy of throwing someone to the dogs in order to gain time. But we want to give the dogs someone who can put up a fight. Poor Lorle would not be much of a match for Gort Bro-Doral and she wouldn't gain us much time. But the Stellar Guardians would. In fact, the Stellar Guardians themselves will commit the overt act—with a little help."

The Guardian Captain was stunned at the very audacity of her plan. He had to admit that its logic was undeniable. But how could she possibly seek to accomplish such an incredible feat as forcing the Guardians into a suicidal attack upon the Delbans? Unless...

Then his worst suspicions were realized as she said, "The Ganser mind-conditioning treatments will not harm your essential ego, Captain Glayne. But, if you struggle against them, your mind will be shattered and you will be left an idiot when the effects wear off."

A cold thrill of fear caressed Glayne's spine as he heard her words. The brutal, tearing fingers of the horrible mind-conditioner devised by the Delban Espionage Chief, Hoteh Ganser, would change his goals and values in the space of only a few hours. What seemed to him irrational now would be the height of reason after his conditioning. As the ramifications of Imperial Terra's plot came clear to him, Glayne realized with increasing urgency that he simply had to overcome the girl.

"You may be sure that your attack on Sterle II will not be in vain," came the girl's brittle tones. "Admiral Bardled will station units of the Imperial Terran Fleet in hyper-space with the purpose of cracking the wavelength of the broadcast power and locating its source.

"Our plan is much cleaner and nobler than yours, is it not, Captain Glayne? You Stellar Guardians are all hard, ruthless fighters. You can take care of yourselves. But poor little Lorle wouldn't have a chance. Don't you agree, Captain? Don't you find it heroic to sacrifice yourself to the Delban dog pack to gain time for the rest of the galaxy?"

Glayne ignored the mockery in her voice. A sudden wave of bitter anger swept over him at the presumptuous manner in which they were all bent upon throwing one another to the dogs. Surely they were not so tactically poverty-stricken that they could not conceive of a better plot that would not demand such a tremendous sacrifice of human life.

SUDDENLY, almost without warning, the tiny spark of rebellion within him blazed up in hot determination. To hell with Garstow and the Stellar Guardian Policy Organ. To hell with Admiral Bardled and the Terran fleet. To hell with everyone. The vague suggestion of a plan was forming in the recesses of his mind, breath-taking in its audacity and possibly, just possibly workable.

But what of the girl? To think about overpowering her was one thing; actually doing it was another. She had already killed one Guardian earlier this evening, he presumed. She would not hesitate to kill another. That meant that he would have to meet cunning with cunning.

"You don't mind if I smoke one last cigar while I am still in control of my essential-ego, do you?" he asked, trying to match her mocking, satirical mood. "I don't believe the Ganser-personality enjoys tobacco as much as the average Guardian Captain."

She alerted instantly, but the Cardy didn't waver the least fraction of an inch. "You are not the average Guardian Captain," she said in a strange, low voice. "But go ahead and smoke."

Fleetingly Glayne wondered what she had meant, then he let the thought flicker away as he concentrated on his cigar. He reached for the radioactive on the instrument panel, flicking it so that its coal gleamed into gradual dull red life. She was watching him like a hawk, he knew, and smiled inwardly. The closer the better. Idly he began to hum a snatch of melody, a curious thing arranged in minors. It was peculiarly suited to his unsteady bass. He waved the radioactive in his hand in slow, sweeping circles in time to his humming.

Smoothly he ignited his cigar, puffing the semi-narcotic smoke in thick clouds. He hummed louder, his voice pushing the deep, wailing dirge into the cabin. It acted like a drug, throwing everything into slow time. It numbed the sensibilities and dulled acute perceptions.

Ever so gently and smoothly Glayne turned his head and glanced at the girl. His scheme had worked. Her eyes automatically followed the circles he described with the radioactive in his hand. She was lulled into a near-hypnotic condition.

In a single jump, Glayne seized the hand in which she held the Cardy gun. She reacted instantly, but not quite fast enough to wrest the weapon from his hand. Like a spring under great pressure she exploded into writhing, clawing, kicking, biting action. Her savage ferocity so startled Glayne that he nearly lost the weapon to her. As he sought to fend her off with one hand and throw the weapon away with the other, he felt her nails sink agonizingly into the side of his face. Gasping, he finally got rid of the weapon, then drew back his fist and slugged her with a short, jabbing punch.

Panting, he recovered from the struggle. Suddenly he became aware of the peculiar angle of flight of the air-jet. It was shrieking down on its stubby fins toward the planet's surface. Somehow the Terran girl had kicked off the robot control. As he righted the craft and reoriented the course, he became aware of the girl's brooding eyes on him.

"You are very clever, Captain Glayne," she said. "Perhaps one might even say courageous. A heavy planet man like you should not risk himself with such reckless bravery in a physical struggle with a small planet individual."

Glayne was stung by her rebuke, but he was even more startled at her bitterness. She was an espionage agent and she knew the risks and hazards involved. Certainly she was not whining at her defeat.

"How do you propose to fake the overt act, Captain?" she continued in a light, conversational tone.

Glayne was grimly aware of the accusation in her words but he said nothing. She had a right to be bitter, he realized. Ironically, she was going to get her way after all, though she didn't know it yet. He grinned mirthlessly at her, the cigar clenched between his teeth.

She was beautiful, but especially so in the resentment that was mirrored in her features. Glayne was suddenly very sorry that she had killed the Guardian agent he was supposed to meet. Otherwise he would have liked very much to have known her.

CHAPTER FOUR

THE NINE-HUNDRED-FOOT bulk of the Stellar class cruiser *Algol* loomed hugely over the little air-jet as Glayne maneuvered it into the gaping reception maw in the cruiser's belly. The craft's slight lurch as it came to rest just inside the lock awoke the Terran girl who had fallen asleep.

Glayne sighed, glancing at her. She stared back at him coolly. He shook his head and said, "That green outfit of yours will just have to go, Lieutenant Chodred. Crew's morale, you know."

Her eyes widened in sudden dismay. "But...but surely you don't want me to—"

He grinned. "You will have to wear a crew jumper." Glancing again at her graceful figure, he made a mental note—it would have to be an over-size jumper several sizes over.

Stiffly they climbed from the little air-jet and propelled themselves weightlessly to the elevator. Seconds later its door slid open and they were on the navigation bridge. Glayne took the girl's arm and escorted her around the bulking computers and auxiliary boards to the Captain's Station.

Graysen, the grizzled old Executive Officer, snapped to attention and delivered a brisk salute. Glayne acknowledged it absently, his attention absorbed primarily in a hasty inspection of the bridge. Then he became aware of the intent stares of Graysen and the other officers. Those who were not gawking at Niala Chodred were staring hard at his cheek, obviously striving not to laugh.

Puzzled, Glayne felt his cheek, then glanced at his hand. There was blood on it. He suddenly recalled the two long red welts inflicted by the Terran agent's fingernails and realized that his officers were drawing the obvious inferences. Abruptly he was stung with chagrin and pictured the juicy tidbit of gossip that he had just supplied gunroom scuttlebutt throughout the Guardian Fleet. Exasperated at his own lack of foresight, he stared back at his officers, browbeating them into submission with his stony gaze.

"Morning, Captain," drawled Graysen, breaking the embarrassed silence.

"Good morning, Commander," returned Glayne. "Stoke her up. Set an orbit for Sterle II. Incidentally, this is Lieutenant Niala Chodred of Imperial Terran Espionage. I met her instead of our own agent. He had an unfortunate accident with a Cardy gun—so I'm told."

Glayne glanced significantly at the girl. Graysen nodded understandingly and raised a quizzical eyebrow in Niala's direction. She looked from one to the other, mystified.

Then sudden understanding registered on her features. "Glayne!" she cried in a horrified tone. "I didn't kill him! Terran Espionage had nothing to do with his death. He was murdered by the Delbans and we found out by bribing one of Kairn's men that he was supposed to make contact with an unknown Guardian big gun at the Yarga. We knew he was to meet you but the Delbans didn't. That's the only reason you escaped them, Captain Glayne. The Delbans murdered your contact agent but I had nothing to do with it. You must believe me!"

Glayne smiled cynically at her and said, "Of course, Lieutenant Chodred, we believe you." He brusquely turned his back on her and said to Graysen, "You will have to move in with one of the other officers, Commander. Just temporarily, of course."

"Aye, sir," replied Graysen.

PRESENTLY the navigation bridge was filled with hurrying men. The orbit computers began to clatter noisily and somewhere within the depths of the ship a keening whine indicated that the huge driver atomics were being warmed.

"What acceleration, Captain?" Graysen asked, appearing with a sheaf of orbit calculations.

Glayne was on the point of saying three G's out of deference to Niala Chodred and her light planet birth. But he thrust her from his mind as he realized that speed was of the utmost importance. High acceleration meant speed and speed meant time saved. Time to carry out his bold scheme, time to locate and sabotage the mysterious Delban power broadcast, time to build the mesh antennae and energize the Stellar Guardian fleet...

His face hardened grimly. "Five G's," he said shortly.

Doubt flickered for an instant across Graysen's face as he glanced at the girl. Then he shrugged and turned away to comply with the order.

Silently Glayne took Niala Chodred's arm and descended to the next deck. As the first traces of a floor appeared under their feet, he opened the door to Graysen's quarters. It was furnished with the Spartan simplicity of a typical warrior. Trophies and a few rather gruesome battle prints decorated the bulkheads. Niala examined the room curiously but preserved a hurt silence.

He showed her the acceleration hammocks and how to use the anti-thrust drugs in their small surettes.

"If you need me," he said, "I will be in the cabin at the end of the corridor."

She looked at him with mock surprise. "What? No connecting door? Really, Captain, you've shattered all my girlish illusions about the Stellar Guardians."

Glayne paused, his hand on the door stud. He turned around and said, "I want to wake up tomorrow without suffering an accident with a Cardy gun." He closed the door behind him.

By the time he reached the navigation bridge again, the *Algol* had built up to five G's. To Glayne, accustomed to the heavy Dorleb planets, this was a little more than twice normal.

Young Brodis, the ship's Intelligence Officer, approached him and saluted. "I beg your pardon, sir. Communications just handed these over to me—I thought you might be interested." He extended a sheaf of flimsies to Glayne.

The big Guardian examined them, eyes narrowed. They were transcripts of an official Lode news bulletin. Rapidly he read:

Intelligence Chief Kairn announced tonight the death of Carling Clawdor, allegedly an espionage agent of the Stellar Guardians. It is believed that he was to contact another agent or agents at the Yarga nightclub this evening. Prior to his death by Cardy burns, Clawdor accused Delban agents.

Intelligence Chief Kairn also revealed that a raid carried out on the Yarga nightclub failed to apprehend the Guardian agents. Just before their arrival a spectacular gun battle took place. Investigation is still proceeding, Kairn announced, indicating that…

Silently Glayne handed the flimsies back to Brodis, chewing his lower lip. It was incredible that Kairn should reveal such confidential information. Obviously the Lorle Intelligence Chief was taking no chances on provoking an incident with which the Delbans could twist into a pretext for war. But an even more important fact came clear to Glayne: Niala Chodred had not murdered Clawdor. He was very glad that she was innocent of the Guardian agent's death. Unconsciously he framed the apology he would make to her as he climbed with an effort into the Captain's Dome and lowered himself into its gimbal-slung shock seat.

Far off to his left the globe of Lorle IV shrunk visibly. Again the mental picture of the Delban warships streaking over those short horizons in fast orbits flashed across his mind and he imagined them pouring their inconceivable torrents of energy into the unprotected cities. At least, he thought, he wouldn't be guilty of that crime. But what was the real chance of the wild scheme and its attendant insubordination that he had conceived in the air-jet?

For a long time he pondered it. No matter how much he rationalized, it was still insubordination and it lay heavily on his mind. Suddenly he was shaky and he realized that he held the fate of the civilized galaxy in his hands. If he blundered, would that not be a greater crime than the mere sacrifice of Lorle? Glayne could not resolve the question and he was vaguely glad that that decision was no longer in his hands and he could not turn back if he wanted to.

THE *Algol* emerged from sub-space four hundred million kilometers below the plane of the ecliptic in the Sterle System. With her identity signals broadcasting at full power, she changed course, veering "upward" toward the second planet of Sterle's small brood of five.

The faint beams of the distant red dwarf sun shed a sickly glow on the navigation bridge through the huge glassene ports. Shortly after her arrival the *Algol* was picked up by two fast and deadly Delban destroyers of the Planet class. Almost delicate in their unobtrusiveness, they slipped in on either side of the *Algol* and escorted her swiftly to the capital planet of the Delban Empire, Sterle II.

"There's one consolation, anyway," Graysen remarked to his chief as they stood before the glassene ports. "They don't seem to have fitted out their whole fleet with receiving antennae yet."

Glayne nodded, flipping on the small auxiliary battle screen at his side. Expertly he manipulated the viewer until one of the rakish Delban warships ballooned up mightily on its plate. The tell-tale coppery mesh antenna was absent.

"That is fortunate," Glayne grunted dourly. "But there is the possibility that these ships may be too small for the installation."

The Delbans began to decelerate and the *Algol's* pilot hastily imitated them. Faintly Glayne made out the tiny red ball that was Sterle II. Uneasily Glayne realized that he had better go over the plan once more with Niala Chodred. Next to himself, the Terran girl's part was the most important. He grunted at Graysen to take over and descended to her quarters. He knocked twice perfunctorily and entered the room.

Niala smiled up at him, pleased at his visit. "How much longer now, Captain?"

Glayne looked down at her, marveling at the failure of her absurdly huge jumper in concealing the long, smooth curves of her body. Her hair was a varied mass of copper and gold, which gleamed with a subtle display of half tones. In the cabin's fluorescents Glayne noted for the first time that she had once been the owner of a saddle of freckles across her nose. Now only one or two were left, which contrasted deliciously with the smoothness of her face. Glayne felt a sudden desire to jet down on Sterle Capital like the legendary buccaneers and ransack the best dress shops to outfit her properly.

"Well?" she said.

"Huh?" said Glayne foolishly. Then he collected his wandering thoughts and replied, "Oh, yes. We're being escorted in now. We'll be down in a couple of hours. I wanted to make a last minute check of the plan."

"Ahh," she replied, stretching with devastating effect in the heavy jumper. "We've done this so many times, Captain. But really they're very entertaining."

"I'm glad you like them," said Glayne dryly. "You should because the plan is substantially the one you would have had me carry out under a Ganser-personality."

She colored, then regained control of her vascular motors and recited the plan in a sing-song monotone, "We jet down at Sterle Capital. You and I attend the informal reception. Commander Graysen remains with the *Algol* along with Lieutenant Harbin. But precisely at twenty-one hundred Standard, Harbin and twenty men leave the ship, ostensibly on liberty. At twenty-one fifteen, you and I attempt to maneuver Gort Bro-Doral and General Ganser together in conversation. At that moment Lieutenant Harbin will land on the roof of the palace, attacking the guards there. Then we will hustle the two Delbans into the elevator, take them to the roof, and escape with Harbin in the flier. In the meantime Graysen will have blasted off in the *Algol;* we will intercept him twenty miles over Topo Gulf."

"Exactly," Glayne said. "Everything is going well so far. We've just received permission to land a liberty party so we don't have to worry about that anymore."

He took some hand-drawn maps from the case in his hand. "Brodis and I made these from memory and a little inside information—one of the palace, one of the roof, and one of the grounds. The whole thing depends upon whether they are using an old style one-way shield. If so, we can get out all right. Otherwise we're finished."

She nodded and bent over the maps. Glayne bit the end off of a cigar, then lit it meticulously. He smiled quizzically at the girl. "How's your courage?" he asked.

Her wide green eyes looked up thoughtfully into his. "I've seen some shoe-string deals pulled before, but Captain, I'll have to award you the prize—never one as thin and short as this."

Glayne felt a sudden fear and a sudden hunger as he looked at her. He could not bear the thought of failure—and the consequent fate of Niala Chodred. His cheek twitched nervously and he reached for her, gathering her into his powerful arms and drawing her face to his. Her breath was hot against his cheek and he could feel her heart pounding heavily against his chest. Willingly she responded to his kisses.

"Here's to luck," he breathed.

"And plenty of it," she replied.

CHAPTER FIVE

TRY AS HE MIGHT, GLAYNE could never accustom himself to these Sectors that lay far out on the edge of galaxy. Neighboring stars were hundreds of light years apart while the great belt of stars that was in the Main Galaxy revealed itself only as a faint haze twenty thousand light years distant. He could not shake off the loneliness that settled over him like a shroud, separating him from everything he knew. He was accustomed to the vast star clouds of Sagittarius; it was there he had spent the first ten years of his Guardianship.

A dry and thirsty wind seemed to suck the moisture from his body as he waited by the after lock with Niala. It swept across the hard surface of the Spaceport and sang dolefully around the mass of the grounded *Algol*, it even seemed to characterize the Delbans themselves. A lonely people out on this forsaken edge of the galaxy, they hungered and thirsted after wealth and power. The Guardian sympathized with them to some extent, yet at the same time realized the awful threat to civilization they represented with the mysterious, titanic broadcast power at their disposal.

Again Glayne felt inner qualms as he considered the odds against them. Grimly he crushed them out and touched with almost superstitious reverence the tiny blaster at his hip—for ornamental purposes only. More confidently he hefted the weight of the heavy Cardy at his armpit.

The small surface-jet, which had set out for the *Algol* immediately after the mushrooming blasts of its landing jets subsided, now drew up at the tiny waiting dock formed by the *Algol's* after lock. The lack of formality, Glayne knew, was as blatant an insult as the Delbans could manage. He smiled mirthlessly to himself. They couldn't please him more if they tried. The less pomp and ceremony attached to him, the more smoothly his plan would work.

A single Delban emerged from the surface-jet, evidently a civilian judging from his dress. He was incredibly tall and thin and made Glayne very uncomfortable because he had to tilt his head back to get a good look at him.

"Captain Glayne," began the emissary in a high, sighing nasal, "on behalf of His Imperial Excellency, Ruler of Ten Thousand Suns, Master of the Cosmos, and Supreme Overlord of the Delban Empire, Gort Bro-Doral, I humbly welcome you to Sterle II," He bowed very low.

Glayne, nervously anticipating almost anything, could hardly restrain his laughter at this comic pomposity. It was quite out of place in the desolate, curiously-deserted spaceport. He and Niala entered the rear compartment of the surface car and sunk back in the luxurious cushions. Their Delban guide tooled it with expert ease from the spaceport and down a traffic artery toward the bright blob on the horizon that was Sterle Capital.

In minutes, it seemed, they were pausing for the first guard check along the private road that led to the Bro's fabulous palace. Glayne had been there once before, five years ago. They passed two more guard checks. For a minute Glayne thought they were safely on the palace grounds, only to be disillusioned by another, and this time very close, guard check.

The weapons detector emitted a raucous buzz when they came into its field. Suspiciously the guards stared at them, their weapons leveled. Seeing the tiny toy at Glayne's hip, they smiled and passed them on with contemptuous nods.

What a hell of a mess, he thought to himself. It was too late to back out. In another hour Harbin would be on his way to the palace—and right into a hive of trigger-happy guards. One faint consolation was their contempt, which would render them more vulnerable to the surprise attack he planned. But on the whole it looked pretty grim. He suppressed his unhappy thoughts as the surface-jet drew up at last beneath a gigantic, arched entrance.

Niala squeezed his hand bravely, casting a quick smile at him.

Heartened by her display of courage, he climbed from the little jet car and followed the escorting Delban down a long series of luxuriously furnished corridors. Eventually they turned off into an enormous reception room brilliantly illuminated by chandeliers of priceless Tharna crystals. Tremendous tapestries hung along the wall, depicting ancient, pre-spaceship battle scenes. A score or so of guests stood about the huge room, all of them quite obviously in very advanced stages of drunkenness. Quite cheerfully they spilled drinks on the priceless *jrik* carpets or on the equally priceless marl Shanzi-wood furnishings.

GLAYNE was puzzled by all the intoxication. As he speculated, it suddenly occurred to him that they were celebrating. Quite obviously they believed that they had won a victory of some sort in the diplomatic call by the Stellar Guardian *Algol*. Glayne had to agree that it was a logical conclusion and resolved to exploit their mistaken belief as far as possible.

The first person to be presented to Glayne and Niala was General Hoteh Ganser. He was hopelessly drunk. Glayne knew the pop-eyed Delban Espionage Chief only by reputation; he was rather disappointed at the dried and withered figure he cut. Nevertheless he was pleased to see the Delban in an intoxicated condition; he could be more easily handled.

"The Bro will arrive presently," their guide informed them. Affairs of state prevented his presence at the moment.

Meanwhile they were introduced to a number of curious and intoxicated guests—high ranking, Glayne gathered from the monotonous repetition of titles.

Then General Ganser was before them again, accompanied by another Delban in a brilliant uniform surmounted by a gaudy, flowing cape. He was aristocratic and condescending in his demeanor and a smile played about his eyes and dry lips.

"May I present His Excellency, Gort Bro-Doral...Captain Glayne of the Stellar Guardians," introduced Ganser. His eyes were owlish with forced dignity. Gort Bro-Doral waved him away with a careless sweep of his arm and bowed politely to Glayne.

"I think we met several years ago, Captain. Am I right?"

Glayne nodded politely.

"But of course. Won't you and your...er...lady have a drink?"

Glayne colored angrily. Yes, they would have a drink. He glanced casually at his wrist-chromo. Twenty minutes...just twenty minutes before Harbin would be down on the roof.

He sipped slowly at the huge cup of *borse* that the Bro had personally ladled out for him, letting its blue-green smoothness ease his parched throat and his nervousness. Niala, at his sign, slipped away and was immediately surrounded by a crowd of the outlanders, General Ganser at the head. They knew a good thing when they saw it, Glayne reflected wryly.

Gort Bro-Doral eyed him with amusement across the mammoth *borse* bowl. "Now really, Captain, why did you come here? Surely not to inform us of the decision of your sacred Policy Organ?" The Ruler of Ten Thousand Suns emitted an odd, explosive noise that corresponded to laughter.

To the Delban leader's question Glayne replied cautiously, "The Guardians have landed on their feet in every major crisis for the last thousand years. Perhaps we want to land feet-first this time."

"That is quite understandable, Captain," replied Gort Bro-Doral, cautious in his turn.

"When one side in a battle has unlimited strength," Glayne continued, "the wise man has no difficulty in deciding whom he will support. That is similar to our own position, Your Excellency;"

Again Bro-Doral produced his strange, whinnying laugh. "Really, Captain, you amaze me. The future Delban Empire cannot tolerate such things as mercenary armies and space fleets—nor do we need such organizations to win our battles now. But, if you could bring yourself to the point of forgetting your traditions and other related paraphernalia of which you are so fond, then there is a possibility that you might be absorbed into the Delban Space Navy. Of course, you would have to submit to our commands—but that's understandable…"

Glayne exulted inwardly. The Bro simply saw them begging for a crumb of the spoils—he enjoyed his power to humiliate the Stellar Guardians. But what he didn't see, contrary to the old adage, was going to trim his scrawny neck. Where were Niala and Ganser? A minute to go!

"Your conditions are rather harsh, Your Excellency," he said, looking around for Niala. "But perhaps tomorrow…?"

"Yes. Tomorrow by all means, Captain. And it will be a formal occasion this time." Again Bro-Doral produced his explosive laugh, glancing obliquely at Glayne from beneath lowered eyelids. Amusement at the Guardian's plight bubbled in the depths of his otherwise fathomless black eyes.

A SUDDEN series of shocks made the floor shudder and Glayne's heart jumped to his throat. Harbin had struck! Out of the corner of his eye he perceived Niala thrusting a big, black Cardy into Ganser's back, concealing it beneath his cape. Glayne drew his own and thrust it into Bro-Doral's ribs.

"Keep laughing, damn you!" Glayne instructed. "Walk to the roof elevator—casually." Glayne's eyes flickered rapidly about the room. Niala was right behind him with the staggering and nonplussed General Ganser. He thrust his weapon into the fold of his jumper before it could be seen. Repeated tremors shook the floor—Harbin must be digging them out with a secondary Kellander, he thought fleetingly.

"You must be insane!" choked the Master of the Cosmos. "The roof guards—the palace guards and my own personal men will blast you down before you can set a foot outside this room."

"*Just—keep—laughing!*" Glayne said, emphasizing every word. One or two of the guests looked at them curiously as they approached the massive doors, then turned away indifferently. The trembling had ceased. That meant that Harbin had cleared away the immediate defenses—but Glayne knew it would be a race with the reinforcements.

The doors were opened before them by attendants—slowly and with agonizing dignity. Two hawk-eyed Delban guards glanced at them sharply as they entered the corridor that led to the Bro's private apartment and the crucial fifth level roof elevator. Ever so slowly they moved down the corridor. It was a snail's pace to Glayne. Gort Bro-Doral laughed—or gasped in his sickly, explosive manner. He gestured. He spoke to Glayne, waving his arms in a deprecating manner. And all the while the Guardian looked innocently into the Delban's tormented features, his hand clinging wetly to the Cardy in the folds of his jumper.

They met no more guards in the corridor; evidently the rest of them had hastened to the roof. But the first two were still eyeing them. Glayne could feel their stares burning into his back. Twenty feet separated them from the waiting elevator…fifteen…ten. Niala had drawn abreast with General Ganser; the sick, the pale, the fuzzy-minded Intelligence Chief whose cunning was known throughout the Galaxy.

There was a sudden commotion behind them. Glayne cast a glance over his shoulder and saw the corridor rapidly filling with uniformed and heavily-armed Delbans. They commanded him to stop; he smiled back. They brandished their weapons; he waved back gaily, herding the prisoners into the open elevator. They rushed after him; he drew his Cardy gun, crouched, and fired with murderous effect. Then he lunged into the elevator and jabbed the roof stud.

Swiftly it rose. Glayne turned to the two Delbans. The Ruler of Ten Thousand Suns was in a blue funk but General Ganser had pulled himself together a bit. His heavily-veined, crimson eyes blazed furiously at the kidnapers.

"Be careful with the General," Glayne warned. "He is dangerous when sober."

She managed a weak smile and thereby jumped another ten points in Glayne's esteem. The elevator sighed to a stop and the heavy door slid open, letting the dry wind pluck at them. Glayne turned his blaster on the controls, fusing them into tangled slag. Then he crept to the open door, crouched, and surveyed the palace roof in the pale, rosy illumination shed by one of Sterle's just-risen moons.

On his left, not a hundred yards away, lay the flier from the *Algol*. Three gunners from the crew were operating a portable Kellander, firing along the edge of the anti-energy shield which had been generated from the flier to prevent other Delban roof emplacements from destroying the little assault force. The rest of the attacking group manned Delban energy projectors that were still in operating condition, sending a heavy fire into possible concentration points for an enemy counterattack. Bodies—mostly Delban—sprawled everywhere.

"We'll have to run for it," Glayne said. "They've erected an anti-shield between us and the flier. Once we gain that, we're safe."

Niala nodded and prodded the two prisoners out of the elevator. Bending low, they ran diagonally across the roof toward the shimmering ovoid that was the anti-shield. They had not gone more than forty steps before a counterattacking wave of Delban palace guards suddenly appeared on their right. Cursing, Glayne doubled about and increased his pace in order not to be cut off. "Glayne! Slow down...I can't keep up," the girl panted.

The Guardian glanced anxiously back at her just in time to be struck full force by General Ganser's flying body. They went down together in a wild tangle of thrashing arms and legs. The Delban, in spite of his dissipation, was tough and wiry; his long fingers sought Glayne's throat and clung to it with a vise-like grip. In vain the Guardian battered his body with sledge-hammer blows of his fists. Somewhere he had lost his gun. A black film threatened to engulf his consciousness as he struggled against the strangling grip of General Ganser. Vaguely he felt the roof on which he lay tremble from the impact of the energy beams that smashed into it.

From far away he heard Niala scream. It was a bitter spur to his flagging strength. Summoning every last reserve, he tore Ganser's clutching hands from his throat and flung him down to the roof. Not done yet, the Delban snatched up Glayne's weapon, which had fallen in the first seconds of the combat, and lifted it to fire. Furiously Glayne launched his booted foot at Ganser in a savage kick. Bones crunched as it caught him full in the face and the impact sent him spinning.

Glayne scooped up the Cardy gun and searched desperately for Niala. The Delban palace guard continued to storm the little Guardian stronghold, but the fire of the defenders took horrible effect on their ranks. In the darkness he saw Niala's crumpled form on the roof. And almost immediately afterwards he saw Gort Bro-Doral fleeing to the safety of his attacking soldiers. Holding his breath, Glayne tried a long range shot. But it was to no avail. The Supreme Overlord had made good his escape.

ANXIOUSLY Glayne bent over the girl who was just beginning to stir. There was a nasty welt on her forehead.

"I'm all right," she gasped, rising to her feet. "Where's Bro-Doral? Did he get away?"

Glayne nodded grimly. "Yes, but never mind. We've got this one. Hurry!"

Grunting, he swung Ganser's supine form to his shoulder and ran panting to the edge of the anti-shield. He halted a pace before the shimmering field and pulled a dark-colored disc from his pocket. Set beforehand to the shield frequency that Harbin would use, its purpose was to nullify a small section long enough for them to slip through.

Hastily his fingers flipped the trigger and it began to vibrate furiously in his hand. Instantly an irregular opening flickered in the lethal shimmer of the shield. Glayne shoved the girl through, then darted after her with Ganser over his shoulder.

Harbin waved joyously at them from the flier turret, his youthful face wreathed in smiles. "We can't hold them much longer," he shouted. "They're nullifying the shield with field scramblers. Hurry!"

Right behind Glayne as he steered Niala through the lock and leaped in behind her came the portable Kellander crew, still firing as they backed the gun into the flier. With a clang the locks slammed shut and the flier's driver engines thundered. With a single motion of his arm, Harbin released the anti-shield and fed the pent-up driver power to the jets. With a tremendous heave that crushed Glayne back rigidly in his seat the flier blasted up from the palace roof.

Harbin flung the flier around in a screaming turn and thundered low over the vast forest preserves that surrounded the palace. The tall, scraggly trees seemed to brush against the ship's stubby fins as Harbin sought to evade enemy pursuit. Grunting with effort, Glayne clambered up to the nose of the craft and sank back into a shock seat beside the pilot.

Grimly the Guardian Captain peered ahead at the huge, featureless ovoid of grey which was fast rushing down upon them. It was the palace defense shield. If it was the new type, then they were licked because nothing could get in or out. But the two-way shields were dangerous and unnecessary as protection for a natural siege position like Gort Bro-Doral's palace. Hence Glayne had concluded that the Delbans would keep their old style shield.

Or had he made a mistake in his reasoning? Glayne tensed unconsciously as the tiny flier flashed toward the grey ovoid. It was all or nothing. And suddenly the flier slashed through it like so much paper.

Glayne suppressed a sigh of relief at the vindication of his logic. Now the flier was hurtling over Sterle Capital. Harbin, in an effort to avoid enemy detectors, was almost flying down the very streets. Their wild gamble almost looked as if it would pay off. Glayne hoped fervently that Graysen had managed to evade the two Delban escort destroyers that had accompanied them to the spaceport. The *Algol* would be a sitting duck over Topo Gulf until the flier arrived.

But after that, Glayne thought grimly, they were clear. No matter how much power the Delbans could receive from their astounding transmitter, they could not withstand a sustained ten G thrust like his crew of heavy planet men. Then he thought of Niala, accustomed to Terran Standard. He bit his lip. She would just have to take it; there was no other way.

The flier had left Sterle Capital far behind and was climbing rapidly into the stratosphere. Evidently the surprise attack had disorganized the Delban patrols and drawn them like flies to the city. At any rate, not one was in sight as their flier streaked over Topo Gulf.

Feverishly Harbin doubled the flier back and forth, searching the conic broadcast beam of the *Algol,* undetectable behind her inert screen. Finally a welcome series of dots and dashes crackled from the receiver and Harbin brought the flier around in a screaming turn to follow the directional beam. Cautiously he slowed the craft as the intensity of the signals increased. Suddenly the reception maw gaped at them out of grey nothingness—and the flier shuddered to a stop at the *Algol's* landing dock.

Hastily Glayne jumped out of the flier and hurried to the navigation bridge, dropping Niala in her quarters along the way. Harbin would take General Ganser—the precious, indispensable Ganser—to Surgery for facial repairs.

Graysen nodded at him, as taciturn as ever. "Your orbit, Captain?"

"Anywhere," Glayne replied. "Anywhere, just so long as we get far enough out of this system to drop into sub-space." He rubbed his bristly chin for a moment, thinking. "Make it eight G's," he added.

Graysen acknowledged and turned away. Almost immediately the inert screens were dropped and a floor began to build under Glayne's feet. By the time he had mounted to the Captain's Station, he was panting with effort. Automatically he jabbed an anti-thrust surette into his arm and felt his muscles relax instantaneously under the influence of the magic drug.

The inter-ship communicator phones gurgled over his head for a couple of seconds, then Brodis' voice issued from the speaker, "The General is floating up to his ears in verchromynal, Captain. They're putting his face back together right now. Give the word and I'll go to work on him, thrust or no thrust."

"No," Glayne replied. "We'll make subspace in a few hours. Then we'll have all the time we need to pump him. And, Lieutenant…"

"Sir?"

"Prepare the General's very own treatments for him."

Brodis paused for an appreciable instant, then said, "Right, Captain," and cut off.

Glayne watched the globe of Sterle II diminish in his battle screen with deep satisfaction. The first step in his plan had been carried off with miraculous good fortune. Now the most pressing necessity was speed. Once the *Algol* was sufficiently far from mass to drop into sub-space, the mysterious power source of the Delbans would be only a couple of hours distant at the most. With Ganser under control and acting as a safe conduct, Glayne saw success dangling just within his fingers.

Yet deep within his nether-mind he felt a twinge of foreboding—as if he had forgotten some vital factor in his calculations. The dim awareness was almost on the threshold of prescience, but it was too indistinct for him to make out clearly. Uneasily he sought to ignore it but could not.

CHAPTER SIX

IN SUB-SPACE, time crept along in low gear. Glayne was aware of the fact that five hours in sub-space corresponded to about forty minutes in flat, normal space due to the difference in time rates. But time was time, whether fast or slow. General Hoteh Ganser also realized that time was passing; in fact, he exerted every effort to increase the length of time the *Algol* would have to remain in subspace.

Sullenly he stared at Brodis and Glayne as they stood over him. There was a hint of amusement in the depths of his peculiar, crimson eyes.

"You deserve congratulations in the success of your attack, Captain Glayne," he said mockingly. "A touch of bravado here, a bit too audacious there…but, all in all, quite well executed. His Excellency will remember it for a long time. In fact, your success now will add to his delight at witnessing your Vibra-Death later."

Glayne suppressed an involuntary shudder. What a fertile imagination the Delban had!

"Shut up!" snapped Brodis with disgust in his voice. "You might as well make it easier for yourself, Ganser. Relax your mind barriers or we will smash them down and drag the information from you. Either way, we'll get it in the end."

Ganser sneered at the young Guardian.

"I can loosen him up with some physical persuasion, Captain," suggested Brodis hopefully.

Ganser made an obscene remark that brought Brodis to his feet, enraged. The young officer was on the verge of clobbering him with a meaty fist, but Glayne stopped him.

"Such an old veteran as the General is certain to have taken the precaution of having automatic anesthesia cultures introduced into his blood stream," he said. "He would like nothing better than to have you strike him because the sustained trauma of physical pain would trigger the anesthesia and make him unconscious for as long as forty-eight hours."

Ganser made a mocking bow to Glayne.

The Guardian Captain rubbed his cheek wearily. Nothing else but the Ganser conditioner probe now, he realized. He caught Brodis' eye and moved his head slightly in the direction of the gleaming mass of coils and the huge helmet that was the Ganser conditioner.

Brodis nodded. With the aid of a couple of the technicians he set the helmet down carefully over the General's bald pate.

"Have you ever tried these wonderful treatments of yours, General?" Brodis inquired with clinical detachment. "They eliminate all your worries in instants, I understand. They can even make a new man of you, I'm told."

Ganser remained obstinately silent as the massive helmet was adjusted about his head and clamped to the chair in which he was secured. In spite of himself Glayne admired the Delban's strength of will. He, if anyone, should know the mental anguish of the conditioner. But now it was dog eat dog, kill or be killed, and the devil take the hindmost. He nodded imperceptibly to Brodis who was waiting for the signal to begin.

Hours passed and Glayne cursed each inexorable minute. He and Brodis and the four grey-faced technicians were wet with perspiration. Ganser drooped in the chair, but his crimson eyes still blazed with fanatical hatred.

"Lord, what barriers..." whispered Brodis. He stared with fascination at the indomitable Delban.

"What is the power source?" Glayne asked repeatedly, holding his face impassive through sheer force of will. "You want to help us, Guardian. Tell us about the broadcast power."

The conditioned self was slowly beginning to take shape in Ganser's mind. It offered a new set of values, new goals and desires, uppermost of which was to give all possible aid to the Stellar Guardians. Thus the Ganser-personality they were so painstakingly superimposing upon the Delban was almost that of a Stellar Guardian. Gradually they saw it appear in the Delban's crimson eyes.

"The Tane Jewel," he whispered. "Found it in space...no bigger than a Terran grapefruit. Engineers...found way to drain its power potential ...almost infinite."

The Tane! The Flame-Jewel of the Elder Tane!

GLAYNE was stunned. He remembered the legends he had heard of the incredible Tane—weird creatures who had ruled the Galaxy long before the existence of protein life forms. He even recalled the tales of their fabulous Second Universe in which they had sought refuge in order to maintain an artificial stasis and escape extermination. Ever since the discovery of the Tane legends, scientists had speculated about the Second Universe and the titanic source of power it represented. And now it had been found by the Delban Empire and was at the disposal of Gort Bro-Doral.

What had Ganser called it? A *Jewel*—and no larger than a grapefruit! Incredulously Glayne snapped a glance at one of the technicians who was watching the jerking movements of the lie detector stylus on its graphed scroll. The man looked up and nodded, his mouth a tight line across his face.

Glayne turned back to the Delban prisoner. "Where is the power broadcast from, Guardian?" he asked urgently.

"Tjadlinn," muttered Ganser, under the control of a pseudo-Guardian personality. "Jorger Sun...deep helio orbit. The planetless Jorger Sun—remember, we were commissioned to clear it of meteor drift. Later *they* built the Tjadlinn discoid around the Jewel..."

Glayne smiled mirthlessly. So the Delbans had planted the Jewel right under their noses. Yet what more logical place! He recalled the job he had supervised there five years before. The Delbans were going to build a power research station in an orbit about the planetless sun—a practice common in many Sectors.

Glayne tensed as he leaned toward Ganser to ask a third question. It was the crucial one and the others knew it. There was a hushed silence as Glayne asked:

"What is the frequency of the Jewel power broadcast? What do you know about the design of the mesh receiving antennae? Tell us, Guardian. We need your help."

Silence followed Glayne's question. It lengthened and became unbearable.

At last: "The mesh antennae are manufactured at the secret Karkara Fleet Station on Scone III. It is defended by Jewel powered Kellander batteries in addition to secondary auxiliary projectors. The approach code is not available to me. Neither is there information available on broadcast frequencies or antenna design."

Glayne smashed his fist against his leg in violent disappointment. The facts were simply not available in Ganser's mind, so the pseudo-Guardian personality naturally failed to produce them. Again Glayne felt a twinge of respect for the Delban. If anyone knew the technical secrets of the Jewel broadcast, it should have been Ganser. But the Delban's wily cunning had thwarted them. He had carefully avoided all technical knowledge of the Jewel, anticipating an attempt to drain his mind.

There was only one course open to him now. Attack Tjadlinn! He looked at his wrist-chrono. Twelve hours they had spent in this nether-space! It was inconceivable. Glayne swore to himself and thought furiously.

According to Ganser, the mass of the Tjadlinn discoid was too slight to maintain an interstellar telephone; only message craft connected it with the rest of Bro-Doral's empire. That was a break, thought Glayne. In spite of the time they had spent in sub-space, they might still reach Jorger Sun before a warning came from Sterle II. With Ganser under their control and posing as a guide, they could bluff through the outer defenses of the Jewel station. Once inside, they would have to take the breaks as they came.

His shoulders suddenly sagged at the appalling decision he would have to make. Once within the discoid, he would be cut off from outside communication and could not warn the fleet if anything went wrong. On the other hand, the fleet had to be standing by or there was no possible chance of success. Desperately he sought for alternatives to his scheme but none presented themselves. The Terran Combine's last chance rested within his own hands, he realized grimly. An immediate decision had to be made. But if he failed...

With sudden resolve he crushed out his burning doubts and turned to Brodis. "Take the fastest flier we have, dope yourself up with verchromynal, and go to the Stellar Guardian Communication Station at Zandrome. They generate enough power there to push a message over the interstellar telephone to Dorleb in thirty-five minutes. Contact Admiral Garstow. Give him all the information we have and tell him that Scone III will be without Jewel power in forty-eight hours. Have him advise Admiral Bardled of the Terran Fleet that his aid is essential. Inform Garstow that every available fleet unit must be at Scone III in forty-eight hours. Hurry!"

Brodis reached the door in one jump and was halfway down the corridor in another. Glayne watched him go, bleakly phrasing the rest of the message under his breath. *Garstow,* he thought, *you will be slaughtered if there's one tiny slip on my part. It's good you don't know about it.*

Then Glayne shrugged and went up to the navigation bridge.

JORGER SUN was barely visible through the glassene observation ports. But it blew up hugely in Glayne's auxiliary battle screen—a white dwarf of brilliant intensity and a temperature equal to that of the greatest white super-giants in the main galaxy. It was incredibly *alone* out on the furthest reaches of the vast, trailing arms of the galaxy.

The *Algol* was decelerating as it flashed toward Jorger Sun. Somewhere behind it was the Tjadlinn discoid built around the fabulous Tane Jewel. It would look strange, Glayne knew, if they were detected in a maximum ten G deceleration thrust while on an official inspection tour—especially with their low-gravity guide, General Ganser, aboard.

Commander Graysen approached, shifting his weight from one gnarled leg to the other in the space-man's shuffling gait. His leathery face widened in a rare grin as he reached Glayne. "I should have retired after that last cruise," he wheezed. "Here is Harbin for last minute instructions, Captain."

Glayne nodded to the younger officer.

"Harbin, you will take over when Commander Graysen and I leave with the landing party. If you are fired upon while we are inside the discoid, clear out fast. Take the *Algol* to Scone III as quickly as possible. Warn Admiral Garstow that my plan has failed and that it would be best to disperse all fleet units. Under no conditions are you to attempt battle. Do you understand?"

"Aye, sir!" snapped the youngster. His face worked for an instant, but he suppressed his protest and brought himself under control.

"Destination in sight, Captain Glayne," called the pilot over the communicator.

"Cut deceleration to four G's." To Graysen, "How is Ganser?"

"In excellent shape—even his face. According to Psych he is completely under control."

Glayne turned back to his screen and stared at the expanding Tjadlinn discoid. Instinctively he looked for the slim and deadly Jewel-powered cruisers that would be waiting for them if a warning had reached Tjadlinn. But of course he saw nothing. If they were there, they would be masked by inert detector screens, waiting for him to approach so closely that no amount of frantic acceleration could tear him from their grasp.

The discoid was a huge thing of beralloy, all of ten kilometers in diameter. About halfway from the center he could make out the landing dock as Ganser had indicated. He could also make out the evil snouts of Kellander projectors sprouting in dusters on Tjadlinn's metallic surface. Even as he watched, they wheeled about ominously, coming to bear on the decelerating *Algol*. Were they simply taking precautions, Glayne wondered, or were they cagily waiting for him to climb right down the barrels of their projectors?

As he stood alone before the battle screen he suddenly felt a small hand touch his. He looked around. It was Niala Chodred, subdued and somewhat apprehensive. She looked up at him intently, forcing him to meet her eyes.

"I believe you are planning to leave me behind in the ship when you land at Tjadlinn, aren't you?"

Glayne winced at the slight accusation in her eyes. A sudden wave of nervous irritation welled up in him and he was on the verge of hurling a curse at her and driving her back to her quarters. But the tenderness in her eyes made him feel guilty because of his hasty mood and he relented.

"Yes," he said. "I'm very sorry. The ship is unsafe enough as it is, but down there..." He gestured at the image of Tjadlinn in the screen. "...down there will be fighting and certainly many casualties."

"But if I am present," she pointed out logically, "they will be much less likely to suspect you of hostile intentions."

"How do you think I would feel if you were killed down there?" Glayne asked, avoiding her eyes.

"How do you think I would feel if *you* were?" she countered.

Glayne turned to her, about to point out another difficulty, then said nothing. Suddenly she was in his arms and he felt his senses swim at her touch. For a timeless instant he forgot everything but the warm, laughing, green-eyed Niala whom he held in his arms.

CHAPTER SEVEN

TJADLINN WAS GIGANTIC. It rotated on its central axis once every forty hours and completed a revolution about Jorger Sun once every eighty-five years. The orbit was like that of a comet; at perihelion its velocity approached seventy miles per second. Now it had begun its journey away from the sun, swinging out into the infinite blackness of the lonely void.

Grimly the Guardian Captain looked at his crewmen, sturdy big-planet men like himself. There were six of them. Glayne wondered how many would be left when they returned—if they ever did return. He looked at the girl and wondered if she would return. She smiled at him as the artificial planetoid loomed hugely over their tiny landing launch. He felt no regret that she was along—his mind ignored all such feelings of that nature now. Instead it was concentrated to the highest degree of receptivity, sorting and classifying the sense impressions that came to it.

The massive beralloy portals of the outer air-lock gaped open at them and the launch jetted inside. Then they closed with a thunderous clang and the inner doors slid open in an oddly obsequious fashion. They were much less ponderous than the outer doors, Glayne noted. A moment later the launch came to rest and General Hoteh Ganser, Chief of Delban Intelligence, stalked out of the cabin followed by representatives of the Stellar Guardians, now allied with the Delban Empire.

There was a group of high-ranking Delban Army and Fleet officers awaiting them as they stepped from the launch. They bowed ceremoniously to Ganser, then to Glayne and his party as they were introduced. The Guardian smiled, he bowed, he clicked his heels solemnly—but all the time his hand was casually resting inside of the fold of his jumper on the Cardy gun there.

The only name Glayne remembered was that of the commander of Tjadlinn discoid: Admiral Selzi-Narfid, Right Royal Protector of the Emperor's Hunting Preserves. But he was not notable because of his absurd title; rather, it was the hint of amusement that Glayne fancied he saw flickering in the depths of his jet black eyes.

It was Selzi-Narfid who turned to Ganser and said, "I'm sure you must be weary after your arduous journey, Your Excellency. Won't you and Captain Glayne and his party partake of some refreshment?"

Glayne frowned. That was not so good. They could not afford to waste time eating and drinking because the message craft might bring the warning from Sterle II at any minute. Yet how could they refuse?

Evidently this same train of thought flashed through the conditioned intellect of General Ganser. For just an instant he paused before saying yes, they would be delighted.

Again Selzi-Narfid bowed and this time Glayne was positive he saw mockery in the Tjadlinn commander's eyes. Following him, they entered a large mono-car poised on its single, gleaming span by gyros. It started with a jolt, picked up speed, and was presently bulleting down the tunnel, the walls a blur on either side. To Glayne it almost seemed as if they were moving downhill.

"You will notice the gravity attraction increasing as we progress," began Selzi-Narfid. "That is because we are approaching the Jewel. It is considerably more comfortable in my quarters close to the center. On the periphery of the discoid one has almost no weight because of the distance from the Jewel.

"No one knows the exact mass of the Tane Jewel. Probably around two hundred million tons, it is thought. Naturally it is not safe to approach too closely—the inverse square law, you know. Within a few meters the attraction is so tremendous that we have great difficulty in anchoring the power drain machinery. But you will see for yourself in the Jewel Chamber."

The mono-car sighed to a halt and Selzi-Narfid ushered them graciously into a tapestried corridor. Glayne noticed that the gravity was just about Terran Standard. He also noticed that Selzi-Narfid, in spite of his flow of suave conversation, was worried. Suddenly a peculiar sensation of wrongness flared up in Glayne's mind and he knew that his battle-trained, preternatural intuition was at work. His hand tightened on the Cardy and his eyes flickered everywhere but could discover nothing.

At the wide entrance stage the Admiral held back, gesturing for Ganser, Glayne, and the others to precede him.

The small hairs on the back of Glayne's neck arose as they entered the luxurious suite of the Tjadlinn commander. Something was definitely very wrong.

THEN sick dismay scalded up in the pit of his stomach. He saw what was wrong. It was Gort Bro-Doral who faced them, a Cardy gun in his hand.

Calmly the Delban Overlord fired at Ganser. The energy beam lashed into the pseudo-Guardian, making a big, ragged hole where his belly had been.

Glayne could do nothing more than stare helplessly. He did not even think to resist when the room filled with armed Delbans who went about the job of disarming them in a very silent and efficient fashion.

"Such a pity," remarked Gort Bro-Doral, glancing down at Ganser's charred and crumpled body. "Hoteh was my right hand, but the poor wretch was just too thorough. His own mind conditioning device caught him in the end." He produced his sickly, explosive laugh and inclined his head to one of the armed Delbans. "Take it away," he murmured.

"How did you get here so quickly?" Glayne said, asking the question uppermost in his mind. He was bewildered to think of the incredible acceleration the low-gravity Delban must have undergone to have beaten the Guardian ship.

"Another of the wonders of the glorious Tane Jewel," replied Bro-Doral with amused condescension. "Theoretically it was always possible to project material bodies into sub-space directly from planetary mass in the same way that the immaterial waves of an interstellar telephone message are cast directly into sub-space. Heretofore, however, there has never been sufficient power to form a shield around the material object strong enough to prevent its being completely crushed by the brutal space warp in the presence of mass. That difficulty vanishes when one has the unlimited power of the Tane Jewel at his disposal."

Glayne understood. Ganser, who had meticulously avoided all technical knowledge, did not know this. Consequently they had walked straight into a trap. Glayne's shoulders sagged as he looked around, savoring the taste of defeat. Tough old Graysen stood at his side, impotently balling his fists. His carefully picked crewmen were behind him, arms above their heads. They looked grim and ready for anything. But Niala...

Glayne fought down the painful lump in his throat. It made no difference. They had the *Algol* too. So it mattered not at all whether she came along or stayed behind, he told himself. They had only one thing to look forward to—and that would be unpleasant. Surreptitiously he touched the massive ring on his hand. It contained a single blaster charge. Shakily he resolved to use it on Niala when it came to that.

Bro-Doral whinnied. "I have your day planned for you, Captain," he said. "I have often been accused of lacking a sense of justice, but you will see for yourself that such a charge wrongs me. Your men will be executed as humanly as possible. You and the esteemed Graysen will be given a chance to witness the destruction of your ship. And then—" the Delban snickered, "—the Vibra-Death! The girl...I'm not sure. Yes, it will take some thought. But you may be sure that it will be interesting."

Bro-Doral's sadism was too much for Glayne. With a snarl of animal hatred he leaped at the Delban Overlord, brushing aside his Cardy gun and reaching for his throat. The force of his lunge carried them back a few steps and the Bro tripped. Glayne, blazing with blind rage, lifted his foot to crush the Bro like a worm. At that instant a cold beam lanced into his back. Its icy fingers played along his spine and paralyzed him with numbness. Helplessly his arms fell to his sides and two of the armed Delbans came up behind him, supporting him to prevent his falling.

Gort Bro-Doral clambered up from the floor. His heavily-veined eyes were red with insane ferocity. He thrust his contorted face close to Glayne's own and said, "Guardian, you will now be extended another privilege. You will be permitted to see the girl writhing in the agonies of the Vibra-Death!"

Bro-Doral turned to one of his men. "Take those crewmen away—execute them," he said. "Keep the girl here under guard while I show the two officers around."

Glayne was horrified at the fruits of his unthinking attack on the Bro. It was almost as if he himself had pulled the switch which would subject Niala to the most infamous nerve torture ever devised. Dully he realized that he could not even lift his hand to administer a merciful death with the clean, fast energy beam of his ring.

"The paralysis will wear off in a minute or two, Captain," observed Bro-Doral. He had completely regained his self-control. "Since you have exerted so much useless effort to destroy our Tane Jewel, I think you ought to at least be permitted to see it. But after that…" He sighed expressively. "…after that, we will procrastinate no longer."

Even before the effects of the cold beam had worn off completely, Bro-Doral nodded to his men and they took him by the arms and escorted him from the room. In despair, Glayne tried to jerk his head around to see the girl. For the briefest of instants he saw her smiling bravely at him. Then his view was cut off by the door as the guards maneuvered his still half paralyzed frame around it.

In a couple of moments Glayne was able to move under his own power. He turned to find Graysen staring anxiously at him, alert for the slightest command. Glayne nodded imperceptibly and examined the guards. There were six of them. He noticed wryly that they held cold-beam weapons in their long-fingered fists while the ones that really produced the fatal damage—the Cardys—hung in holsters at their sides. Trust them not to risk killing their prisoners when so many more delightful methods presented themselves, he thought bitterly.

AS HE and Graysen were led side-by-side down a maze of corridors, their weight gradually increased. Along with it was the sensation of going downhill. Glayne's mind operated rapidly and with cold precision but the Delbans showed not the slightest weakness. Not even the increase in gravity seemed to annoy them. Nevertheless, Glayne resolved, he would risk everything on a sudden attack when they got as close to the jewel as possible. There the conditions would be ideal for him. With eyes narrowed, he tried desperately to remember the turns they had taken through the winding corridors of the beralloy discoid.

As they progressed, Glayne saw the tough, all-metal walls were more heavily buttressed with the massive beralloy supports. Selzi-Narfid saw the direction of his glance and said, "Those were necessary when we maneuvered the Jewel into the center of the discoid. You have no idea of what such a tremendous mass in a body the size of the Jewel can do when it is not balanced."

Glayne listened to the Admiral with just a part of his mind. His main attention was devoted to photographing mentally the warren of passages. Here and there he saw groups of Delban technicians, none of them armed.

Good, thought Glayne.

They reached the entrance stage of the Jewel Chamber. The beralloy walls here were neatly a meter thick. In single file the party crawled through the narrow opening that dilated ponderously in the entrance stage. Two very weary-looking guards snapped to attention as they passed, but almost immediately slumped back into their somnolent positions, exhausted by their abnormally increased weight.

Better yet; thought Glayne.

"This is the Jewel Chamber, Captain. It is the very heart of Tjadlinn," puffed Selzi-Narfid after he had crawled through the dilated entrance stage.

Glayne stared about the vaulted room curiously. It was shaped like the inside of an oval, thick at the center but tapering off to nothing at the sides. They were standing on a balcony, which was heavily buttressed and ran all the way around the Chamber past several other massive portals. In the exact center of the Chamber a kind of a nest was formed by the tremendously thick beralloy girders. Something burned there with a cold, golden brilliance that filtered through the interstices of the girders and etched them sharply in banded shadows about the heavy walls.

An uncanny sensation possessed Glayne as he gazed at the Jewel. A vague dread passed over him and he found himself wondering if the Elder Tane Gods would emerge from their crypt and wreak hideous vengeance on mere mortals for disturbing their sleep. Uneasily he crushed the fantasy that was rioting up in his mind and determined to look for something more practical.

He concentrated on the power drain machinery that hung in clusters from the massive girders. Obviously those mechanisms were far more delicate than their supports and could be sabotaged with comparatively little work. As he calculated he gradually became aware of Bro-Doral who was speaking:

"—were remarkable creatures. As you know, Tane legends exist in every part of the known galaxy. They even possessed immortality—but they lost it for all practical purposes when they failed to adjust their bodies to the expanding universe.

"While the universe expands, quanta emission frequencies remain constant. You are familiar, of course, with the shift in the wavelength of the cadmium spectrum, taken over the centuries. Ages ago, emission frequencies were so long, relatively speaking, that energy liberation from protein organisms was impossible. That definitely rules out protein construction for the Tane—but just what they were composed of is unknown. At any rate, their bodies couldn't stand the shortened emission frequencies that overloaded their muscles. They exploded. Like a plague. Billions and billions of them must have died before they discovered the answer to the strange death that was striking among them. And billions more must have died before their marvelous science was able to build the Second Universe, as the legends call it."

Gort Bro-Doral gestured at the Jewel, which shed its cold, brilliant light about the Chamber.

"They enclosed themselves in that tiny ovoid crypt you see there," he went on. That was countless ages ago. Somehow they had managed to construct shields capable of withstanding the spatial expansion of the universe. Who knows—they may still live in their static crypt?

"As millions and millions of years passed, the Tane Jewel—the Second Universe, as the legends call it—slowly dwindled in size when considered in relation to our own universe. As it dwindled, its energy potential grew. Now its accumulated charge is so titanic that it defies conception.

"Someday those beautiful engines of the Tane Gods would have run down and the shield would have collapsed. Then our own universe would have been destroyed. The sudden release of such a vast energy potential would have caused a concussion that would literally warp our flat space into the fourth-dimensional sub-space.

"Now that can't happen. We are draining off that infinite potential and broadcasting it—flooding it—through sub-space to be received everywhere there is a Delban receiving antenna. The power is limitless. We Delbans will be the rulers of the universe just as the Tane Gods were of old. There is no limit to our power…"

Bro-Doral's eyes blazed with a pure lust for power as he stared exultantly at the green brilliance of the Tane Jewel. His mouth was slack and he breathed heavily from the effort of his speech. Selzi-Narfid, too, was tired. Wearily he rested against the support rail of the balcony. The guards blinked their large pop-eyes from fatigue, shuffling from one foot to another to promote circulation. Most of them had placed their weapons in holsters as Bro-Doral talked. That is, all except one. He still held his weapon loosely in his fingers at his side. Slowly and gently Glayne poised, gathering his strength.

"Isn't it beautiful, Glayne?" mused the Delban Overlord, staring into the tiny radiant sun. "An artifact of the mightiest culture that ever existed. Now we will carry on in their footsteps. We will be the mightiest—"

CHAPTER EIGHT

THEN GLAYNE LEAPED. With one flailing fist he caught the Delban guard on his bony jaw and with the other he snatched the cold beam gun from his limp fingers. Whirling, he played it among the stupefied guards. Then old Grayson exploded into action, seizing Selzi-Narfid and hurling him bodily at Bro-Doral who was in the act of bringing up his Cardy gun. Three of the guards had collapsed and another was crumpling on his knees under Glayne's cold beam. The other two had crouched back in the shadows of the entrance portal, trying to bring their weapons to bear upon Glayne.

Graysen whirled and lunged at them, smashing one down with a single blow. The last guard on his feet, surprised and dismayed by this attack from the rear, fled to the portal and tried to dilate it. But he was too late and sagged in a heap under Glayne's hand weapon.

Scooping up two of the Cardy guns which had fallen to the balcony floor, Glayne shouted, "Pick up an energy gun, Graysen. Cut down the power drain machinery."

Graysen reached for an energy gun in the holster of one of the paralyzed guards. He never even saw Gort Bro-Doral scramble to his feet and fire point blank. His head disappeared as the Delban's beam struck full force. Glayne fired back wildly but he was off balance and missed. Before he could collect himself to fire again, Bro-Doral had fled to another stage and darted through the dilation.

Glayne whirled toward the Delbans. Selzi-Narfid had a broken neck and was obviously dead. The guards were all unconscious and would remain so for a long time.

Glayne turned back to the Jewel, which cast its chill, gold light steadily through the interstices of the surrounding girders. Calmly he leveled the Cardy gun and fired at it. As if it were so much water, the deadly little energy beam washed off the Tane Jewel and fused with the beralloy supports. It was as he had expected. Given several hours, the little hand weapon might have made an impression on the incredibly tough beralloy but Glayne had no time to lose.

As he had seen before, the power drain machinery that hung in clusters from the big beams and transmitted the energy through the heavy busbars looked to be the most fragile. Glayne wondered what would happen if he fired into them. There was only one way to find out. The muscles of his jaw hardened as he depressed the firing stud on the Cardy.

Nothing happened. He let the beam of his energy gun play up and down the clusters of power drains, fusing them into slag. Now the thin, invisible rays of power that the drains extracted from the Jewel no longer existed since they had no place to go. But nothing happened.

Then it occurred to him that nothing would happen in the Jewel Chamber itself. It needed no power for lights—the Jewel provided all the light needed. Heartened, Glayne blasted at every drain in reach, following the balcony around the Chamber.

But even this method, he realized, would take too long. Gort Bro-Doral would soon have squads of men hurrying into the Chamber after him. Grimly he wished he had an energy bomb. With one of those he could finish the job in a few seconds.

Suddenly he remembered an old Guardian trick. Hurriedly he began to tinker with one of the Cardy guns. By jamming a couple of the safety gadgets, it was possible to make the weapon fire out of phase. When the trigger stud was depressed, its tiny miatron coils would build up an unstable load in a couple of seconds, then explode. Quickly he fixed the weapon to his satisfaction, then hurried on around the balcony to find a suitable opening in the girders through which to hurl the ersatz bomb.

Halfway around, he met two panic-stricken Delban technicians. The instant they saw him they turned tail and ran back through the portal. Obviously something must be happening, Glayne thought with grim satisfaction. Then he found a good spot, pressed the firing stud of the doctored Cardy gun, then flung it with all his strength into the remaining power drains. In an instant he had pivoted and lunged for the port of the entrance stage behind him, feeling in the shadow for its dilator stud.

It refused to open!

Obviously Glayne himself had sabotaged its power circuit. Now he was trapped in the Chamber and the ersatz bomb was about to explode. Tensely he crouched as far back in the recess of the port as he could and waited. With a terrific roar the bomb exploded in the confined Chamber, rupturing the membranes of his nose and crushing him violently against the port. Parts of the devastated power drains were hurled against the massive walls, then fell back to the Jewel. One of the heavy busbars had collapsed, ripping festoons of cables from the top of the Chamber, which shorted violently against one another.

Dazed, Glayne pulled himself to his feet. Fortunately he had broken no bones. But one of his ear drums was ruptured and his nose bled unremittingly. He had lost his other Cardy. Hurriedly he felt about, found it, and thrust it into the fold of his tattered jumper.

He turned back to the portal and found that the concussion had dilated it for him. Breathing heavily, he crawled through it into the inky blackness of the passages. On all sides he heard the sound of running footsteps. By touch he staggered into the blackness, realizing that he must keep going uphill, away from the Jewel's attraction.

The exertion cleared his head a bit. He knew he was lost, but he hoped to be able to find his way back to Selzi-Narfid's quarters. There he would find Niala and be oriented with the rest of the discoid.

Figures bumped into him in the blackness, hurrying to the scene of destruction. The Delbans were badly disorganized. Obviously they had not been prepared to cope with such devastation wreaked on their sacred Jewel. Not even to the extent of auxiliary power for lights, he thought as he panted up the black passages.

EVEN as he thought about it, the lights began to flicker weakly in their fluorescent tubes, growing stronger with each passing second. Startled, Glayne crouched back in the shadow of a recess in the wall. That was Luck in all her perversity, he thought grimly. His hand sought the butt of the blaster in his jumper. Fortunately the lights did not wax as brightly as they had when the Jewel was still functioning, but that did not offer much consolation. He would be recognized instantly by the outline of his thick-chested body if he was seen in the corridor.

He noticed that fewer Delbans were passing. He decided to chance it. Tightly grasping the gun in his jumper, he crept from his hiding place and ran on the balls of his feet, dodging and ducking into shadows every time one of the enemy passed. Once he was seen and pursued by a squad of Delban guards. Breathlessly he ran at full tilt through a cross-corridor, up a flight of high steps, and twisted into another of the endless passages of the discoid.

The pull of the Jewel had become very slight. In fact it was much slighter than it had been in Selzi-Narfid's suite. Glayne pushed on, realizing that he was hopelessly lost. His only chance now was to find the mono-rail on which they had ridden from the landing dock to the Tjadlinn commander's suite. It occurred to him that even if he did find Niala, they might never escape Tjadlinn. And it was absolutely imperative that he make contact with Garstow at Scone III. The slightest delay on the part of the Stellar Guardian Admiral in attacking the Karkara Station might give the Delbans the precious time they needed to repair the damage he had affected.

There were two entrance stages, one on either side, in the corridor through which he was hurrying. He tried one and found it was locked. He was more fortunate with the other. It creaked open slowly when he flipped the dilator stud. Tensely, hand on the Cardy gun in his jumper, he crept through the port. It was the landing dock!

Glayne's heart jumped with delight as he crouched back in a shadow and examined the place. Not a hundred meters away was the launch that had brought his party from the *Algol*. His eyes drank it in avidly and a plan for escape formed rapidly in his mind. A message craft of some sort was preparing to leave, he saw. As soon as the inner lock door closed behind it, he would smash the launch through it and the air pressure would fling him out of the discoid. How very simple!

Then the impact of the realization that he would have to leave Niala Chodred behind struck him. He was stunned by its very violence.

Leave Niala? Abandon her to Gort Bro-Doral and his sadistic vengeance for the sabotage Glayne himself had performed? No! That was out of the question. But what of the Terran Combine? What did the life of Citizen Niala Chodred mean against the lives of the trillions who made up that Combine to which she had sworn allegiance? Viewed in that light, it was obvious that the life of one person was a cheap price to pay for security of the Combine against the Tane Jewel.

Glayne crouched in the shadow and buried his face in his hands. In an agony of indecision he prodded his weary mind to discover an alternative to the horrible dilemma. But he could find none. He would have to decide between Niala, the laughing, green-eyed Niala, and the ideal of human progress, which he had sworn the Guardian Oath to protect.

Dully he realized that the power of the abstract was too strong. He would forsake Niala. The pain redoubled itself as he made his decision but he set his face in a granite-mask against it. Unfortunately it was not so easy to quell the agony that burned within him.

Grimly he stood up. He saw that the time had come for action. The message craft was slowly jetting down the cinder blastway toward the lock door. Glayne tensed for an instant, then raced for the launch, covering ten meters at a stride in the light gravity. Three Delban mechanics caught sight of him as he rounded the stubby fins and leaped for the lock. In mid-stride he whipped out his Cardy gun and brought them down in charred heaps.

A guard squad saw him and fired. Their beams sang dangerously close, smashing into the beralloy side of the launch. They crunched down the blastway in pursuit as Glayne jumped through the open lock, slammed it shut, and darted to the controls. The atomic driver engine coughed and surged into life. He let it scream up beyond audibility, then fed power to the jets. The blast washed over the guards who were closest to the launch and the others fell back hastily before its searing heat.

The inner lock of the entrance port had slid shut behind the message craft. It was now or never, Glayne realized. He opened the atomic driver wide and the stubby launch shuddered for an instant, then lunged for the lock. The sudden thrust created constricting hands about Glayne's chest and he fought precariously on the edge of blacking out. For a brief instant Glayne was aware of the huge outer doors swinging shut before him—and then the air pressure struck them and flung the launch bodily through the narrow space left between them.

The launch tumbled crazily end-over-end until Glayne straightened it out and oriented himself with Tjadlinn and

Jorger Sun. He had just sighted the tiny gleaming speck of the *Algol* a dozen kilometers distant when something struck the launch a terrific blow. Almost instantly the telltales indicated air was escaping. Dismayed, Glayne shot a glance over his shoulder at the receding discoid. He discovered that they were firing at him with the secondary Kellander batteries, using auxiliaries to power the miatrons. Feverishly he changed course, zigzagging wildly away from the discoid.

Due to over confidence, the Delbans had not destroyed the *Algol* immediately. They preferred to play cat and mouse. And now, with the titanic energies of the Jewel no longer available to them, they could not destroy the *Algol*.

The Kellander energy beams slashed dangerously close to the fleeing launch. Not in salvoes but by ones and twos. That meant that their fire control was badly disorganized— and it was that fact which saved Glayne. Harbin had raised the *Algol's* anti-shield when the Delbans had commenced firing but he had not turned tail as Glayne had ordered, realizing that the launch was fleeing in his direction.

Glayne flipped the stud of the shield-nullifier that was matched to the frequency of the *Algol's* anti-shield and darted the launch through it, braking with eye-searing blasts of the forward jets as the huge Reception Deck locks yawned open. With a heavy larch, his battered craft came to rest inside the lip of the gaping outer doors.

CHAPTER NINE

THE *ALGOL'S* OFFICERS formed a silent group beneath the huge glassene dome of the navigation bridge. They looked expectantly at Glayne as the elevator port dilated and he approached them, weary and unshaven, his face covered with blood.

Ignoring their unspoken questions, Glayne said brusquely, glancing at the navigation chrono, "Lieutenant Harbin, Compute an orbit for Scone III. Get the ship under way immediately...drop into sub-space at three ten to the seventh kilos from Jorger Sun. Thrust—eight G's."

He was about to turn on his heel when Harbin's hesitant voice stopped him.

"Sir...what...what about Commander Graysen and the others?"

Glayne stared at the youngster bleakly. "Graysen is dead," he said with a flat voice. "So is Ganser. And I presume that our escort has been executed."

Harbin's youthful jaw tightened. "And Lieutenant Chodred?"

The lines about Glayne's mouth deepened. He let his gaze travel over Harbin's troubled face and the impassive faces of the rest of the ship's officers. He saw accusation in their eyes along with resentment and veiled hostility. He knew what they were thinking. Why should he be the only one to return? Why had he abandoned the others? And now they wanted to know what had happened to the girl. So he told them.

"She is still alive." Bitterly he wondered why Fate had designated her to be the only one left to face Gort Bro-Doral's vengeance. He looked up again at the silent cluster of officers. "If your curiosity is satisfied, gentlemen, suppose we get on with the war?"

"If Tjadlinn is without Jewel power," persisted Harbin stubbornly, "why can't we attack? We might be able to rescue Lieutenant Chodred. It's the least we could do—"

"Follow my orders!" Glayne cut in savagely. He turned on his heel and mounted to his shock seat in the Captain's Station. Yes, he thought bitterly, they could attack Tjadlinn, incur heavy damage on the discoid—perhaps even accomplish a miraculous rescue of Niala. But weighed against that was the possibility that the *Algol* might be heavily damaged or destroyed by the highly potent secondary Kellanders of the discoid. Unless he got through to Garstow, the conservative Grand Admiral of the Stellar Guardians was likely to delay his attack on Karkara—and such a delay would be suicidal.

Gradually a floor began to build under his feet and the *Algol* got under way. As the thrust increased, the discoid began to shrink in the distance. Glayne stared at its image grimly in the battle screen. He didn't say farewell because he knew he would be back. He rubbed his bristly cheek. He saw success now. He felt it on the tips of his clutching fingers. But something else was beyond his grasp now—something that made success dry and unpalatable. He covered his eyes with his hand as the thought stabbed him...the laughing, green-eyed Niala...

THE Stellar Guardian fleet lay motionless across forty thousand kilometers of space when the *Algol* reached the rendezvous at Scone III. Admiral Garstow's anxious face formed rapidly in the featureless gray surface of Glayne's ship-to-ship communicator screen.

"Give me a fast, verbal report on the Jewel, Glayne," ordered the Admiral.

The Guardian Captain complied, rapidly sketching the main details of his sabotage and providing a rough outline of the Delban defense of the discoid.

When he finished, Garstow nodded thoughtfully. "Do you think it advisable to risk an immediate attack on the discoid on the chance that we can knock it out before they repair the power drains?"

Glayne frowned, then said, "No. It's too long a chance. They will mass their fleet at Tjadlinn immediately. Under normal circumstances we could lick them, but if they repair that Jewel faster than I expect, then we'll be sitting ducks."

Garstow nodded again. "Lieutenant Brodis informed me of the plan you had in mind of attacking the Karkara Fleet Station on Scone III and thereby acquiring the Jewel power-receiving antennae. On the whole, I think that is the shrewder move. Since you've managed this show up to now, Captain, I think you might as well organize the attack."

"Thank you, sir," Glayne replied. "I'll take my own cruiser division in first to clear away what little resistance they'll put up. That will be the simplest part about it. The real difficulty will come when we install the antennae. As Brodis probably told you, we were unable to get any technical information from General Ganser."

Garstow rubbed his fleshy nose thoughtfully and then said, "It's in your hands, Captain." Then he cut out.

Rapidly Glayne organized the attack, placing his own cruiser division at the point of the spearhead. Smoothly the. Stellar Guardian striking force flashed down on Scone III. As Glayne had anticipated, their sudden assault was little more than an armed landing. The Delbans were caught completely off guard. They put up a fanatical resistance with the auxiliary powered Kellander secondary batteries, but the superior weight of Glayne's miatron blasters soon crushed every last shred of opposition.

As soon as the *Algol* had jetted down on the immense spaceport of the Karkara Fleet Station, a group of technicians in addition to the landing party raced off to confiscate an antennae unit for the big ship. Glayne set up an operations unit in the glassene dome of the *Algol* to assign landing patterns to the other Guardian fleet units. The heaviest Ouster and Galactic class warships he assigned to fast orbits about Scone to defend the ships that had already landed.

After he saw that landing operations were proceeding smoothly he descended to the engine room of the *Algol* to see how the installation of the antenna was progressing. Massive cables snaked across the deck in confusions, waiting to be hooked into the heavy buses that the technicians were jockeying into place. Outside on the hull, gangs of men were welding in the mesh antenna. Fuming, he looked at his wrist-chrono repeatedly.

"How much longer?" he asked Harbin impatiently.

"Thirty minutes at the most, sir," replied Harbin stiffly, refusing to meet Glayne's eyes.

Glayne rubbed his bristly cheek thoughtfully as he turned away. The young officer was determined to give him the silent treatment along with the rest of the officers in his crew. Word would spread; soon the whole fleet would hear of his cowardly negligence. He smiled thinly as he made his way back up to the navigation bridge. He had seen it happen before. There were just two ways to escape it. One was retirement. The other involved a Cardy gun placed at the temple...

The red light of his personal communicator was blinking intermittently when he regained the bridge. It was Garstow.

"Glayne!" he barked abruptly. "Bardled is on his way in with the fleet of Imperial Terra. And a dozen other Sectors have massed their fleets and are on the way, too."

"Excellent," said Glayne. "We're working faster now. We've put the Delban technicians to work and repaired the damage to their assembly lines. We ought to be able to handle a thousand ships an hour. How long before Bardled will arrive?"

"Four hours...maybe six."

"I'm lifting in a few minutes," Glayne said. "When Bardled arrives, install the units in his heavy ships first.

Those tubs will smash the Tjadlinn anti-shield if anything will."

Rapidly Glayne went on to sketch his plan of attack. When he finished, Garstow nodded ponderously. "Then we will subspace as soon as we pick up the power broadcast. A sound strategy, Captain. Good luck." His face faded from the screen.

THE FIRST of the big Cluster class battleships were easing down on vast fingers of flame when Harbin reported that the work of installation was complete. In quick succession the other cruisers of his division reported readiness and he gave the command to blast off.

The *Algol* was almost two hundred million kilos below Scone System's plane of ecliptic when the hastily installed antenna unit began to pick up the first surges of power from the Tane Jewel. Cautiously the *Algol's* pilot experimented with it, accustoming himself to unlimited power at his finger tips. One by one, the ship's atomic drivers fell silent as the pilot gained confidence.

"Raise the anti-shield, Lieutenant Harbin," Glayne said crisply over his inter-ship phone. "We'll sub-space right now."

Harbin's image stared at him incredulously from the communicator screen for an instant but he fought down the words that trembled on his lips.

"Aye, sir," he snapped.

Glayne was grimly amused at his anxiety but said nothing to relieve it. They were dangerously close to mass, he knew, but if Gort Bro-Doral could blast into sub-space directly from Sterle II with a shield supported by Jewel power, then he ought to be able to get away with it at two hundred million kilos from mass.

Briefly Glayne communicated his intent to the commanders of the thirty other cruisers in his division and their anti-shields began to build. At his curt command they dropped smoothly into sub-space, their shield generators heating up slightly as the sudden strain hit them.

They plunged on through sub-space, building up to incredible velocities in that nether dimension where such commonplace things as mass and light did not exist. Glayne's mind worked rapidly, analyzing his plan of battle for any defects. Obviously the enemy would mass his fleet at the all-important Tjadlinn. If his calculations were correct, his cruiser division would pop into normal space right among them. If they struck fast enough, they could disorganize the Delbans sufficiently for Garstow and Bardled to get in among them with the heavy units of their fleets. And that, he knew, would be the end of the Delban Grand Fleet.

The discoid was another matter. Paradoxically, it contained within it the very source of the power which they would use to destroy it. The only possible way the Delbans could deprive them of the Jewel power would be to turn off the non-directional broadcast entirely. That, however, would leave them open to an attack by the regular miatron batteries of the heavy Guardian and Terran battleships. They could not possibly hope to beat off such an attack with their Kellander secondaries. Hence, Glayne reasoned, they would keep up the power broadcast at all costs.

Satisfied with his plan, Glayne let his mind relax and drift where it wanted. Abruptly it turned to thoughts of Niala Chodred and he winced at the pain which filled him. Grimly, he realized that if the silent treatment by his fellow officers failed to ruin him, the bitter acid of remorse that burned his soul would certainly accomplish the job.

CHAPTER TEN

ONE INSTANT THE FLEET of the Delban Empire was assembling about the vital Tjadlinn discoid in an orderly fashion. An instant later all hell broke loose amid its massed ranks.

Glayne's cruiser division popped out of sub-space at two hundred kilometers per second and flailed through the Delbans like a giant scythe. His eyes glued to the small battle screen in front of him, Glayne clipped off rapid commands over the ship-to-ship communicator that kept him in touch with the rest of his group.

Three Delban warships—one a battleship—had been caught with their shields down and were now exploding enthusiastically in nova-fashion. A dozen others had been heavily damaged by the slashing miatron beams as they vainly sought to lift their shields.

The *Algol* screamed in protest as the pilot flung her around to bore in again. Her armored hide seemed to crawl in squealing agony at the twenty G turn. Glayne panted, on the verge of blacking out. Dimly he glimpsed the strained features of the pilot wracked with spasms of coughing that flung lobs of blood and lung tissue against the terraced banks of instruments at his side...

Then they were among the Delbans again, slashing right and left with Kellander miatron beams. This time the Delbans were ready for them and replied with a vengeance. Torrents of energy smashed at the *Algol's* shield, which shuddered like a live thing under the impact. Behind Glayne a knot of sweating gunnery officers rattled off firing data to waiting Kellander crews before the mammoth battle screen. Somewhere in the bowels of the ship the accumulators were screaming as they fed the Jewel energies from the antenna to the smoking banks of shield generators and the ravenous Kellander condensers. But dominating the ear-splitting crescendo of the *Algol* in full fighting stride was the continuous, ravening thunder of Kellander projectors as they flung their blasts at the Delban warships.

Glayne saw that his division had scattered widely—but, at the same time, the disorganization of the Delbans was even more evident. Unaware that the sudden attack was a feint to draw them away from Tjadlinn, a dozen Delban fleet divisions abandoned the Jewel to join the fray.

As the Guardian Captain scanned the screen, he saw that the tide was fast running in favor of the Delbans. The *Ansa* was finished for the day. A flotilla of swift Delban destroyers had darted in with mines and torpedoes, one of which had gotten through her shield and exploded with a devastating energy concussion against her stern, sheering off plates and jet tubes by it force. The *Altor* and *Astrid* were cornered by a dozen Delban Galactics and Ousters and their shields coruscated in brilliant hues as they trembled on the point of collapse. A third Guardian ship, the *Aesir,* blasted in to offer aid and even as Glayne watched, hurled her energies in a concerted salvo at a point just below the jets of one of the Delban Ousters. Its shield coruscated brilliantly, tottered, and suddenly it was strewing its guts, nova-fashion. Almost immediately the *Aesir* followed her example as a salvo of Galactic beams struck her amidships, rupturing her shield. A torpedo ripped into the bridge of the *Astrid* and she exploded in an eye-searing nova. The *Altor* managed to limp away in the confusion, her beralloy hide mangled and torn from a near miss.

The *Algol* herself was in trouble. Two Delban Stellars were hurling torrents of energy at her shield, making it coruscate in a blaze of overloaded power foci. A pack of destroyers was circling hungrily, looking for a chance to dart in and plant their seeds of destruction. The pilot maneuvered desperately, but the overloaded power lines could not shunt sufficient power through the drivers to pull them out of their difficulty.

Glayne swore, wondering where the rest of the fleet was. It couldn't go on much longer. The *Akkad* had novaed; the *Ashlar* and *Asgard* had disappeared without leaving a trace. Only six of his original thirty were in fighting shape—and even as he watched he had to revise it to five. The *Atlas*, surrounded by a dozen enemies, exploded in nova-fashion as her shield collapsed.

And then the void was suddenly full of great warships bearing the Guardian and Terran insignia, appearing magically in the midst of the Delbans. What had appeared to be triumph suddenly turned into a rout for the Delbans. Badly disorganized, they attempted to flee back to the safety of the mighty Kellander projectors of Tjadlinn.

BUT Glayne's annihilated cruiser division had done its work well; the Delbans, drawn too far from the discoid, were cut off by the fleets that opposed them. They fought desperately and fanatically, but there was only one possible outcome. One after another they exploded nova-fashion as the massed salvos of the tremendous Terran and Guardian battleships swept aside their shields and touched destructive fingers to their beralloy sides.

Glayne's ship-to-ship suddenly crackled into life and Garstow's heavy face appeared on the screen. "My boy," he boomed, "I'm proud of you. Excellent work! We've bagged them all at almost no cost. Bardled tells me he didn't lose a ship."

Glayne gazed stupidly at him for a moment before he could adjust himself to the idea of victory. Then he said quietly, "I have five ships left out of a command of thirty."

"Oh...oh that's too bad," mumbled Garstow, his broad face becoming serious. "What I mean to say is—"

"The chaplain will say what needs to be said," Glayne cut in with unnecessary bitterness. "If you still want me to run this show, then I submit that we attack Tjadlinn without delay."

Admiral Garstow nodded, his face like a deflated balloon.

Quickly Glayne outlined his plan for the assault on the discoid itself. The battle would be fought between the Kellander accumulator and condenser capacity of the massed fleets and the total generator capacity of the mighty anti-shield which the Delbans would raise from the discoid. If the Delban shield capacity was less than the massed strength of the fleet, then the discoid would be destroyed. But if the Delbans held them off, they would try something else.

It took several hours to assemble the scattered and highly numerous Terran and Guardian warships into a closely-integrated formation. Matters were not helped by the appearance of dozens of warships from the fleets of other Sectors. They roamed about searching for enemy stragglers, but succeeded only in getting in the way. Finally, however, Glayne got them organized and the enormous fleet moved ponderously on Tjadlinn.

The Delbans waited behind their featureless gray shield, not firing a single Kellander blast at the advancing fleet. When it reached to within fifty kilometers of the discoid, Glayne gave the order to commence fire.

In the center of the huge discoid the Jewel, the Second Universe of the Elder Tane, blazed with a chill, golden luminescence. It did not waver a fraction as the tremendous energy demands struck it. The power drains fed voraciously of its infinite energies and flooded them into sub-space. The cumbersome mesh antennae on the hulls of the numberless ships in the massed fleet gulped it up and transmitted it to screaming accumulators which in turn fed it to the ravenous Kellander condensers. They, in turn, cast it through the miatron projectors at the shield of Tjadlinn from whence it had emerged.

For minutes on end those titanic torrents of energy blasted at that phenomenal shield. But it held. The inconceivable energies could not crack it. Not even when every single accumulator and condenser in the massed fleets of the Terran Combine labored at peak capacity did the shield so much as tremble. Not even to the extent of a tiny spider web of coruscation along the power foci.

Glayne barked a command to cease fire. He saw that the hail of torpedoes and mines which they had strewn had penetrated the shield. But they had been detonated by roving beams from the Tjadlinn secondaries before they could strike the surface of the discoid. If they could get through that mighty barrier, Glayne reasoned, then so could the *Algol*. He peered into the battle screen, attempting to locate the mammoth landing dock of the discoid through its shimmering grey shield.

He made his decision. Garstow's face came to life on his communicator screen. Briefly he communicated his intention to the Guardian leader. When he had finished, Garstow nodded soberly and mumbled farewell.

When he learned that the *Algol's* Kellander batteries had been rigged to fire by remote control from the pilot's seat, Glayne contacted Harbin.

"Abandon ship!" he ordered laconically when the youngster's face filled the screen.

"Wha—what?" blurted Harbin incredulously.

"I said," Glayne repeated curtly, "abandon ship. Make haste!"

"Aye, sir," said Harbin. His face still mirrored astonishment at it faded from the screen.

CHAPTER ELEVEN

GLAYNE SAT ALONE IN THE pilot's massive shock seat of the *Algol*. The instruments rose about him on all sides in terraced banks with the battle screen directly in front of his eyes. Tentatively he reached for the firing studs, accustoming his fingers to their shape. When he saw that the last of the *Algol's* lifeboats had been picked up he realized that the time had come.

He transferred his gaze to the discoid that was vague and indistinct beneath its anti-energy shield. Fastening his eyes to the armored outer lock doors of the landing dock, he gently fed power to the drivers. The *Algol* shuddered and gradually picked up speed. Glayne dropped the anti-shield, realizing that he would never get through the barrier with the energized shield functioning. But once he was through, it would have to go up quickly or his ship would be shattered by the roving secondaries. Hand hovering tensely over the shield control, he guided the ship toward the landing dock.

His speed increased; at twenty kilometers he was streaking toward the discoid in a free fall, all energy sources quiet. Fifteen-ten-five—and the *Algol* was boring through the energy barrier, stormed and buffeted as it sought to impede the passage of the individual circuits. Suddenly she emerged inside the shield and Tjadlinn was rushing upwards.

Like, lightning Glayne's fingers stabbed at the shield control and fed power to the drivers. He braked the ship crazily to avoid the lashing secondary beams that reached hungrily for him. Once...twice—and yet a third time the

Kellander beams found the cruiser and slashed through her half-formed shield, dealing terrific blows to the plummeting ship.

Then the massive beralloy doors of the landing stage were expanding hugely in his screen and he braked with all the power he could shunt into the straining drivers. Somehow his clutching fingers found the Kellander firing studs and he lashed out repeatedly against the outer lock. It whitened, ran into slag, crusted, and flared again and again as the ravening bolts struck it. Desperately Glayne fought to prevent blackness encroaching on the corners of his vision.

Suddenly a rending, thundering roar filled the *Algol* and she was crashing headlong through the weakened beralloy doors of the landing dock. But even above that deafening roar, Glayne could hear the scream of twisted and tortured metal. Then the big ship stopped moving and all was quiet except for the shriek of air escaping through the crevices around her mangled hull.

Groggily, Glayne shook his head in an effort to shake off the blackout which had engulfed his vision. In spite of his circulation exercises he couldn't see anything. Then a glimmering of the answer occurred to him and with wild surmise he experimentally flicked the firing stud of the ship's Kellanders.

Nothing happened.

Then Glayne understood. Every bit of the ship's power was cut off, including the lights and the battle screen. Obviously the Jewel power was cut off. Evidently the impact of the *Algol's* crash had jarred the delicate power drains so that Tjadlinn was once again without power. But he'd have to make sure.

Heartened, he rose and took a space suit from the locker, checking to see if its light torch was operating. As he turned away, a vague, ridiculous hope struck him. He took a second suit from the locker.

TWISTED and buckled beralloy plates had sheered long, jagged gashes in the equally tough armor of the cruiser, Glayne saw, as he clambered from the emergency lock. A little air still sighed through the huge rent that the cruiser had smashed in the skin of the discoid. The gigantic landing dock was dwarfed by the three hundred meter bulk of the cruiser. Small Delban craft had been flung violently on either side and now littered the walls with their battered bodies. One or two of the Delban technicians had been caught by the crash and were either smeared thinly along the blastway or turned inside out as their bodies exploded from lack of air pressure.

Hurriedly Glayne flashed his torch about, trying to find the mono-car that his party had used to get to Selzi-Narfid's quarters. The car itself was gone but he found the gleaming mono-rail and followed it at a rapid trot. Fortunately the passage was well-equipped with automatic air-locks, one of which had whipped in place when the air pressure dropped suddenly. When he came to the first of these, he found that the dilator was without power. He fumed at the wasted time as he burned around the lock with his torch and triggered the mechanism with his finger.

After he closed it behind him, Glayne picked up his jogging pace down the monorail passage. He felt a kind of grim, ruthless hatred when he thought of Bro-Doral. He hoped wistfully that he would find the sneering sadist before Garstow's energy beams ripped the discoid to pieces.

He wondered what had happened to Niala Chodred. During the battle he had consciously held his thoughts away from her and the dull ache of her memory. A chill loathing spread through him as he thought of the Vibra-Death. He knew of the agonies of that nerve torture; it produced not one slow death but thousands. More passionately than ever he longed to find the Bro.

Suddenly Glayne felt the floor of the discoid tremble under his feet. At first he ignored it, but it grew persistently stronger and he realized that the fleet was again hurling its energy beams at the discoid—but this time they were penetrating because there was no shield to stop them. He quickened his pace, rounded a long curve, and found that he had reached his goal.

He vaulted the high curbing and pounded down the tapestried corridor to the wide entrance stage. The dilator stud refused to operate, so Glayne burned into the lock to operate the stud. He discovered that the port itself was locked and a sudden unreasoning hope blazed up in him. With rapid movements he burned the lock out altogether and threw his weight against the door. With a wheeze it dilated and he staggered into the luxurious apartment, stumbling from the force of his own momentum.

He was scrambling to his feet when something hit him. It was soft with rounded contours, which he perceived even through the unsympathetic thickness of his spacesuit. And it had blondish-red hair and green eyes.

It was Niala.

"Glayne...oh, Glayne," she murmured clinging lightly to him.

"But...but you're not hurt," he stammered, his mind striving to adjust to the realization of a hope which it had long rejected.

"I thought they had killed you," she sobbed happily. "But you got away."

"Yes, he did," remarked a third voice, familiar and hated. "It was unfortunate."

Glayne whirled. Gort Bro-Doral stood inside the entrance stage, a black Cardy gun in his hand.

"Without you in the audience, Captain, I didn't see much point in amusing myself with the girl. But now that you have returned, Glayne—"

The big Guardian crouched to spring at the Delban, gathering his legs under him.

"I shouldn't do that, Captain," Bro-Doral observed sharply, waving the Cardy menacingly. "Life is too sweet to throw it away so rashly, isn't it? Besides, such refined methods require time and I fear your leader, Admiral Garstow, doesn't propose to give us that commodity."

It was true, Glayne realized. The energy beams of the assaulting fleets were smashing tremendous blow at the discoid so that it shuddered violently. The shocks increased in strength even as he turned his attention to them. Somewhere deep in Tjadlinn air was escaping with a screaming whistle where the skin was ruptured.

"You seem to have no idea how hideous Death is, Glayne," said the Delban, approaching them slowly. "Out here on the periphery of the galaxy we like to make some sort of a ceremony of his coming, you see, he is always hovering around us." The Delban produced his explosive, nasal snicker. "Death is a fascinating subject; I have often wondered why you people in the Main Galaxy ignore him. Ever present, you know. And always waiting for you to step into his dark embrace."

Glayne watched Bro-Doral narrowly. He was but a couple of meters away. As the blows of the Kellander beams smashing into the discoid increased, he became more preoccupied with his subject and his grip on the Cardy grew lax. Glayne's hand tightened imperceptibly on the spare spacesuit.

"—out here on the Edge," Bro-Doral was saying, "Life is considered only a prelude to Death. Personally—"

GLAYNE lunged, flinging the extra spacesuit to one side. Bro-Doral alerted instantaneously, but his Cardy wavered for a fraction of an instant toward the empty space suit. Before he could recover from his mistake, Glayne's flying body had struck him. The two went down together in a thrashing tangle. Glayne's movements were hampered by the bulky spacesuit and he felt his desperate grip on the Delban slipping. Out of the corner of his eye he saw Bro-Doral extending his long fingers for the Cardy that he had dropped. Frantically he sought to restrain the Delban's long arm, missed, and saw the Delban slither from his grasp and reach for the gun.

Glayne scrambled to his feet just in time to see Niala snatch up the weapon a split second ahead of Bro-Doral. For a brief instant the Ruler of Ten Thousand Suns stared into the muzzle of Death. Then it wrapped him in its dark embrace forever as Niala fired.

Glayne retrieved the spacesuit and hurriedly helped her don it. The screaming whistle of escaping air formed a mad symphony with the rumbling crashes of corridors and whole levels caving in upon themselves. They raced from the apartment, through the tapestried corridor to the mono-rail, which twisted like a live thing under the impact of the blasting energy beams. Jolt after jolt shook the discoid as torpedoes and mines exploded with devastating energy concussions deep within its entrails.

It was uphill all the way as the tremendous mass of the Tane Jewel dragged at their flagging steps. Niala fell a half a dozen times from the smashing shocks that shook the discoid. Glayne helped her to her feet, only to be thrown down himself the next instant by the concussion of an energy torpedo. Huge seams opened in the tough beralloy sides of the mono-rail passage as the mammoth support beams fractured.

Panting, they finally reached the point where the air-lock had fallen in place automatically. Glayne pushed at the port, expecting it to dilate. It didn't move a fraction of a centimeter. A rapid examination showed that it was sprung. Feverishly he felt for his torch to cut it down.

But it was gone!

He suddenly felt sick, realizing that he had lost it in the struggle with Bro-Doral. Now he would never be able to find it again. They were trapped. Waves of defeat swept over him as he crouched in the darkness...

Suddenly he heard it new sound in the mad cacophony of destruction that raged about them. It was the tortured scream of rending, snapping beralloy. And along with it came the sensation of increased weight.

The Tane Jewel!

The huge beams that had anchored it in place had evidently collapsed under the impact of the assault and now the Jewel was falling freely through space, crashing through everything that stood in its path. And it was falling toward them!

Glayne's weight grew unbearable as it approached. Vaguely he could make out its steady gold brilliance behind him in the passage. Grimly he clung to a projection in the wall with one arm and hung onto Niala with the other.

Then the miraculous happened.

The air-lock door, which had been sprung, now dilated under its own tremendous weight and the air pressure that remained in the passage flung Glayne and Niala through the lock.

Summoning the last reserves of his diminishing strength, Glayne put his arm around her body and half-supported her, half-dragged her up the few remaining steps of the mono-rail passage to the landing dock. Forty meters separated him from the emergency lock of the *Algol*. Thirty meters. His straining muscles groaned in anguish. Twenty meters. Niala was unconscious and her slight form was an unbearable weight to him as he dragged her with painfully slow steps. Ten…Five…he reached the lock.

He heaved her bodily into the lock and clambered in himself. Then through the inner door and across to the elevator. His muscles were a symphony of agony. Slowly, slowly the elevator climbed. As it ascended his weary mind wandered. He imagined he was back on the navigation bridge of the *Algol* again, surrounded by his loyal crewmen. He saw visions of Niala in his arms, both of them soaring through space, the brightly glowing Tane Jewel in her hand. And then he saw Graysen again, alive and well. But the screaming calamity about them brought him back to his senses. The discoid was splitting and breaking up around the *Algol*—or was it wedging the cruiser more firmly than ever in the vice grip of the beralloy outer portals? The elevator door quivered for a moment, and then dilated in a series of little shudders. Ever so slowly Glayne crawled across the bridge deck, dragging the girl. A shock seat…a surette of verchromynal into the blue vein inside her elbow.

The crescendo of destruction reached new heights. The Tane Jewel was following him, splashing its insidious yellow radiance through the glassene window of the navigation bridge. It dogged his footsteps…closer…closer. The pilot's seat. The surette. Blackness encroached upon his vision. Dimly he was aware of his arm; it moved instinctively …slowly…slowly. The regular driver atomics began to shriek. His arm made another movement, flicking jet studs. Power suddenly sang in the forward jet chambers and ejected itself in a great, mushrooming flame. The *Algol* lurched backwards…another lurch…straining…a third. And the *Algol* was suddenly free.

The yawning pit of blackness closed its gaping maw on Glayne and he slid down, down, down...

IT OCCURRED to Glayne, when he woke up, that his quarters in the *Algol* had a changed appearance. He climbed from his acceleration hammock and bounded to the shower.

"Terran Standard!" he snorted to himself. "What the hell is Harbin doing puttering along like that?"

As he dried himself from the tingling shower he tried to put his finger on the change that had come over his quarters. For one thing, he couldn't find what he wanted. But an even worse defect was the absence of his dust.

Flag officers in the Stellar Guardians were generally conceded some slight idiosyncrasy through which they could assert their individuality in a service where individuality was otherwise rigorously suppressed. Glayne's own idiosyncrasy was dust. After five long years as a Dorleb training-cadet without a speck of dust to his name, Glayne felt he had earned his right to wallow in a bit of dust. But now it was all gone. His quarters were spotless.

He had finished dressing when a cautious knock sounded on his entrance portal; then it dilated before he could answer. Harbin's face appeared in the opening.

"Oh! I'm sorry, sir. Didn't think you were awake yet," Harbin said apologetically.

"Forget it," grunted Glayne. "Come in."

Harbin entered the room and fidgeted nervously for a moment. "Sir," he finally burst out, "I...we're sorry about that unpleasantness. I want to apologize on behalf of—"

Glayne snorted and cut him off with a wave of his arm. "What I want to know," he said with deceptive calmness, "is, where the hell is my dust?"

Harbin grinned. "Lieutenant Chodred. I advised her against it—told her it was one of your peculiarities. But she wouldn't listen."

"What 'she' is this?" inquired a new voice, pleasantly husky.

Glayne turned and saw Niala leaning in the entrance stage. "You know damned well whom we are talking about," he said ominously. "Why did you take away my dust?"

"Oh, is that all?" she laughed. It was a deliciously cool and tinkling laugh. Harbin foresaw an imminent explosion. Being a discreet warrior who longs to fight another day, he fled from the room.

But it never quite jelled. Glayne extended his arms to the laughing, green-eyed Niala. But she stood her ground.

"No," she teased. "Not when you have a beard like that."

Glayne swore and reached for his depilatory. He was going to set a new galactic speed record for shaving.

THE END

If you've enjoyed this book, you will not want to miss these terrific titles...

ARMCHAIR SCI-FI & HORROR DOUBLE NOVELS, $12.95 each

D-131 **COSMIC KILL** by Robert Silverberg
BEYOND THE END OF SPACE by John W. Campbell

D-132 **THE DARK OTHER** by Stanley Weinbaum)
WITCH OF THE DEMON SEAS by Poul Anderson

D-133 **PLANET OF THE SMALL MEN** by Murray Leinster
MASTERS OF SPACE by E. E. "Doc" Smith & E. Everett Evans

D-134 **BEFORE THE ASTEROIDS** by Harl Vincent
SIXTH GLACIER, THE by Marius

D-135 **AFTER WORLD'S END** by Jack Williamson
THE FLOATING ROBOT by David Wright O'Brien

D-136 **NINE WORLDS WEST** by Paul W. Fairman
FRONTIERS BEYOND THE SUN by Rog Phillips

D-137 **THE COSMIC KINGS** by Edmond Hamilton
LONE STAR PLANET by H. Beam Piper & John J. McGuire

D-138 **BEYOND THE DARKNESS** by S. J. Byrne
THE FIRELESS AGE by David H. Keller, M. D.

D-139 **FLAME JEWEL OF THE ANCIENTS** by Edwin L. Graber
THE PIRATE PLANET by Charles W. Diffin

D-140 **ADDRESS: CENTAURI** by F. L. Wallace
IF THESE BE GODS by Algis Budrys

ARMCHAIR SCIENCE FICTION & HORROR CLASSICS, $12.95 each

C-58 **THE WITCHING NIGHT**
by Leslie Waller

C-59 **SEARCH THE SKY**
by Frederick Pohl and C. M. Kornbluth

C-60 **INTRIGUE ON THE UPPER LEVEL**
by Thomas Temple Hoyne

ARMCHAIR SCI-FI & HORROR GEMS SERIES, $12.95 each

G-15 **SCIENCE FICTION GEMS, Vol. Eight**
Keith Laumer and others

G-16 **HORROR GEMS, Vol. Eight**
Algernon Blackwood and others

A HARBINGER OF EARTH'S DOOM

It started with a strange blinking light on faraway Venus. Soon there was a mysterious visitor hovering in the skies over mother Earth—a visitor that was the forerunner of a possible invasion from space. And then it was war— Interplanetary war.

No one on Earth could have imagined how it was all going to turn out, but in the cloud-shrouded depths of Venus two Americans were perhaps Earth's best hope. These two fearless fighters stood up to a planet that had literally run amok, trying to find and destroy a horrible weapon that might spell the end of mankind.

So from Earth and Sub-Venus there soon converged a titanic offensive of justice, brought against the ruthless and seemingly unstoppable man-things of Torg…

ABOUT CHARLES W. DIFFIN:

Charles Diffin was born on March 25th, 1884. In addition to being a well-known writer of science fiction tales for the pulp magazines in the 1930s, he also went on to become an engineer and eventually a salesman of airplanes. As a young man, Diffin's knowledge of science was fairly deep, having graduated with a degree in analytical chemistry from the University of Buffalo in New York.

Starting in late 1929, Diffin began writing science fiction and horror stories, which were eagerly gobbled up by editor Harry Bates over at the Clayton Magazines publishing group. Diffin's first sci-fi tale, "Spawn of the Stars," appeared in the February, 1930 issue of *Astounding Stories*. Diffin was soon one of Bates' regular contributors, often writing in the swashbuckling style of Edmond Hamilton.

Diffin wrote several novels during his short sci-fi writing career, all of which were serialized in *Astounding*, including "The Pirate Planet," "Two Thousand Miles Below," "Brood of the Dark Moon," and "Blue Magic." Diffin also wrote a number of tales for *Astounding's* sister magazine, *Strange Tales of Mystery and Terror*. Charles Diffin passed away on May 15th, 1966.

THE PIRATE PLANET

By
CHARLES W. DIFFIN

ARMCHAIR FICTION
PO Box 4369, Medford, Oregon 97501-0168

For more information about Armchair Books and products, visit our website at…

www.armchairfiction.com

Or email us at…

armchairfiction@yahoo.com

CHAPTER ONE

LIEUTENANT McGuire threw open his coat with its winged insignia of the air force and leaned back in his chair to read more comfortably the newspaper article.

A strange light blinks on Venus, and over old Earth hovers a mysterious visitant—dread harbinger of interplanetary war.

He glanced at Captain Blake across the table. The captain was deep in a game of solitaire, but he looked up at McGuire's audible chuckle.

"Gay old girl!" said Lieutenant McGuire and smoothed the paper across his knees. "She's getting flirtatious."

The captain swore softly as he gathered up his cards. "Not interested," he announced; "too hot to-night. Keep her away."

"Oh, she's far enough away," McGuire responded; "about seventy million miles. Don't get excited."

"What are you talking about?" The captain shuffled his cards irritably.

"Venus. She's winking at us, the old reprobate. One of these star-gazers up on Mount Lawson saw the flashes a week or so ago. If you'll cut out your solitaire and listen, I'll read you something to improve your mind." He ignored the other's disrespectful remark and held the paper closer to see the paragraphs.

"Is Venus Signaling?" inquired the caption which Lieutenant McGuire read. "Professor Sykes of Mt. Lawson Observatory Reports Flashes.

"The planet Venus, now a brilliant spectacle in the evening sky, is behaving strangely according to a report from the local observatory on Mount Lawson. This sister star, most like Earth of all the planets, is now at its eastern elongation, showing like a half-moon in the big telescopes on Mt. Lawson. Shrouded in impenetrable clouds, its surface has never been seen, but something is happening there. Professor Sykes reports seeing a distinct flash of light upon the terminator, or margin of light. It lasted for several seconds and was not repeated.

"No explanation of the phenomenon is offered by scientists, as conditions on the planet's surface are unknown. Is there life there? Are the people of Venus trying to communicate? One guess is as good as another. But it is interesting to recall that our scientists recently proposed to send a similar signal from Earth to Mars by firing a tremendous flare of magnesium.

"Venus is now approaching the earth; she comes the nearest of all planets. Have the Venusians penetrated their cloak of cloud masses with a visible light? The planet will be watched with increased interest as it swings toward us in space, in hope of there being a repetition of the unexplained flash."

"There," said Lieutenant McGuire,"—doesn't that elevate your mind? Take it off this infernally hot night? Carry you out through the cool reaches of interplanetary space? If there is anything else you want to know, just ask me."

"Yes," Captain Blake agree, "there is. I want to know how the game came out back in New York—and you don't know that. Let's go over and ask the radio man. He probably has the dope."

"Good idea," said McGuire; "maybe he has picked up a message from Venus; we'll make a date." He looked vainly for the brilliant star as they walked out into the night. There were clouds of fog from the nearby Pacific drifting high overhead. Here and there stars showed momentarily, then were blotted from sight.

The operator in the radio room handed the captain a paper with the day's scores from the eastern games. But Lieutenant McGuire, despite his ready amusement at the idea, found his thoughts clinging to the words he had read. "Was the planet communicating?" he pictured the great globe—another Earth—slipping silently through space, coming nearer and nearer.

Did they have radio? he wondered. Would they send recognizable signals—words—or some mathematical sequence to prove their reality? He turned to the radio operator on duty.

"Have you picked up anything peculiar," he asked, and laughed inwardly at himself for the asking. "Any new dots and dashes? The scientists say that Venus is calling. You'll have to be learning a new code."

The man glanced at him strangely and looked quickly away.

"No, sir," he said. And added after a pause: "No new dots and dashes."

"Don't take that stuff too seriously, Mac," the captain remonstrated. "The day of miracles is past; we don't want to commit you to the psychopathic ward. Now here is something real: the Giants won, and I had ten dollars on them. How shall we celebrate?"

The radio man was listening intently as they started to leave. His voice was hesitating as he stopped them; he seemed reluctant to put his thoughts into words.

"Just a minute, sir," he said to Captain Blake.

"Well?" the captain asked. And again the man waited before he replied. Then—

"Lieutenant McGuire asked me," he began, "if I had heard any strange dots and dashes. I have not; but...well, the fact is, sir, that I have been getting some mighty queer sounds for the past few nights. They've got me guessing.

"If you wouldn't mind waiting. Captain; they're about due now—" He listened again to some signal inaudible to the others, then hooked up two extra head-sets for the officers.

"It's on now," he said. "If you don't mind—"

McGuire grinned at the captain as they took up the ear-phones. "Power of suggestion," he whispered, but the smile was erased from his lips as he listened. For in his ear was sounding a weird and wailing note.

No dots or dashes, as the operator had said, but the signal was strong. It rose and fell and wavered into shrill tremolos, a ghostly, unearthly sound, and it kept on and on in a shrill despairing wail. Abruptly it stopped.

The captain would have removed the receiver from his ear, but the operator stopped him. "Listen," he said, "to the answer."

There was silence, broken only by an occasional hiss and crackle of some far distant mountain storm. Then, faint as a whisper, came an answering, whistling breath.

It, too, trembled and quavered. It went up—up—to the limit of hearing; then slid down the scale to catch and tremble and again ascend in endless unvarying ups and downs of sound. It was another unbroken, unceasing, but always changing vibration.

"What in thunder is that?" Captain Blake demanded.

"Communication of some sort, I should say," McGuire said slowly, and he caught the operator's eyes upon him in silent agreement.

"No letters," Blake objected; "no breaks; just that screech." He listened again. "Darned if it doesn't almost seem to say something," he admitted.

"When did you first hear this?" he demanded of the radio man.

"Night before last. I didn't report it. It seemed too—too—"

"Quite so," said Captain Blake in understanding, "but it is some form of broadcasting on a variable wave; though how a thing like that can make sense—"

"They talk back and forth," said the operator; "all night, most. Notice the loud one and the faint one; two stations sending and answering."

Captain Blake waved him to silence. "Wait—wait!" he ordered. "It's growing louder!"

In the ears of the listening men the noise dropped to a loud grumble; rose to a piercing shriek; wavered and leaped rapidly from note to note. It was increasing; rushing upon them with unbearable sound. The sense of something approaching, driving toward them swiftly, was strong upon Lieutenant McGuire. He tore the headphones from his ears and rushed to the door. The captain was beside him. Whoever—whatever—was sending that mysterious signal was coming near—but was that nearness a matter of miles or of thousands of miles?

They stared at the stormy night sky above. A moon was glowing faintly behind scudding clouds, and the gray-black of flying shadows formed an opening as they watched, a wind-blown opening like a doorway to the infinity beyond, where, blocking out the stars, was a something that brought a breath-catching shout from the watching men.

Some five thousand feet up in the night was a gleaming ship. There were rows of portholes that shone twinkling against the black sky—portholes in multiple rows on the side. The craft was inconceivably huge. Formless and dim of outline in the darkness, its vast bulk was unmistakable.

And as they watched with staring, incredulous eyes, it seemed to take alarm as if it sensed the parting of its concealing cloud blanket. It shot with dizzy speed and the roar of a mighty meteor straight up into the night. The gleam of its twinkling lights merged to a distant star that dwindled, shrank and vanished in the heights.

The men were wordless and open-mouthed. They stared at each other in disbelief of what their eyes had registered.

"A liner!" gasped Captain Blake. "A—a—liner! Mac, there is no such thing."

McGuire pointed where the real cause of their visitor's departure appeared. A plane with engine wide open came tearing down through the clouds. It swung in a great spiral down over the field and dropped a white flare as it straightened away; then returned for the landing. It taxied at reckless speed toward the hangars and stopped a short distance from the men. The pilot threw himself out of the cockpit and raced drunkenly toward them.

"Did you see it?" he shouted, his voice a cracked scream. "Did you see it?"

"We saw it," said Captain Blake; "yes, we saw it. Big as—" He sought vainly for a proper comparison, then repeated his former words: "Big as an ocean liner!"

The pilot nodded; he was breathing heavily.

"Any markings?" asked his superior. "Anything to identify it?"

"Yes, there were markings, but I don't know what they mean. There was a circle painted on her bow and marks like clouds around it, but I didn't have time to see much. I came out of a cloud, and there the thing was. I was flying at five thousand, and they hung there dead ahead. I couldn't believe it; it was monstrous; tremendous. Then they sighted me, I guess, and they up-ended that ship in mid-air and shot straight up till they were out of sight."

It was the captain's turn to nod mutely.

"There's your miracle," said Lieutenant McGuire softly.

"Miracle is right," agreed Captain Blake; "nothing less! But it is no miracle of ours, and I am betting it doesn't mean any good to us. Some other country has got the jump on us."

To the pilot he ordered: "Say nothing of this—not a word—get that? Let me have a written report—full details, but concise as possible."

He went back to the radio room, and the operator there received the same instructions.

"What are you going to do?" the lieutenant questioned.

Captain Blake was reaching for a head-set. "Listen in," he said briefly; "try to link up that impossible ship with those messages, then report at once to the colonel and whoever he calls in. I'll want you along, Mac, to swear I am sober."

He had a head-set adjusted, and McGuire took up the other. Again the room was still, and again from the far reaches of space the dark night sent to them its quavering call.

The weird shrillness cried less loudly now, and the men listened in strained silence to the go and come of that variable shriek. Musical at times as it leaped from one clear note to another, again it would merge into discordant blendings of half-tones that sent shivers of nervous reaction up the listeners' spines.

"Listen," said McGuire abruptly. "Check me on this. There are two of them, one loud and one faint—right?"

"Right," said Captain Blake.

"Now notice the time intervals—there! The faint one stops, and the big boy cuts in immediately. No waiting; he answers quickly. He does it every time."

"Well?" the captain asked.

"Listen when he stops and see how long before the faint one answers. Call the loud one the ship and the faint one the station... There! The ship is through!"

There was pause; some seconds elapsed before the answer that whispered so faintly in their ears came out of the night.

"You are right, sir," the operator said in corroboration of McGuire's remark. "There is that wait every time."

"The ship answers at once," said McGuire; "the station only after a wait."

"Meaning—?" inquired the captain.

"Meaning, as I take it, that there is time required for the message to go from the ship to the station and for them to reply."

"An appreciable time like that," Captain Blake exclaimed, "—with radio! Why, a few seconds, even, would carry it around the world a score of times!"

Lieutenant McGuire hesitated a moment. "It happens every time," he reminded the captain, "it is no coincidence. And if that other station is out in space—another ship perhaps, relaying the messages to yet others between here and—Venus, let us say…"

He left the thought unfinished. Captain Blake was staring at him as one who beholds a fellow-man suddenly insane. But the look in his eyes changed slowly, and his lips that had been opened in remonstrance came gradually in a firm, straight line.

"Crazy!" he said, but it was apparent that he was speaking as much to himself as to McGuire. "Plumb, raving crazy! Yet that ship *did* go straight up out of sight—an acceleration in the upper air beyond anything we know. It might be—" And he, too, stopped at the actual voicing of the wild surmise. He shook his head sharply as if to rid it of intruding, unwelcome thoughts.

"Forget that!" he told McGuire, and repeated it in a less commanding tone. "Forget it, Mac, we've got to render a report to sane men, you and I. What we know will be hard enough for them to believe without any wild guesses.

"That new craft is real. It has got it all over us for size and speed and potential offensive action. Who made it? Who mans it? Red Russia? Japan? That's what the brass hats will be wondering; that's what they will want to find out.

"Not a word!" he repeated to the radio man. "You will keep mum on this."

He took McGuire with him as he left to seek out his colonel. But it was a disturbed and shaken man, instead of the cool, methodical Captain Blake of ordinary days, who went in search of his commanding officer. And he clung to McGuire for corroboration of his impossible story.

THERE was a group of officers to whom Blake made his full report. Colonel Boynton had heard but little when he halted his subordinate curtly and reached for a phone. And his words over that instrument brought a quick conference of officers and a quiet man whom McGuire did not recognize. The "brass hats," as Blake had foreseen, were avid for details.

The pilot of the incoming plane was there, too, and the radio man. Their stories were told in a disconcerting silence, broken only by some officer's abrupt and skeptical question on one point and another.

"Now, for heaven's sake, shut up about Venus," McGuire had been told. But he did not need Captain Blake's warning to hold himself strictly to what he had seen and let the others draw their own conclusions.

Lieutenant McGuire was the last one to speak. There was silence in the office of Colonel Boynton as he finished, a silence that almost echoed from the grim walls. And the faces of the men who gathered there were carefully masked from any expression that might betray their thoughts.

It was the quiet man in civilian attire who spoke first. He sat beside another whose insignia proclaimed him of general's rank, but he addressed himself to Colonel Boynton.

"I am very glad," he said quietly, "very glad. Colonel, that my unofficial visit came at just this time. I should like to ask some few questions."

Colonel Boynton shifted the responsibility with a gesture almost of relief. "It is in your hands. Mr. Secretary," he said. "You and General Clinton have dropped in opportunely. There is something here that will tax all our minds."

The man in civilian clothes nodded assent. He turned to Captain Blake.

"Captain," he said, "you saw this at first hand. You have told us what you saw. I should like greatly to know what you think. Will you give us your opinion, your impressions?"

The captain arose smartly, but his words came with less ease.

"My opinion," he stated, "will be of little value, but it is based upon these facts. I have seen to-night, sir, a new type of aircraft, with speed, climb and ceiling beyond anything we are capable of. I can only regard it as a menace. It may or may not have been armed, but it had the size to permit the armament of a cruiser; it had power to carry that weight. It hung stationary in the air, so it is independent of wing-lift, yet it turned and shot upward like a feather in a gale. That spells maneuverability.

"That combination, sir, can mean only that we are out-flown, out-maneuvered and out-fought in the air. It means that the planes in our hangars are obsolete, our armament so much old iron.

"The menace is potential at present. Whether it is an actual threat or not is another matter. Who mans that ship—what country's insignia she carries—is something on which I can have no opinion. The power is there. Who wields it I wish we knew."

The questioner nodded at the conclusion of Blake's words, and he exchanged quiet, grave glances with the general beside him. Then—

"I think we all would wish to know that, Captain Blake," he observed. And to the colonel, "You may be able to answer that soon. It would be my idea that this craft should be—ah—drawn out, if we can do it. We would not attack it, of course, until its mission is proved definitely unfriendly, but you will resist any offensive from them.

"And now," he added, "let us thank these officers for their able reports and excuse them. We have much to discuss…"

CAPTAIN Blake took McGuire's arm as they went out into the night. And he drew him away where they walked for silent minutes by themselves. The eyes of Lieutenant McGuire roamed upward to the scudding clouds and the glimpse of far, lonely stars; he stumbled occasionally as he walked. But for Captain Blake there was thought only of matters nearby.

"The old fox!" he exclaimed. "Didn't he 'sic us on' neatly? If we mix it with that stranger there will be no censure from the Secretary of War."

"I assumed that was who it was," said McGuire. "Well, they have something to think about, that bunch; something to study over… Perhaps more than they know.

"And that's their job," he concluded after a silence. "I'm going to bed; but I would like a leave of absence to-morrow if that's okay."

"Sure," said Captain Blake, "though I should think you would like to stick around. Perhaps we will see something. What's on your mind, Mac?"

"A little drive to the top of Mount Lawson," said Lieutenant McGuire. "I want to talk to a bird named Sykes."

CHAPTER TWO

LIEUTENANT McGuire, U.S.A., was not given as a usual thing to vain conjectures, nor did his imagination carry him beyond the practical boundaries of accepted facts. Yet his mind, as he drove for hours through the orange-scented hills of California, reverted time and again to one persistent thought. And it was with him still, even when he was consciously concentrating on the hairpin turns of Mount Lawson's narrow road.

There was a picture there, printed indelibly in his mind—a picture of a monstrous craft, a liner of the air, that swung its glowing lights in a swift arc and, like a projectile from some huge gun, shot up and up and still up until it vanished in a jet-black sky. Its altitude when it passed from sight he could not even guess, but the sense of ever-increasing speed, of power that mocked at gravitation's puny force, had struck deep into his mind. And McGuire saw plainly this mystery ship going on and on far into the empty night where man had never been.

No lagging in that swift flight that he had seen; an acceleration that threw the ship faster and yet faster, regardless of the thin air and the lessened buoyancy in an ocean of atmosphere that held man-made machines so close to Earth. That constant acceleration, hour after hour, day after day—the speed would be almost unlimited; inconceivable!

He stopped his car where the mountain road held straight for a hundred feet, and he looked out over the coastal plain spread like a toy world far below.

"Now, how about it?" he asked himself. "Blake thinks I am making a fool of myself. Perhaps I am. I wonder. It's a long time since I fell for any fairy stories. But this thing has got me. A sort of hunch, I guess."

The sun was shining now from a vault of clear blue. It was lighting a world of reality, of houses where people lived their commonplace lives, tiny houses squared off in blocks a mile below. There was smoke here and there from factories; it spread in a haze, and it meant boilers and engines and sound practical machinery of a practical world to the watching man.

What had all this to do with Venus? he asked himself. This was the world he knew. It was real; space was impenetrable; there were no men or beings of any sort that could travel through space. Blake was right—he was on a fool's errand. They couldn't tell him anything up here at the observatory; they would laugh at him as he deserved...

Wondering vaguely if there was a place to turn around, he looked ahead and then up; his eyes passed from the gash of roadway on the mountainside to the deep blue beyond. And within the man some driving, insistent, mental force etched strongly before his eyes that picture and its problem unanswered. There was the ship—he saw it in memory—and it went up and still up; and he knew as surely as if he had guided the craft that the meteor-like flight could be endless.

Lieutenant McGuire could not reason it out—such power was beyond his imagining—but suddenly he dared to believe, and he knew it was true.

"Earthbound!" he said in contempt of his own human kind, and he looked again at the map spread below. "Ants! Mites! That's what we are—swarming across the surface of the globe. And we think we're so damn clever if we lift ourselves up a few miles from the surface!

"Guess I'll see Sykes," he muttered aloud. "He and his kind at least dare to look out into space; take their eyes off the world; be impractical!"

He swung the car slowly around the curve ahead, eased noiselessly into second gear and went on with the climb.

There were domed observatories where he stopped: rounded structures that gleamed silvery in the air; and offices, laboratories. It was a place of busy men. And Professor Sykes, he found, was busy. But he spared a few minutes to answer courteously the questions of this slim young fellow in the khaki uniform of the air service.

"What can I do for you?" asked Professor Sykes.

"No dreamer, this man," thought McGuire as he looked at the short, stocky figure of the scientist. Clear eyes glanced sharply from under shaggy brows; there were papers in his hand scrawled over with strange mathematical symbols.

"You can answer some fool questions," said Lieutenant McGuire abruptly, "if you don't mind."

The scientist smiled broadly. "We're used to that," he told the young officer; "you can't think of any worse ones than those we have heard. Have a chair."

McGuire drew a clipping from his pocket—it was the newspaper account he had read—and he handed it to Professor Sykes.

"I came to see you about this," he began.

The lips of Professor Sykes lost their genial curve; they straightened to a hard line. "Nothing for publication," he said curtly. "As usual they enlarged upon the report and made assumptions and inferences not warranted by facts."

"But you did see that flash?"

"By visual observation I saw a bright area formed on the terminator—yes! We have no photographic corroboration."

"I am wondering what it meant."

"That is your privilege—and mine," said the scientist coldly.

"But it said there," McGuire persisted, "that it might have been a signal of some sort."

"*I* did not say so; that is an inference only. I have told you, Lieutenant..." He glanced at the card in his hand. "...Lieutenant McGuire—all that I know. We deal in facts up here, and we leave the brilliant theorizing to the journalists."

The young officer felt distinctly disconcerted. He did not know exactly what he had expected from this man—what corroboration of his wild surmises—but he was getting nowhere, he admitted. And he resented the cold aloofness of the scientist before him.

"I am not trying to pin you down on anything," he said, and his tone carried a hint of the nervous strain that had been his. "I am trying to learn something."

"Just what?" the other inquired.

"Could that flash have been a signal?"

"You may think so if you wish. I have told you all that I know. And now," he added, and rose from his chair, "I must ask to be excused; I have work to do."

McGuire came slowly to his feet. He had learned nothing; perhaps there was nothing to be learned. A fool's errand! Blake was right. But the inner urge for some definite knowledge drove him on. His eyes were serious and his face drawn to a scowl of earnestness as he turned once more to the waiting man.

"Professor Sykes," he demanded, "One more question. Could that have been the flash of a—a rocket? Like the proposed experiments in Germany. Could it have meant in any way the launching of—a ship—to travel Earthward through space?"

Professor Sykes knew what it was to be harassed by the curious mob, to avoid traps set by ingenious reporters, but he knew, too, when he was meeting with honest bewilderment and a longing for knowledge. His fists were placed firmly on the hips of his stocky figure as he stood looking at the persistent questioner, and his eyes passed from the intent face to the snug khaki coat and the spread wings that proclaimed the wearer's work. A ship out of space—a projectile—this young man had said.

"Lieutenant," he suggested quietly, and again the smile had returned to his lips as he spoke, "sit down. I'm not as busy as I seem. Now tell me, what in the devil have you got in your mind?"

And McGuire told him. "Like some of your dope," he said, "this is not for publication. But I have not been instructed to hush it up, and I know you will keep it to yourself."

He told the clear-eyed, listening man of the previous night's events. Of the radio's weird call and the mystery ship.

"Hallucination," suggested the scientist. "You saw the stars very clearly, and they suggested a ship."

"Tell that to Jim Burgess," said McGuire, "he was the pilot of that plane." And the scientist nodded as if the answer were what he expected.

He asked again about the ship's flight. And he, too, bore down heavily upon the matter of acceleration in the thin upper air. He rose to lay a friendly hand on McGuire's shoulder.

"We can't know what it means," he said, "but we can form our own theories, you and I—and anything is possible.

"It is getting late," he added, "and you have had a long drive. Come over and eat; spend the night here. Perhaps you would like to have a look at our equipment—see Venus for yourself. I will be observing her through the sixty-inch refractor to-night. Would you care to?"

"Would I?" McGuire demanded with enthusiasm. "Say, that will be great!"

THE SUN was dropping toward the horizon when the two men again came out into the cool mountain air.

"Just time for a quick look around," suggested Professor Sykes, "if you are interested."

He took the lieutenant first to an enormous dome that bulged high above the ground, and admitted him to the dark interior. They climbed a stairway and came out into a room that held a skeleton frame of steel. "This is the big boy," said Professor Sykes, "the one hundred-inch reflector."

There were other workers there, one a man standing upon a raised platform beside the steel frame, who arranged big holders for photographic plates. The slotted ceiling opened as McGuire watched, and the whole structure swung slowly around. It was still, and the towering steel frame began to swing noiselessly when a man at a desk touched various controls. McGuire looked about him in bewilderment.

"Quite a shop," he admitted; "but where is the telescope?"

Professor Sykes pointed to the towering latticework of steel. "Right there," he said. "Like everyone else, you were expecting to see a big tube."

He explained in simple words the operation of the great instrument that brought in light rays from sources millions of light years away. He pointed out where the big mirror was placed—the one hundred-inch reflector—and he traced for the wondering man the pathway of light that finally converged upon a sensitized plate to catch and record what no eye had ever seen.

He checked the younger man's flow of questions and turned him back toward the stairs. "We will leave them to their work," he said; "they will be gathering light that has been traveling millions of years on its ways. But you and I have something a great deal nearer to study."

Another building held the big refractor, and it was a matter of only a few seconds and some cryptic instructions from Sykes until the eye-piece showed the image of the brilliant planet.

"The moon!" McGuire exclaimed in disappointed tones when the professor motioned him to see for himself. His eyes saw a familiar half-circle of light.

"Venus," the professor informed him. "It has phases like the moon. The planet is approaching; the sun's light strikes it from the side." But McGuire hardly heard. He was gazing with all his faculties centered upon that distant world, so near to him now.

"Venus," he whispered half aloud. Then to the professor, "It's all hazy. There are no markings—"

"Clouds," said the other. "The goddess is veiled; Venus is blanketed in clouds. What lies underneath we may never know, but we do know that of all the planets this is most like the earth; most probably is an inhabited world. Its size, its density, your weight if you were there—and the temperature under the sun's rays about double that of ours. Still, the cloud envelope would shield it."

McGuire was fascinated, and his thoughts raced wildly in speculation of what might be transpiring before his eyes. People, living in that tropical world; living and going through their daily routine under that cloud-filled sky where the sun was never seen. The margin of light that made the clear shape of a half-moon marked their daylight and dark; there was one small dot of light forming just beyond that margin. It penetrated the dark side. And it grew, as he watched, to a bright patch.

"What is that?" he inquired abstractedly—his thoughts were still filled with those beings of his imagination. "There is a light that extends into the dark part. It is spreading—"

He found himself thrust roughly aside as Professor Sykes applied a more understanding eye to the instrument.

The professor whirled abruptly to his assistant. "Phone Professor Giles," he said sharply; "he is working on the reflector. Tell him to get a photograph of Venus at once; the cloud envelope is broken." He returned hurriedly to his observations. One hand sketched on a waiting pad.

"Markings!" he said exultantly. "If it would only hold... There, it is closing...gone..."

His hand was quiet now upon the paper, but where he had marked was a crude sketch of what might have been an island. It was "L" shaped; sharply bent.

"Whew!" breathed Professor Sykes and looked up for a moment. "Now that was interesting."

"You saw through?" asked McGuire eagerly. "Glimpsed the surface?—an island?"

The scientist's face relaxed. "Don't jump to conclusions," he told the aviator, "we are not ready to make a geography of Venus quite yet. But we shall know that mark if we ever see it again. I hardly think they had time to get a picture. And now there is only a matter of three hours for observation; I must watch every minute. Stay here if you wish. But," he added, "don't let your imagination run wild. Some eruption, perhaps, this we have seen—an ignition of gasses in the upper air—who knows? But don't connect this with your mysterious ship. If the ship is a menace, if it means war, that is your field of action, not mine. And you will be fighting with someone on Earth. It must be that some country has gained a big lead in aeronautics. Now I must get to work."

"I'll not wait," said McGuire. "I will start for the field; get there by daylight, if I can find my way down that road in the dark."

"Thanks a lot." He paused a moment before concluding slowly, "and in spite of what you say, Professor, I believe that we will have something to get together on again in this matter."

The scientist, he saw, had turned again to his instrument. McGuire picked his way carefully along the narrow path that led where he had parked his car. "Good scout, this Sykes!" he was thinking, and he stopped to look overhead in the quick-gathering dark at that laboratory of the heavens, where Sykes and his kind delved and probed, measured and weighed, and gathered painstakingly the messages from suns beyond counting, from universe out there in space that added their bit of enlightenment to the great story of the mystery of creation.

He was humbly aware of his own deep ignorance as he backed his car, slipped it into second, and began the long drive down the tortuous grade. He would have liked to talk more with Sykes. But he had no thought as he wound round the curves how soon that wish was to be gratified.

PART way down the mountainside he again checked his car where he had stopped on the upward climb and reasoned with himself about his errand. Once more he looked out over the level ground below, a vast glowing expanse of electric lights now, that stretched to the ocean beyond. He was suddenly unthrilled by this man-made illumination, and he got out of his car to stare again at the blackness above and its myriad of stars that gathered and multiplied as he watched.

One brighter than the rest winked suddenly out. There was a constellation of twinkling lights that clustered nearby, and they too vanished. The eyes of the watcher strained themselves to see more clearly a dim-lit outline. There were no lights; it was a black shape, lost in the blackness of the mountain sky that was blocking out the stars. But it was a shape, and from near the horizon the pale gleams of the rising moon picked it out in softest of outline; a ghost of a curve that reflected a silvery contour to the watching eyes below.

There had been a wider space in the road that McGuire had passed; he backed carefully till he could swing his car and turn it to head once more at desperate speed toward the mountain top. And it was less than an hour since he had left when he was racing back along the narrow footpath to slam open the door where Professor Sykes looked up in amazement at his abrupt return.

The aviator's voice sounded hoarse as he shouted, "It's here— the ship! It's here! Where's your phone?—I must call the field! It's overhead—descending slowly—no lights, but I saw it!"

He was working with trembling fingers at the phone where Sykes had pointed. "Long distance!" he shouted. He gave a number to the operator. "Make it quick," he implored. "Quick!"

CHAPTER THREE

BACK at Maricopa Flying Field the daily routine had been disturbed. There were conferences of officers, instructions from Colonel Boynton, and a curiosity-provoking lack of explanations. Only with Captain Blake did the colonel indulge in any discussion.

"We'll keep this under our hats," he said, "and out of the newspapers as long as we can. You can imagine what the yellow journals would do with a scarehead like that. Why, they would have us all wiped off the map and the country devastated by imaginary fleets in the first three paragraphs."

Blake regarded his superior gravely. "I feel somewhat the same way, myself. Colonel," he admitted. "When I think what this can mean—some other country so far ahead of us in air force that we are back in the dark ages—well, it doesn't look any too good to me if they mean trouble."

"We will meet it when it comes," said Colonel Boynton. "But, between ourselves, I am in the same state of mind.

"The whole occurrence is so damn mysterious. Washington hasn't a whisper of information of any such construction; the Secretary admitted that last night. It's a surprise, a complete surprise, to everyone.

"But, Blake, you get that new ship ready as quickly as you can. Prepare for an altitude test the same as we planned, but get into the air the first minute possible. She ought to show a better ceiling than anything we have here, and you may have to fly high to say 'Good morning' to that liner you saw. Put all the mechanics on it that can work to advantage. I think they have it pretty well along now."

"Engine's tested and installed, sir," was Blake's instant report. "I think I can take it up this afternoon."

He left immediately to hurry to the hangar where a new plane stood glistening in pristine freshness, and where hurrying mechanics grumbled under their breaths at the sudden rush for a ship that was expected to take the air a week later.

An altitude test under full load! Well, what of it? they demanded one of another; wouldn't another day do as well as this one? And they worked as they growled, worked with swift sureness and skill, and the final instruments took their place in the ship that she might roll from the hangar complete under that day's sun.

Her supercharger was tested—the adjunct to a powerful engine that would feed the hungry cylinders with heavy air up in the heights where the air is thin; there were oxygen flasks to keep life in the pilot in the same thin air. And the hot southern sun made ludicrous that afternoon the bulky, heavily-wrapped figure of Captain Blake as he sat at the controls and listened approvingly to the roaring engine.

He waved good-by and smiled understandingly as he met the eyes of Colonel Boynton; then pulled on his helmet, settled himself in his seat and took off in a thunderous blast of sound to begin his long ascent.

HE HAD long since cracked open the valve of his oxygen flask when the climb was ended, and his goggles were frosted in the arctic cold so that it was only with difficulty he could read his instrument board.

"That's the top," he thought in that mind so light and so curiously not his own. He throttled the engine and went into a long spiral that was to end within a rod of where he had started on the brown sun-baked field. The last rays of the sun were slanting over distant mountains as he climbed stiffly from the machine.

"Better than fifty thousand," exulted Colonel Boynton. "Of course your barograph will have to be calibrated and verified, but it looks like a record, Blake—and you had a full load.

"Ready to go up and give merry hell to that other ship if she shows up?" he asked. But Captain Blake shook a dubious head.

"Fifty thousand is just a start for that bird," he said. "You didn't see them shoot out of sight, Colonel. Lord knows when they quit *their* climb—or where."

"Well, we'll just have a squadron ready in any event," the colonel assured him. "We will make him show his stuff or take a beating— if that is what he wants."

They were in the colonel's office. "You had better go and get warmed up," he told the flyer, "then come back here for instructions." But Blake was more anxious for information than for other comforts.

"I'm all right," he said, "just tired a bit. Let me stretch out here, Colonel, and give me the dope on what you expect of our visitor and what we will do."

He settled back comfortably in a big chair. The office was warm, and Blake knew now he had been doing a day's work.

"We will just take it as it comes," Colonel Boynton explained. "I can't for the life of me figure why the craft was spying around here. What are they looking for? We haven't any big secrets the whole world doesn't know.

"Of course he may not return. But if he does I want you to go up and give him the once over. I can trust you to note every significant detail.

"You saw no wings. If it is a dirigible, let's know something of their power and how they can throw themselves up into the air the way you described. Watch for anything that may serve to identify it and its probable place of manufacture—any peculiarity of marking or design or construction that may give us a lead. Then return and report."

Blake nodded his understanding of what was wanted, but his mind was on further contingencies—he wanted definite instructions.

"And," he asked; "if they attack—what then? Is their fire to be returned?"

"If they make one single false move," said Colonel Boynton savagely, "give them everything you've got. And the 91st Squadron will be off the ground to support you at the first sign of trouble. We don't want to start anything, nor appear to do so. But, by the gods, Blake, this fellow means trouble eventually as sure as you're a flyer, and we won't wait for him to ask for it twice."

They sat in silence, while the field outside became shrouded in night. And they speculated, as best they could from the few facts they had, as to what this might mean to the world, to their country, to themselves. It was an hour before Blake was aware of the fact that he was hungry.

He rose to leave, but paused while Colonel Boynton answered the phone. The first startled exclamation held him rigid while he tried to piece together the officer's curt responses and guess at what was being told.

"Colonel Boynton speaking... McGuire...? Yes, Lieutenant... Over Mount Lawson...? Yes—yes, the same ship, I've no doubt."

His voice was even and cool in contrast to the excited tones that carried faintly to Blake standing by.

"Quite right!" he said shortly. "You will remain where you are; act as observer; hold this line open and keep me informed. Captain Blake will leave immediately for observation. A squadron will follow. Let me know promptly what you see."

He turned abruptly to the waiting man.

"It is back!" he said. "We're in luck! Over the observatories at Mount Lawson; descending, so Lieutenant McGuire says. Take the same ship you had up to-day. Look them over—get up close—good luck!" He turned again to the phone.

There were planes rolling from their hangars before Blake could reach his own ship. Their engines were thundering; men were rushing across the field, pulling on leather helmets and coats as they ran—all this while he warmed up his engine.

A mechanic thrust in a package of sandwiches and a thermos of coffee while he waited. And Captain Blake grinned cheerfully and gulped the last of his food as he waved to the mechanics to pull out the wheel blocks. He opened the throttle and shot out into the dark.

He climbed and circled the field, saw the waving motion of lights in red and green that marked the take-off of the planes of the 91st, and he straightened out on a course that in less than two hours would bring him over the heights of Mount Lawson and the mystery that awaited him there. And he fingered the trigger grip that was part of the stick and nodded within his dark cockpit at the rattle of a machine gun that merged its staccato notes with the engine's roar.

But he felt, as he thought of that monster shape, as some primordial man might have felt, setting forth with a stone in his hand to wage war on a saurian beast.

CHAPTER FOUR

IF COLONEL Boynton could have stood with one of his lieutenants and Professor Sykes on a mountain top, he would have found, perhaps, the answer to his question. He had wondered in a puzzled fashion why the great ship had shown its mysterious presence over the flying field. He had questioned whether it was indeed the field that had been the object of their attention or whether in the cloudy murk they had merely wandered past. Could he have seen with the eyes of Lieutenant McGuire the descent of the great shape over Mount Lawson, he would have known beyond doubt that here was the magnet that drew the eyes of whatever crew was manning the big craft.

It was dark where the two men stood. Others had come running at their call, but their forms, too, were lost in the shadows of the towering pines. The light from an open door struck across an open space beyond which McGuire and Professor Sykes stood alone, stood silent and spellbound, their heads craned back at a neck-wrenching angle. They were oblivious to all discomforts; their eyes and their whole minds were on the unbelievable thing in the sky.

Beyond the fact that no lights were showing along the hull, there was no effort at concealment. The moon was up now to illumine the scene, and it showed plainly the gleaming cylinder with its long body and blunt, shining ends, dropping, slowly, inexorably down.

"Like a dirigible," said McGuire huskily. "But the size, man—the size! And its shape is not right; it isn't streamlined correctly; the air—" He stopped his half-unconscious analysis abruptly. "The air!" What had this craft to do with the air? A thin layer of gas that hung close to the earth—the skin on an apple! And beyond—space! There was the ethereal ocean in which this great shape swam!

The reality of the big ship, the very substance of it, made the space ship idea the harder to grasp. Lieutenant McGuire found that it was easier to see an imaginary craft taking off into space than to conceive of this monstrous shape, many hundreds of tons in weight, being thrown through vast emptiness. Yet he knew; he knew!

And his mind was a chaos of grim threats and forebodings as he looked at the unbelievable reality and tried to picture what manner of men were watching, peering, from those rows of ports.

At last it was motionless. It hung soundless and silent except for a soft roar, a scant thousand feet in the air. And its huge bulk was dwarfing the giant pines, the rounded buildings; it threw the men's familiar surroundings into a new and smaller scale.

He had many times flown over these mountains, and Lieutenant McGuire had seen the silvery domes of the observatories shining among the trees. Like fortresses for aerial defense, he had thought, and the memory returned to him now. What did these new-comers think of them? Had they, too, found them suggestive of forts on the frontier of a world, defenses against invasion from out there?

Or did they know them for what they were? Did they wish only to learn the extent of our knowledge, our culture? Were they friendly, perhaps?—half-timid and fearful of what they might find?

A star moved in the sky, a pin-point of light that was plain in its message to the aviator. It was Blake, flying high, volplaning to make contact and learn from the air what this stranger might mean. The light of his plane slanted down in an easy descent; the flyer was gliding in on a long aerial toboggan slide. His motor was throttled; there was only the whistle of torn air on the monoplane's wings. McGuire was with the captain in his mind, and like him he was waiting for whatever the stranger might do.

Other lights were clustered where the one plane had been. The men of the 91st had their orders, and the fingers of the watching, silent man gripped an imaginary stick while he wished with his whole heart that he was up in the air. To be with Blake or the others! His thoughts whipped back to the mysterious stranger; the great shape was in motion; it rose sharply a thousand feet in the air.

The approaching plane showed clear in the moon's light. It swung and banked, and the vibrant song of its engine came down to the men as Blake swept in a great circle about the big ship. He was looking it over, but he began his inspection at a distance, and the orbit of his plane made a tightening spiral as he edged for a closer look. He was still swinging in the monotonous round when the ship made its first forward move.

It leaped in the air; it swept faster and faster. And it was moving with terrific speed as it crashed silently through the path of the tiny plane. And Blake, as he leaned forward on the stick to throw his plane downward in a power dive, could have had a vision, not of a ship of the air, but only of a shining projectile as the great monster shrieked overhead.

McGuire trembled for the safety of those wings as he saw Blake pull his little ship out of the dive and shoot upward to a straight climb.

"But— That's dodging them!" he exulted. "that's flying! I wonder, did they mean to wipe him out or were they only scared off?"

His question was answered as, out of the night, a whistling shriek proclaimed the passage of the meteor ship that drove unmistakably at the lone plane. And again the pilot with superb skill waited until the last moment and threw himself out of the path of the oncoming mass, though his own plane was tossed and whirled like an autumn leaf in the vortex that the enemy created. Not a second was lost as Blake opened his throttle and forced his plane into a steep climb.

"Atta-boy!" said McGuire, as if words could span across to the man in the plane. "Altitude, Blake—get altitude!"

The meteor had turned in a tremendous circle; so swift its motion that it made an actual line of light as the moon marked its course. And the curved line straightened abruptly to a flashing mark that shot straight toward the struggling plane.

This time another sound came down to the listening ears of the two men. The plane tore head on to meet the onslaught, to swing at the last instant in a frantic leap that ended as before in the maelstrom of air back of the ship. But the muffled roar was changed, punctured with a machine-gun's familiar rattle, and the stabbing flashes from Blake's ship before he threw it out of the other's path were a song of joy to the tense nerves of the men down below.

This deadly rush could only be construed as an attack, and Blake was fighting back. The very speed of the great projectile must hold it to its course; the faster it went the more difficult to swerve it from a line. This and much more was flashing sharply in McGuire's mind. But—Blake!—alone against this huge antagonist...! It was coming back. Another rush like a star through space...

And McGuire shouted aloud in a frenzy of emotion as a cluster of lights came falling from on high. No lone machine gun now that tore the air with this clattering bedlam of shots—the planes of the 91st Squadron were diving from the heights. They came on a steep slant that seemed marking them for crashing death against the huge cylinder flashing past. And their stabbing needles of machine-gun fire made a drumming tattoo, till the planes, with the swiftness of hawks, swept aside, formed to groups, tore on down toward the ground and then curved in great circles of speed to climb back to the theater of action.

LIEUTENANT McGuire was rigid and quivering. He should go to the phone and report to the colonel, but the thought left him as quickly as it came. He was frozen in place, and his mind could hold only the scene that was being pictured before him.

The enemy ship had described its swift curve, and the planes of the defenders were climbing desperately for advantage. So slowly they moved as compared with the swiftness of the other!

But the great ship was slowing; it came on, but its wild speed was checked. The light of the full moon showed plainly now what McGuire had seen but dimly before—a great metal beak on the ship, pointed and shining, a ram whose touch must bring annihilation to anything it struck.

The squadron of planes made a group in the sky, and Blake's monoplane, too, was with them. The huge enemy was approaching slowly, was it damaged? McGuire hardly dared hope...yet that raking fire might well have been deadly; it might be that some bullets had torn and penetrated to the vitals of this ship's machinery and damaged some part.

It came back slowly, ominously, toward the circling planes. Then, throwing itself through the air, it leaped not directly toward them but off to one side.

Like a stone on the end of a cord it swung with inconceivable speed in a circle that enclosed the group of planes. Again and again it whipped around them, while the planes, by comparison, were motionless. Its orbit was flat with the ground; then tilting, more yet, it made a last circle that stood like a hoop in the air. And behind it as it circled it left a faint trace of vapor. Nebulous!—milky in the moonlight!—but the ship had built a sphere, a great globe of the gas, and within it, like rats in a cage, the planes of the 91st Squadron were darting and whirling.

"Gas!" groaned the watching man. "Gas! What is it? Why don't they break through?"

The thin clouds of vapor were mingling now and expanding. They blossomed and mushroomed, and the light of the moon came in pale iridescence from their billowing folds.

"Break through!" McGuire had prayed—and he stood in voiceless horror as he saw the attempt.

The mist was touching here and there a plane; they were engulfed, yet he could see them plainly. And he saw with staring, fear-filled eyes the clumsy tumbling and fluttering of unguided wings as the great eagles of the 91st fell roaring to earth with no conscious minds guiding their flight.

The valleys were deep about the mountain, and their shadowed blackness opened to receive the maimed, stricken things that came fluttering or swooping wildly to that last embrace, where, in the concealing shadows, the deeper shadows of death awaited...

There was a room where a telephone waited; McGuire sensed this but dumbly, and the way to that room was long to his stumbling feet. He was blinded; his mind would not function; he saw only those fluttering things, and the moonlight on their wings, and the shadows that took them so softly at the last.

One plane whistled close overhead. McGuire stopped where he stood to follow it with unbelieving eyes. That one man had lived, escaped the net—it was inconceivable! The plane returned; it was flying low, and it swerved erratically as it flew. It was a monoplane, a new ship.

Its motor was silenced; it stalled as he watched, to pancake and crash where the towering pines made a cradle of great branches to cushion its fall.

No thought now of the colonel waiting impatiently for a report; even the enemy, there in the sky was forgotten. It was Blake in that ship, and he was alive—or had been—for he had cut his motor. McGuire screamed out for Professor Sykes, and there were others, too, who came running at his call. He tore recklessly through the scrub and undergrowth and gained at last the place where wreckage hung dangling from the trees. The fuselage of a plane, scarred and broken, was still held in the strong limbs.

Captain Blake was in the cockpit, half hanging from the side. He was motionless, quiet, and his face shone white and ghastly as they released him and drew him out. But one hand still clung with a grip like death itself to a hose that led from an oxygen tank. McGuire stared in wonder and slowly gathering comprehension.

"He was fixed for an altitude test," he said dazedly; "this ship was to be used, and he was to find her ceiling. He saw what the others were getting, and he flew himself through on a jet of pure oxygen—" He stopped in utter admiration of the quickness of thought that could outwit death in an instant like that.

They carried the limp body to the light. "No bones broken so far as I can see," said the voice of Professor Sykes. "Leave him here in the air. He must have got a whiff of their devilish mist in spite of his oxygen; he was flying mighty awkwardly when he came in here."

But he was alive!—and Lieutenant McGuire hastened with all speed now to the room where a telephone was ringing wildly and a colonel of the air force must be told of the annihilation of a crack squadron and of a threat that menaced all the world.

IN THAT far room there were others waiting where Colonel Boynton sat with receiver to his ear. A general's uniform was gleaming in the light to make more sober by contrast the civilian clothing of that quiet, clear-eyed man who held the portfolio of the Secretary of War.

They stared silently at Colonel Boynton, and they saw the blood recede from his face, while his cool voice went on unmoved with its replies.

"...I understand," he said; "a washout, complete except for Captain Blake; his oxygen saved him... It attacked with gas, you say...? And why did not our own planes escape...? Its speed!—yes, we'll have to imagine it, but it is unbelievable. One moment—" He turned to those who waited for his report.

"The squadron," he said with forced quiet, though his lips twitched in a bloodless line, "—the 91st—is destroyed. The enemy put them down with one blow; enveloped them with gas." He recounted the essence of McGuire's report, then turned once more to the phone.

"Hello, Lieutenant—the enemy ship—where is it now?"

He listened—listened—to a silent receiver; silent save for the sound of a shot—a crashing fall—a loud, panting breath. He heard the breathing close to the distant instrument; it ended in a choking gasp; the instrument was silent in his ear...

He signaled violently for the operator, ordered the ringing of any and all phones about the observatory, and listened in vain for a sound or syllable in reply.

"A plane," he told an orderly, "at once! Phone the commercial flying field near the base of Mount Lawson. Have them hold a car ready for me...I shall land there!"

CHAPTER FIVE

TO CAPTAIN alone, of all those persons on the summit of Mount Lawson, it was given to see and to know and be able to relate what transpired there and in the air above. For Blake, although he appeared like one dead, was never unconscious throughout his experience.

Driving head on toward the ship, he had emptied his drum of cartridges before he threw his plane over and down in a dive that escaped the onrush of the great craft by a scant margin, and that carried him down in company with the men and machines of the squadron that dived from above.

He turned as they turned and climbed as they climbed for the advantage that altitude might give. And he climbed faster; his ship outdistanced them in that tearing, scrambling rush for the heights. The squadron was spiraling upward in close formation with his plane above them when the enemy struck.

He saw that great shape swing around them, terrible in its silent swiftness, and, like the others, he failed to realize at first the net she was weaving. So thin was the gas and so rapid the circling of the enemy craft, they were captured and cut off inside of the gaseous sphere before the purpose of the maneuver was seen or understood.

He saw the first faint vapor form above him; swung over for a steep bank that carried him around the inside of the great cage of gas and that showed him the spiraling planes as the first wisps of vapor swept past them.

He held that bank with his swift machine, while below him a squadron of close-formed fighting craft dissolved before his eyes into unguided units. The formations melted; wings touched and locked; the planes fell dizzily or shot off in wild, ungoverned, swerving flight. The air was misty about him; it was fragrant in his nostrils; the world was swimming...

It was gas, he knew, and with the light-headedness that was upon him, so curiously like that of excessive altitudes, he reached unconsciously for the oxygen supply. The blast of pure gas in his face revived him for an instant, and in that instant of clear thinking his plan was formed. He threw his weight on stick and rudder, corrected the skid his ship was taking, and, with one hand holding the tube of life-giving oxygen before his face, he drove straight down in a dive toward the earth.

There were great weights fastened to his arm, it seemed, when he tried to bring the ship from her fearful dive. He moved only with greatest effort, and it was force of will alone that compelled his hands to do their work. His brain, as he saw the gleaming roundness of observatory buildings beneath him, was as clear as ever in his life, but his muscles—his arms and legs—refused to work; even his head; he was slowly sinking beneath a load of utter fatigue.

The observatories were behind him; he must swing back; he could not last long, he knew; each slightest movement was intolerable effort.

Was this death? he wondered; but his mind was so clear! There were the buildings, the trees! How thickly they were massed beyond—

He brought every ounce of will power to bear...the throttle! and a slow glide in...he was losing speed...the stick—must—come—back! The crashing branches whipped about him, bending, crackling—and the world went dark...

THERE were stars above him when he awoke, and his back was wrenched and aching. He tried to move, to call, but found that the paralysing effect of the gas still held him fast. He was lying on the ground, he knew; a door was open in a building beyond, and the light in the room showed him men, a small group of them, standing silent while someone—yes, it was McGuire—shouted into a phone.

"...The squadron," he was saying. "...Lost! Every plane down and destroyed... Blake is living but injured..." And then Blake remembered. And the tumbling, helpless planes came again before his eyes while he cursed silently at this freezing grip that would not let him cover his face with his hands to shut out the sight.

The figure of a man hurried past him, nor saw the body lying helpless in the cool dark. McGuire was still at the phone. And the enemy ship—?

His mind, filled with a welter of words as he tried to find phrases to compass his hate for that ship. And then, as if conjured out of nothing by his thoughts, the great craft itself came in view overhead in all its mighty bulk.

It settled down swiftly; it was riding on an even keel. And in silence and darkness it came from above. Blake tried to call out, but his paralyzed throat made no sound. Doors opened in silence, swinging down from the belly of the thing to show in the darkness square openings through which shot beams of brilliant yellow light.

There were cages that lowered—great platforms in slings—and the platforms came softly to rest on the ground. They were moving with life; living beings clustered upon them thick in the dark. Oh God! for an instant's release from the numbness that held his lips and throat to cry out one word...! The shapes were passing now in the shelter of darkness, going toward the room... He could see McGuire's back turned toward the door.

Man-shapes, tall and thin, distorted humans, each swathed in bulging garments; horrible staring eyes of glass in the masks about their heads, and each hand ready with a shining weapon as they stood waiting for the men within to move.

McGuire must have seen them first, though his figure was half concealed from Blake where he was lying. But he saw the head turn; knew by the quick twist of the shoulders the man was reaching for a gun. One shot echoed in Blake's ears; one bulging figure spun and fell awkwardly to the ground; then the weapons in those clumsy hands hissed savagely while jets of vapor, half liquid and half gas, shot blindingly into the room. The faces dropped from his sight...

There had been the clamor of surprised and shouting men; there was silence now. And the awkward figures in the bloated casings that protected their bodies from the gas passed in safety to the room. Blake, bound in the invisible chains of enemy gas, struggled silently, futilely, to pit his will against this grip that held him. To lie there helpless, to see these men slaughtered! He saw one of the creatures push the body of his fallen comrade out of the way. It was cast aside with an indifferent foot.

They were coming back. Blake saw the form of McGuire in unmistakable khaki. He and another man were carried high on the shoulders of some of the invaders. They were going toward the platforms, the slings beneath the ship… They passed close to Blake, and again he was unnoticed in the dark.

A clamor came from far buildings, a babel of howls and shrieks, inhuman, unearthly. No phrases or syllables, but to Blake it was familiar…somewhere he had heard it…and then he remembered the radio and the weird wailing note that told of communication. These things were talking in the same discordant din.

They were gathering now on the platforms slung under the ship. A whistling note from somewhere within the great structure and the platforms went high in the air. They were loaded, he saw, with papers, books, and instruments taken from the observatories. Some made a second trip to take up the loot they had gathered. Then the black doorways closed; the huge bulk of the ship floated high above the trees; it took form, dwindled smaller and smaller, then vanished from sight in the star-studded sky.

Blake thought of their unconscious passenger—the slim figure of Lieutenant McGuire. Mac had been a close friend and a good one; his ready smile; his steady eyes that could tear a problem to pieces with their analytic scrutiny or gaze far into space to see those visions of a dreamer!

"Far into space." Blake repeated the words in his mind. And: "Good-by Mac," he said softly; "you've shipped for a long cruise, I'm thinking." He hardly realized he had spoken the words aloud.

LYING there in the cold night he felt his strength returning slowly. The pines sang their soothing, whispered message, and the faint night noises served but to intensify the silence of the mountain. It was some time before the grind of straining gears came faintly in the air to announce the coming of a car up the long grade. And still later he heard it come to a stop some distance beyond. There were footsteps, and voices calling; he heard the voice of Colonel Boynton. And he was able to call out in reply, even to move his head and turn it to see the approaching figures in the night.

Colonel Boynton knelt beside him. "Did they get you, old man?" he asked.

"Almost," Blake told him. "My oxygen—I was lucky. But the others—" He did not need to complete the sentence. The silent canyons among those wooded hills told plainly the story of the lost men.

"We will fight them with gas masks," said the colonel; "your experience has taught us the way."

"Gas-tight uniforms and our own supplies of oxygen," Blake supplemented. He told Boynton of the man-things he had seen come from the ship, of their baggy suits, their helmets... And he had seen a small generator on the back of each helmet. He told him of the small, shining weapons and their powerful jets of gas. Deadly and unescapable at short range, he well knew.

"They got McGuire," Blake concluded; "carried him off a prisoner. Took another man, too."

For a moment Colonel Boynton's quiet tones lost their even steadiness. "We'll get them," he said savagely, and it was plain that it was the invaders that filled his mind; "we'll go after them, and we'll get them in spite of their damn gas, and we'll rip their big ship into ribbons—"

Captain Blake was able to raise a dissenting hand. "We will have to go where they are, Colonel, to do that."

Colonel Boynton stared. "Well?" he demanded. "Why not?"

"We can't go where *they* went," said Blake quite simply. "I laughed at McGuire; told him not to be a fool. But I was a bit of a fool I'm afraid—the blind one; we all were, Colonel. That thing came here out of space. It has gone back; it is far beyond our air. I saw it go up out of sight, and I know. Those creatures were men, if you like, but no men that we know—not those shrieking, wailing devils! And we're going to hear more from them, now that they've found their way here!"

CHAPTER SIX

A SCORE of bodies where men had died in strangling fumes in the observatories on Mount Lawson; one of the country's leading astronomical scientists vanished utterly; the buildings on the mountain top ransacked; papers and documents blowing in vagrant winds; tales of a monster ship in the air, incredibly huge, unbelievably swift—

There are matters that at times are not allowed to reach the press, but not happenings like these. And the papers of the United States blazed out with headlines to tell the world of this latest mystery.

Then came corroboration from the far corners of the world. The mystery ship had not visited one section only; it had made a survey of the whole civilized sphere, and the tales of those who had seen it were no longer laughed to scorn but went on the wires of the great press agencies to be given to the world. And with that the censorship imposed by the Department of War broke down, and the tragic story of the destruction of the 91st Air Squadron passed into written history. The wild tale of Captain Blake was on every tongue.

An invasion from space! The idea was difficult to accept. There were scoffers who tried to find something here for their easy wit. Why should we be attacked? What had that other world to gain? There was no answer ready, but the silent lips of the men who had fallen spoke eloquently of the truth. And the world, in wonder and consternation, was forced to believe.

Were there more to come? How meet them? Was this war— and with whom? What neighboring planet could reasonably be suspected. What had science to say?

The scientists! The scientists! The clamor of the world was beating at the doors of science and demanding explanations and answers. And science answered.

A conference was arranged in London; the best minds in the realms of astronomy and physics came together. They were the last to admit the truth that would not be denied, but admit it they must. And to some of the questions they found their answer.

It was not Mars, they said, though this in the popular mind was the source of the trouble. Not Mars, for that planet was far in the heavens. But Venus!—misnamed for the Goddess of Love. It was Venus, and she alone, who by any stretch of the imagination could be threatening Earth.

What did it mean? They had no answer. The ship was the only answer to that. Would there be more?—could we meet them?—defeat them? And again the wise men of the world refused to hazard a guess.

But they told what they knew; that Venus was past her eastern elongation, was approaching the earth. She of all the planets that swung around the sun came nearest to Earth—twenty-six million miles in another few weeks. Then whirling away she would pass to the western elongation in a month and a half and drive out into space. Venus circled the sun in a year of 225 days, and in 534 days she would again reach her eastern elongation with reference to the earth, and draw near us again.

They were reluctant to express themselves, these men who made nothing of weighing and analyzing stars a million of light years away, but *if* the popular conception was correct and *if* we could pass through the following weeks without further assault, we could count on a year and a half before the menace would again return. And in a year and a half—well, the physicists would be working—and we might be prepared.

Captain Blake had made his report, but this, it seemed, was not enough. He was ordered to come to Washington, and, with Colonel Boynton, he flew across the country to tell again his incredible story.

IT WAS a notable gathering before which he appeared. All the branches of the service were represented; there were men in the uniform of admirals and generals; there were heads of Departments. And the Secretary of War was in charge.

He told his story, did Blake, before a battery of hostile eyes. This was not a gathering to be stampeded by wild scareheads, nor by popular clamor. They wanted facts, and they wanted them proved. But the gravity with which they regarded the investigation was shown by their invitation to the representatives of foreign powers to attend.

"I have told you all that happened," Blake concluded, "up to the coming of Colonel Boynton. May I reiterate one fact? I do not wonder at your questioning my state of mind and my ability to observe correctly. But I must insist, gentlemen, that while I got a shot of their gas and my muscles and my nervous system were paralyzed, my brain was entirely clear. I saw what I saw; those creatures were there; they entered the buildings; they carried off Lieutenant McGuire and another man.

"What they were or who they were I cannot say. I do not know that they were men, but their insane shrieking in that queer unintelligible talk is significant. And that means of communication corresponds with the radio reception of which you know.

"If you gentlemen know of any part of this earth that can produce such a people, if you know of any people or country in this world that can produce such a ship—then we can forget all our wild fancies. And we can prepare to submit to that country and that people as the masters of this earth. For I must tell you, gentlemen, with all the earnestness at my command, that until you have seen that ship in action, seen its incredible speed, its maneuverability, its lightning-like attack and its curtain of gas, you can have no conception of our helplessness. And the insignia that she carries is the flag of our conquerors."

Blake got an approving nod from the Secretary of War as he took his seat. That quiet man rose slowly from his chair to add his words. He spoke earnestly, impressively.

"Captain Blake has hit the nail squarely on the head," he stated. "We have here in this room a representative gathering from the whole world. If there is any one of you who can say that this mystery ship was built and manned by your people, let him speak, and we will send you at once a commission to acknowledge your power and negotiate for peace."

The great hall was silent, in a silence that held only uneasy rustlings as men glanced one at another in wondering dismay.

"The time has come," said the Secretary with solemn emphasis, "when all dissensions among our peoples must cease. Whatever there is or ever has been of discord between us fades into insignificance before this new threat. It is the world, now, against a power unknown; we can only face it as a united world.

"I shall recommend to the President of the United States that a commission be appointed, that it may co-operate with similar bodies from all lands. I ask you, gentlemen, to make like representations to your governments, to the end that we may meet this menace as one country and one man; meet it, God grant, successfully through a War Department of the World."

IT WAS was a brave gesture of the President of the United States; he dared the scorn and laughter of the world in standing behind his Secretary of War. The world is quick to turn and rend with ridicule a false prophet. And despite the unanswerable facts, the scope and power of the menace was not entirely believed. It was difficult for the conscious minds of men to conceive of the barriers of vast space as swept aside and the earth laid open to attack.

England was slow to respond to the invitation of the President; this matter required thought and grave deliberation in parliament. It might not be true; the thought, whether spoken or unexpressed, was clinging to their minds. And even if true—even if this lone ship had wandered in from space—there might be no further attack.

"Why," they asked, "should there be more unprovoked assaults from the people of another planet? What was their object? What had they to gain...? Perhaps we were safe after all." The answer that destroyed all hope came to them borne in upon a wall of water that swept the British coast.

The telescopes of the world were centered now on just one object in the heavens. The bright evening star that adorned the western sky was the target for instruments great and small. It was past the half-moon phase now, and it became under magnification a gleaming crescent, a crescent that emitted from the dark sphere it embraced vivid flashes of light. Sykes' report had ample corroboration; the flash was seen by many, and it was repeated the next night and the next.

What was it? the waiting world asked. And the answer came not from the telescopes and their far-reaching gaze but from the waters of the Atlantic. In the full blaze of day came a meteor that swept to the earth in an arc of fire to outshine the sun. There must have been those who saw it strike—passengers and crews of passing ships—but its plunge into the depths of the Atlantic spelled death for each witness.

The earth trembled with the explosion that followed. A gas— some new compound that united with water to give volumes tremendous—that only could explain it. The ocean rose from its depths and flung wave after wave to race outward in circles of death.

Hundreds of feet in height at their source—this could only be estimated—they were devastating when they struck. The ocean raged over the frail bulwark of England in wave upon wave, and, retreating, the waters left smooth, shining rock where cities had been. The stone and steel of their buildings was scattered far over the desolate land or drawn in the suction of retreating waters to the sea.

Ireland, too, and France and Spain. Even the coast of America felt the shock of the explosion and was swept by tidal waves of huge proportions. But the coast of Britain took the blow at its worst.

The world was stunned and waiting—waiting!—when the next blow fell. The flashes were coming from Venus at regular intervals, just twenty hours and nineteen minutes apart. And with exactly the same time intervals the bolts arrived from space to lay waste the earth.

They struck where they would; the ocean again; the Sahara; in the mountains of China; the Pacific was thrown into fearful convulsions; the wheat fields of Canada trembled and vanished before a blast of flaming gas…

Twenty hours and nineteen minutes! Where it would strike, the next star-shell, no man might say; that it surely would come was a deadly and nerve-shattering certainty. The earth waited and prayed under actual bombardment.

Some super-gun, said science with conviction; a great bore in the planet itself, perhaps. But it was fixed, and the planet itself aimed with an accuracy that was deadly; aimed once as each revolution brought its gun on the target. Herein, said science, lay a basis for hope.

If, in that distant world, there was only one such bore, it must be altering its aim as the planet approached; the gun must cease to bear upon the earth. And the changing sweep of the missiles' flight confirmed their belief.

Each meteor-shell that came rushing into Earth's embrace burned brilliantly as it tore into the air. And each flaming arc was increasingly bent, until—twenty hours and nineteen minutes had passed—twenty minutes—thirty—another hour…and the peoples of Earth dropped humbly to their knees in thankful prayer, or raised vengeful eyes and clenched fists toward the heavens while their quivering lips uttered blasphemous curses. The menace, for the time, had passed; the great gun of Venus no longer was aiming toward the earth.

"No more ships," was the belief; "not this time." And the world turned to an accounting of its losses, and to wonder—wonder—what the planet's return would bring. A year and one half was theirs; one year and a half in which to live in safety, in which to plan and build.

A column, double leaded, in the *London Times* voiced the feeling of the world. It was copied and broadcast everywhere.

"Another attack," it concluded, "is not a probability—it is a certainty. They are destroying us for some reason known only to themselves. Who can doubt that when the planet returns there will be a further bombardment; an invasion by armed forces in giant ships; bombs dropped from them miles high in the air. This is what we must look forward to—death and destruction dealt out by a force we are unable to meet.

"Our munitions factories may build larger guns, but can they reach the heights at which these monster ships of space will lie, with any faint probability of inflicting damage? It is doubtful.

"Our aircraft is less than useless; its very name condemns it as inept. Craft of the air!—and we have to war against space ships which can rise beyond the thin envelope of gas that encircles the earth.

"The world is doomed—utterly and finally doomed; it is the end of humankind; slavery to a conquering race at the very best, unless—

"Let us face the facts fairly. It is war—war to the death—between the inhabitants of this world and of that other. We are men. What they are God alone can say. But they are creatures of mind as are we; what they have done, we may do.

"There is our only hope. It is vain, perhaps—preposterous in its assumption—but our sole and only hope. We must meet the enemy and defeat him, and we must do it on his own ground. To destroy their fleet we must penetrate space; to silence their deadly bombardment we must go out into space as they have done, reach their distant world as they have reached ours, and conquer as we would have been conquered.

"It is a tenuous hope, but our only one. Let our men of mundane warfare do their best—it will be useless. But if there be one spark of God-given genius in the world that can point the way to victory, let those in authority turn no deaf ear.

"It is a battle now of minds, and the best minds will win. Humanity—all humankind—is facing the end. In less than one year and a half we must succeed—or perish. And unless we conquer finally and decisively, the story of man in the history of the universe will be a tale that is told, a record of life in a book that is ended—closed—and forgotten through all eternity."

CHAPTER SEVEN

A BREATH of a lethal gas shot from the flying ship had made Captain Blake as helpless as if every muscle were frozen hard, and he had got it only lightly, mixed with the saving blast of oxygen. His heart had gone on, and his breathing, though it became shallow, did not cease; he was even able to turn his eyes. But to the men in the observatory room the gas from the weapons of the attacking force came as a devastating, choking cloud that struck them senseless as if with a blow. Lieutenant McGuire hardly heard the sound of his own pistol before unconsciousness took him.

It was death for the men who were left—for them the quick darkness never lifted—but for McGuire and his companion there was reprieve.

He was lying flat on a hard floor when remembrance crept slowly back to his benumbed brain. An odor, sickish-sweet, was in his nostrils; the breath of life was being forcibly pumped and withdrawn from laboring lungs; a mask was tight against his face. He struggled to throw it off, and someone bending over removed it.

Someone! His eyes stared wonderingly at the grotesque face like a lingering phantasm of fevered dreams. There were others, he saw, and they were working over a body not far away upon the floor. He recognized the figure of Professor Sykes. Short, stocky, his clothes disheveled—but Sykes, unmistakably, despite the mask upon his face.

He, too, revived as McGuire watched, and, like the flyer, he looked wonderingly about him at his strange companions. The eyes of the two met and held in wordless communication and astonishment.

THE unreal creatures that hovered near withdrew to the far side of the room. The walls beyond them were of metal, white and gleaming; there were doorways. In another wall were portholes—round windows of thick glass that framed circles of absolute night. It was dark out beyond them with a blackness that was relieved only by sharp pin-points of brilliance—stars in a night sky such as McGuire had never seen.

Past and present alike were hazy to the flyer; the spark of life had been brought back to his body from a far distance; there was time needed to part the unreal from the real in these new and strange surroundings.

There were doorways in the ceiling, and others in the floor near where he lay; ladders fastened to the wall gave access to these doors. A grotesque figure appeared above the floor and, after a curious glance at the two men, scrambled into the room and vanished through the opening in the ceiling. It was some time before the significance of this was plain to the wondering man—before he reasoned that he was in the enemy ship, aimed outward from the earth, and the pull of gravitation and the greater force of the vessel's constant acceleration held its occupants to the rear walls of each room. That lanky figure had been making its way forward toward the bow of the ship. McGuire's mind was clearing; he turned his attention now to the curious, waiting creatures, his captors.

There were five of them standing in the room, five shapes like men, yet curiously, strangely, different. They were tall of stature, narrow across the shoulders, muscular in a lean, attenuated fashion.

But their faces! McGuire found his eyes returning in horrified fascination to each hideous, inhuman countenance.

A colorless color, like the dead gray of ashes; a skin like that of an African savage from which all but the last vestige of color had been drained. It was transparent, parchment-like, and even in the light of the room that glowed from some hidden source, he could see the throbbing lines of blood-vessels that showed livid through the translucent skin. And he remembered, now, the fingers, half-seen in his moments of awakening—they were like clinging tendrils, colorless, too, in that ashy gray, and showed the network of veins as if each hand had been flayed alive.

The observer found himself analyzing, comparing, trying to find some earthly analogy for these unearthly creatures. Why did he think of potatoes sprouting in a cellar? What possible connection had these half-human things with that boyhood recollection? And he had seen some laboratory experiments with plants and animals that had been cut off from the sunlight—and now the connection was clear; he knew what this idea was that was trying to form.

These were creatures of the dark. These bleached, drained faces showed skin that had never known the actinic rays of the sun; their whole framework proclaimed the process that had been going on through countless generations. Here was a race that had lived, if not in absolute darkness, then in some place where sunlight never shone—a place of half-light—or of clouds.

"Clouds!" The exclamation was startled from him. And: "Clouds!" he repeated meditatively; he was seeing again a cloud-wrapped world in the eye-piece of a big refracting telescope. "Blanketed in clouds," Professor Sykes had said. The scientist himself was speaking to him now in bewildered tones.

"Clouds?" he inquired. "That's a strange remark to make. Where are we, Lieutenant McGuire? I remember nothing after you fired. Are we flying—in the clouds?"

"A long, long way beyond them, is my guess," said McGuire grimly. It was staggering what all this might mean; there was time needed for fuller comprehension. But the lean bronzed face of the flyer flushed with animation, and in spite of the terrors that must surely lie ahead he felt strangely elated at the actuality of an incredible adventure.

Slowly he got to his feet to find that his muscles still were reluctant to respond to orders; he helped the professor to arise. And from the group that drew back further into the far end of the room came a subdued and rasping tumult of discordant sound.

One, seemingly in charge, held a weapon in his hand, a slender tube no thicker than a common wire; and ending in a cylinder within the creature's hand. He pointed it in threatening fashion while his voice rose in a shrill call. McGuire and Professor Sykes stood quiet and waited for what the next moment might have in store, but McGuire waved the weapon aside in a gesture that none could fail to read.

"Steady," he told his companion. "We're in a ticklish position. Do nothing to alarm them."

From up above them came an answering shrill note. Another of the beings was descending into the room.

"Ah!" said Lieutenant McGuire softly, "the big boss, himself. Now let's see what will happen."

If there had seemed something of timidity in the repulsive faces of the waiting creatures, this newcomer was of a different type. He opened flabby thin lips to give one sharp note of command. It was as sibilant as the hissing of a snake. The man with the weapon returned it to a holder at his side; the whole group cringed before the power and authority of the new arrival.

The men that they had seen thus far were all garbed alike; a loose-fitting garment of one piece that was ludicrously like the play rompers that children might wear. These were dull red in color, the red of drying blood, made of strong woven cloth. But this other was uniformed differently.

McGuire noted the fineness of the silky robe. Like the others this was made of one piece, loosely fitting, but its bright vivid scarlet made the first seem drab and dull. A belt of metal about his waist shone like gold and matched the emblem of precious metal in the turban on his head.

All this the eyes of the flyer took in at a glance; his attention only momentarily diverted from the ashen face with eyes narrow and slitted, that stared with the cold hatred of a cat into those of the men.

He made a sound with a whistling breath. It seemed to be a question directed to them, but the import of it was lost.

"An exceedingly queer lot," Professor Sykes observed. "And this chap seems distinctly hostile."

"He's no friend of mine," said McGuire as the thin, pendulous lips repeated their whistling interrogation.

"I can't place them," mused the scientist. "Those facial characteristics... But they must be of some nationality, speak some tongue."

He addressed himself to the figure with the immobile, horrid face.

"We do not understand you," he said with an ingratiating smile. *"Comprenez vous Francaise...? Non...?"* German, perhaps, or Spanish? *"Sprecken sie Deutsche? Usted habla Española...?"*

He followed with a fusillade of questions in strange and varying tongues. "I've even tried him with Chinese," he protested in bewilderment and stared amazed at his companion's laughter.

There had to be a reaction from the strain of the past hours, and Lieutenant McGuire found the serious questioning in polyglot tongues and the unchanging feline stare of that hideous face too much for his mental restraint. He held his sides, while he shook and roared with laughter beyond control, and the figure before him glared with evident disapproval of his mirth.

There was a hissing order, and two figures from the corner sprang forward to seize the flyer with long clinging fingers. Their strength he had overestimated, for a violent throw of his body twisted him free, and his outstretched hands sent the two sprawling across the room. Their leader took one quick step forward, then paused as if hesitating to meet this young adversary.

"Do go easy," Professor Sykes was imploring. "We do not know where we are nor who they are, but we must do nothing to antagonize them."

McGuire had reacted from his hilarious seizure with an emotional swing to the opposite extreme. "I'll break their damn necks," he growled, "if they get rough with me." And his narrow eyes exchanged glare for glare with those in the face like blood and ashes before him.

The cold cat eyes held steadily upon him while the scarlet figure retreated. A louder call, shrill and vibrant, came from the thin lips, and a swarm of bodies in dull red were scrambling into the room to mass about their scarlet leader. Above and behind them the face under its brilliant turban and golden clasp was glaring in triumph.

The tall figures crouched, grotesque and awkward; their long arms and hands with grasping, tendril-like fingers were ready. McGuire waited for the sharp hissing order that would throw these things upon him, and he met the attack when it came with his own shoulders dropped to the fighter's pose, head drawn in close and both fists swinging free.

There were lean fingers clutching at his throat, a press of blood-red bodies thick about him, and a clustering of faces where color blotched and flowed.

The thud of fists in blows that started from the floor was new to these lean creatures that clawed and clung like cats. But they trampled on those who went down before the flyer's blows and stood upon them to spring at his head; they crowded in in overwhelming numbers while their red hands tore and twined about his face.

It was no place now for long swings; McGuire twisted his body and threw his weight into quick short jabs at the faces before him. He was clear for an instant and swung his heavy boot at something that clung to one leg; then met with a rain of hooks and short punches the faces that closed in again. He saw in that instant a wild whirl of bodies where the stocky figure of Professor Sykes was smothered beneath his taller antagonists. But the professor, if he was forgetting the science of the laboratory, was remembering that of the squared circle—and the battle was not entirely one sided.

McGuire was free; the blood was trickling down his face from innumerable cuts where sharp-nailed fingers had sunk deep. He wiped the red stream from his eyes and threw himself at the weaving mass of bodies that eddied about Sykes in frantic struggle across the room.

The face of the professor showed clear for a moment. Like McGuire he was bleeding, and his breath came in short explosive gasps, but he was holding his own! The eyes of McGuire glimpsed a wildly gesticulating, shouting figure in the rear. The face, contorted with rage, was almost the color of the brilliant scarlet that the creature wore. The blood-stained man in khaki left his companion to fight his own battle, and plunged headlong at a leaping cluster of dull red, smashed through with a frenzied attack of straight rights and lefts, and freed himself to make one final leap at the leader of this unholy pack.

He was fighting in blind desperation now; the two were out-numbered by the writhing, lean-bodied creatures, and this thing that showed in blurred crimson before him was the directing power of them all. The figure symbolized and personified to the raging man all the repulsive ugliness of the leaping horde. The face came clear before him through the mist of blood, and he put the last ounce of his remaining strength and every pound of weight behind a straight, clean drive with his right fist.

His last conscious impression was of a red, clawing hand that was closed around the thick butt of a tube of steel…then down, and still down, he plunged into a bottomless pit of whirling, red flashes and choking fumes…

There were memories that were to occur to Lieutenant McGuire afterward—visions, dim and hazy and blurred, of half-waking moments when strange creatures forced food and water into his mouth, then held a mask upon his face while he resisted weakly the breathing of sweet, sickly fumes that sent him back to unconsciousness.

There were many such times; some when he came sufficiently awake to know that Sykes was lying near him, receiving similar care. Their lives were being preserved. How, or why, or what life might hold in store he neither knew nor cared; the mask and the deep-drawn fumes brought stupor and numbness to his brain.

A window was in the floor beside him when he awoke—a circular window of thick glass or quartz. But no longer did it frame a picture of a sky in velvet blackness; no unwinking pin-points of distant stars pricked keenly through the night; but, clear and dazzling, came a blessed radiance that could mean only sunshine. A glowing light that was dazzling to his sleep-filled eyes, it streamed in golden—beautiful—to light the unfamiliar room and show motionless upon the floor the figure of Professor Sykes. His torn clothing had been neatly arranged, and his face showed livid lines of healing cuts and bruises.

McGuire tried gingerly to move his arms and legs; they were still functioning though stiff and weak from disuse. He raised himself slowly and stood swaying on his feet, then made his uncertain way to his companion and shook him weakly by the shoulder.

Professor Sykes breathed deeply and raised leaden lids from tired eyes to stare uncomprehendingly at McGuire. Soon his dark pupils ceased to dilate, and he, too, could see their prison and the light of day.

"Sunlight!" he said in a thin voice, and he seemed to know now that they were in the air; "I wonder—I wonder—if we shall land— what country? Some wilderness and a strange race—a strange, strange race!"

He was muttering half to himself; the mystery of these people whom he could not identify was still troubling him.

McGuire helped the other man to his feet, and they clung to each to the other for support as they crossed to kneel beside the floor-window and learn finally where their captors meant to take them.

A wilderness, indeed, the sight that met their eyes, but a wilderness of clouds—no unfamiliar sight to Lieutenant McGuire of the United States Army air service. But to settle softly into them instead of driving through with glistening wings—this was new and vastly different from anything he had known.

Sounds came to them in the silence, penetrating faintly through thick walls—the same familiar wailing call that trembled and quavered and seemed to the listening men to be guiding them down through the mist.

Gone was the sunlight, and the clouds beyond the deep-set window were gloriously ablaze with a brilliance softly diffused. The cloud bank was deep, and they felt the craft under them sink slowly, steadily into the misty embrace. It thinned below them to drifting vapor, and the first hazy shadows of the ground showed through from far beneath. Their altitude, the flyer knew, was still many thousands of feet.

"Water," said McGuire, as his trained eyes made plain to him what was still indistinct to the scientist. "An ocean—and a shoreline—" More clouds obscured the view; they parted suddenly to show a portion only of a clear-cut map.

IT STRETCHED beyond the confines of their window, that unfamiliar line of wave-marked shore; the water was like frozen gold, wrinkled in countless tiny corrugations and reflecting the bright glow from above. But the land,—that drew their eyes!

Were those cities, those shadow-splashed areas of gray and rose...? The last veiling clouds dissolved, and the whole circle was plain to their view.

The men leaned forward, breathless, intent, till the scientist, Sykes—the man whose eyes had seen and whose brain recorded a dim shape in the lens of a great telescope—Sykes drew back with a quivering, incredulous breath. For below them, so plain, so unmistakable, there lay a distant island, large even from this height, and it formed on this round map a sharp angle like a great letter "L."

"We shall know that if we ever see it again," Professor Sykes had remarked in the quiet and security of that domed building surmounting the heights of Mount Lawson. But he said nothing now, as he stared at his companion with eyes that implored McGuire to arouse him from this sleep, this dream that could never be real. But McGuire, lieutenant one-time in the forces of the U.S.A., had seen it too, and he stared back with a look that gave dreadful confirmation.

The observatory—Mount Lawson—the Earth!—those were the things unreal and far away. And here before them, in brain-stunning actuality, were the markings unmistakable—the markings of Venus. And they were landing, these two, in the company of creatures wild and strange as the planet—on Venus itself!

CHAPTER EIGHT

MILES underneath the great ship, from which Lieutenant McGuire and Professor Sykes were now watching through a floor-window of thick glass, was a glittering expanse of water—a great ocean. The flickering gold expanse that reflected back the color of the sunlit clouds passed to one side as the ship took its station above the island, a continent in size, that had shown by its shape like a sharply formed "L" an identifying mark to the astronomer.

They were high in the air; the thick clouds that surrounded this new world were miles from its surface, and the things of the world that awaited were tiny and blurred.

Airships passed and repassed far below. Large, some of them—as bulky as the transport they were on; others were small flashing cylinders, but all went swiftly on their way.

It must have come—some ethereal vibration to warn others from the path—for layer after layer of craft were cleared for the descent. A brilliant light flashed into view, a dazzling pin-point on the shore below, and the great ship fell suddenly beneath them. Swiftly it dropped down the pathway of light; on even keel it fell down and still down, till McGuire, despite his experience in the air, was sick and giddy.

The light blinked out at their approach. It was some minutes before the watching eyes recovered from the brilliance to see what mysteries might await, and then the surface was close and the range of vision small.

A vast open space—a great court paved with blocks of black and white—a landing field, perhaps, for about it in regular spacing other huge cylinders were moored. Directly beneath in a clear space was a giant cradle of curved arms; it was a mammoth structure, and the men knew at a glance that this was the bed where their great ship would lie.

The pavement seemed slowly rising to meet them as their ship settled close. Now the cradle was below, its arms waiting. The ship entered their grasp, and the arms widened, then closed to draw the monster to its rest. Their motion ceased. They were finally beyond the last faint doubt, at anchor on a distant world.

A shrill cackle of sound recalled them from the thrill of this adventure, and the attenuated and lanky figure, with its ashen, blotchy face that glared at them from the doorway, reminded them that this excursion into space was none of their desire. They were prisoners—captives from a foreign land.

A long hand moved its sinuous fingers to motion them to follow, and McGuire regarded his companion with a hopeless look and a despondent shrug of his shoulders.

"No use putting up a fight," he said; "I guess we'd better be good."

He followed where the figure was stepping through a doorway into a corridor beyond. They moved, silent and depressed, along the dimly lighted way; the touch of cold metal walls was as chilling to their spirits as to their flesh.

But the mood could not last; the first ray of light from the outside world sent shivers of anticipation along their spines. They were landing, in very fact, upon a new world; their feet were to walk where never man had stood; their eyes would see what mortal eyes had never visioned.

Fears were forgotten, and the men clung to each other not for the human touch but because of an ecstasy of intoxicating, soul-filling joy in the sheer thrill of adventure.

They were gripping each other's hand, round-eyed as a couple of children, as they stepped forward into the light.

Before them was a scene whose blazing beauty of color struck them to frozen silence; their exclamations of wonder died unspoken on their lips. They were in a city of the stars, and to their eyes it seemed as if all the brilliance of the heavens had been gathered for its building.

The spacious, open court itself stood high in the air among the masses of masonry, and beyond were countless structures. Some towered skyward; others were lower; and all were topped with bulbous towers and graceful minarets that made a forest of gleaming opal light. Opalescence everywhere!—it flashed in red and gold and delicate blues from every wall and cornice and roof.

"Quartz?" marveled Sykes after one long drawn breath. "Quartz or glass?—what are they made of? It is fairyland!"

A jewelled city! Garish, it might have been, and tawdry, in the full light of the sun. But on these weirdly unreal structures the sun's rays never shone; they were illumined only by the soft golden glow that diffused across this world from the cloud masses far above.

McGuire looked up at that uniform, glowing, golden mass that paled toward the horizon and faded to the gray of banked clouds. His eyes came slowly back to the ramp that led downward to the checkered black and white of the court. Beyond an open portion the pavement was solidly massed with people.

"People!—we might as well call them that," McGuire had told Sykes; "they are people of a sort, I suppose. We'll have to give them credit for brains. They've beaten us a hundred years in their inventions."

He was trying to see everything, understand everything, at once. There was not time to single out the new impressions that were crowding upon him. The air—it was warm to the point of discomfort; it explained the loose, light garments of the people; it came to the two men laden with strange scents and stranger sounds.

McGuire's eyes held with hungry curiosity upon the dwellers in this other world; he stared at the gaping throng from which came a bedlam of shrill cries. Lean colorless hands gesticulated wildly and pointed with long fingers at the two men.

The din ceased abruptly at a sharp, whistled order from their captor. He stood aside with a guard that had followed from the ship, and he motioned the two before him down the gangway. It was the same scarlet one who had faced them before, the one whom McGuire had attacked in a frenzy of furious fighting, only to go down to blackness and defeat before the slim cylinder of steel and its hissing gas. And the slanting eyes stared wickedly in cold triumph as he ordered them to go before him in his march of victory.

McGuire passed down toward the masses of color that were the ones who waited. There were many in the dull red of the ship's crew; others in sky-blue, in gold and pink and combinations of brilliance that blended their loose garments to kaleidoscopic hues. But the figures were similar in one unvarying respect: they were repulsive and ghastly, and their faces showed bright blotches of blood vessels and blue markings of veins through their parchment-gray skins.

The crowd parted to a narrow, living lane, and lean fingers clutched writhingly to touch them as they passed between the solid ranks.

McGuire had only a vague impression of a great building beyond, of lower stories decorated in barbaric colors, of towers above in strange forms of the crystal, colorful beauty they had seen. He walked toward it unseeing; his thoughts were only of the creatures round about.

"What damned beasts!" he said. Then, like his companion, he set his teeth to restrain all show of feeling as they made their way through the lane of incredible living things.

THEY followed their captor through a doorway into an empty room—empty save for one blue-clad individual who stood beside an instrument board let into the wall. Beyond was a long wall, where circular openings yawned huge and black.

The one at the instrument panel received a curt order, the weird voice of the man in red repeated a word that stood out above his curious, wordless tone. "Torg," he said, and again McGuire heard him repeat the syllable.

The operator touched here and there among his instruments, and tiny lights flashed; he threw a switch, and from one of the black openings like a deep cave came a rushing roar of sound. It dropped to silence as the end of a cylindrical car protruded into the room. A door in the metal car opened, and their guard hustled them roughly inside. The one in red followed while behind him the door clanged shut.

Inside the car was light, a diffused radiance from no apparent source, the whole air was glowing about them. And beneath their feet the car moved slowly but with a constant acceleration that built up to tremendous speed. Then that slackened, and Sykes and McGuire clung to each other for support while the car that had been shot like a projectile came to rest.

"Whew!" breathed the lieutenant; "that was quick delivery." Sykes made no reply, and McGuire, too, fell silent to study the tremendous room into which they were led. Here, seemingly, was the stage for their next experience.

A vast open hall with a floor of glass that was like obsidion, empty but for carved benches about the walls; there was room here for a mighty concourse of people. The walls, like those they had seen, were decorated crudely in glaring colors, and embellished with grotesque designs that proclaimed loudly the inexpert touch of the draughtsman. Yet, above them, the ceiling sprang lightly into vaulted, sweeping curves. McGuire's training had held little of architecture, yet even he felt the beauty of line and airy gracefulness of treatment in the structure itself.

The contrast between the flaunting colors and the finished artistry that lay beneath must have struck a discordant note to the scientist. He leaned closer to whisper.

"It is all wrong some way—the whole world! Beauty and refinement—then crude vulgarity, as incongruous as the people themselves—they do not belong here."

"Neither do we," was McGuire's reply; "it looks like a tough spot that we're in."

He was watching toward a high, arched entrance across the room. A platform before it was raised some six feet above the floor, and on this were seats—ornate chairs, done in sweeping scrolls of scarlet and gold. A massive seat in the center was like the fantastic throne of a child's fairy tale. From the corridor beyond that entrance came a stir and rustling that rivetted the man's attention.

A trumpet peal, vibrant and peculiar, blared forth from the ceiling overhead, and the red figures of the guards stood at rigid attention with lean arms held stiffly before them. The one in scarlet took the same attitude, then dropped his hands to motion the two men to give the same salute.

"You go to hell," said Lieutenant McGuire in his gentlest tones. And the scarlet figure's thin lips were snarling as he turned to whip his arms up to their position. The first of a procession of figures was entering through the arch.

Sykes, the scientist, was paying little attention. "It isn't true," he was muttering aloud; "it can't be true. Venus! Twenty-six million miles at inferior conjunction!"

He seemed lost in silent communion with his own thoughts. Then he said, "But I said there was every probability of life; I pointed out the similarities—"

"Hush!" warned McGuire. The eyes of the scarlet man were sending wicked looks in their direction. Tall forms were advancing through the arch. They, too, were robed in scarlet, and behind them others followed.

The trumpet peal from the dome above held now on a long-drawn, single note, while the scarlet men strode in silence across the dais and parted to form two lines. An inverted "V" that faced the entrance—they were an assembly of rigid, blazing statues whose arms were extended like those on the floor below.

The vibrant tone from on high changed to a crashing blare that shrieked discordantly to send quivering protest through every nerve of the waiting men. Those about them were shouting, and again the name of Torg was heard, as, in the high arch, another character appeared to play his part in a strange drama.

Thin like his companions, yet even taller than them, he wore the same brilliant robes and, an additional mark of distinction, a head-dress of polished gold. He acknowledged the salute with a quick raising of his own arms, then came swiftly forward and took his place upon the massive throne.

Not till he was seated did the others on the platform relax their rigid pose and seat themselves in the semicircle of chairs. And not till then did they so much as glance at the men waiting there before them—the two Earth-men, standing in silent, impassive contemplation of the brilliant scene and with their arms held quiet at their sides. Then every eye turned full upon the captives, and if McGuire had seen deadly malevolence in the face of their captor he found it a hundred-fold in the inhuman faces that looked down upon them now.

The inquiring mind of Professor Sykes did not fail to note the character of their reception. "But why," he asked in whispers of his fellow-prisoner, "—why this open hatred of us? What possible animus can they have against the earth or its people?"

The figure on the throne voiced a curt order; the one who had brought them stepped forward. His voice was raised in the same discordant, singing tone that leaped and wandered from note to note. It conveyed ideas—that was apparent; it was a language that he spoke. And the central figure above nodded a brief assent as he finished.

Their captor took an arm of each in his long fingers and pushed them roughly forward to stand alone before the battery of hard eyes.

NOW the crowned figure addressed them directly. His voice quavered sharply in what seemed an interrogation. The men looked blankly at each other.

Again the voice questioned them impatiently. Sykes and McGuire were silent. Then the young flyer took an involuntary step forward and looked squarely at the owner of the harsh voice.

"We don't know what you are saying," he began, "and I suppose that our lingo makes no sense to you—" He paused in helpless wonderment as to what he could say. Then—

"But what the devil is it all about?" he demanded explosively. "Why all the dirty looks? You've got us here as prisoners—now what do you expect us to do? Whatever it is, you'll have to quit singing it and talk something we can understand."

He knew his words were useless, but this reception was getting on his nerves—and his arm still tingled where the scarlet one had gripped him.

It seemed, though, that his meaning was not entirely lost. His words meant nothing to them, but his tone must have carried its message. There were sharp exclamations from the seated circle. The one who had brought them sprang forward with outstretched, clutching hands; his face was a blood-red blotch. McGuire was waiting in crouching tenseness that made the red one pause.

"You touch me again," said the waiting man, "and I'll knock you into an outside loop."

The attacker's indecision was ended by a loud order from above. McGuire turned as if he had been spoken to by the leader on the throne. The thin figure was leaning far forward; his eye were boring into those of the lieutenant, and he held the motionless pose for many minutes. To the angry man, staring back and upward, there came a peculiar optical illusion.

The evil face was vanishing in a shifting cloud that dissolved and reformed, as he watched, into pictures. He knew it was not there, the thing he saw; he knew he was regarding something as intangible as thought; but he got the significance of every detail.

He saw himself and Professor Sykes; they were being crushed like ants beneath a tremendous heel; he knew that the foot that could grind out their lives was that of the one on the throne.

THE cloud-stuff melted to new forms that grew clearer to show him the earth. A distorted Earth—and he knew the distortion came from the mind of the being before him who had never seen the earth at first hand; yet he knew it for his own world. It was turning in space; he saw oceans and continents; and before his mental gaze he saw the land swarming with these creatures of Venus. The one before him was in command; he was seated on a huge throne; there were Earth people like Sykes and himself who crept humbly before him, while fleets of great Venusian ships hovered overhead.

The message was plain—plain as if written in words of fire in the brain of the man. McGuire knew that these creatures intended that the vision should be true—they meant to conquer the earth. The slim, khaki-clad figure of Lieutenant McGuire quivered with the strength of his refusal to accept the truth of what he saw. He shook his head to clear it of these thought wraiths.

"Not—in—a—million—years!" he said, and he put behind his words all the mental force at his command. "Try that, old top, and they'll give you the fight of your life—" He checked his words as he saw plainly that the thin cruel face that stared and stared was getting nothing from his reply.

"Now what do you think about that?" he demanded of Professor Sykes. "He got an idea across to me—some form of telepathy. I saw his mind, or I saw what he wanted me to see of it. It's taps, he says, for us, and then they think they're going across and annex the world."

He glanced upward again and laughed loudly for the benefit of those who were watching him so closely. "Fine chance!" he said; "a fat chance!" But in the deeper recesses of his mind he was shaken.

For themselves there was no hope. Well, that was all in a lifetime. But the other—the conquest of the earth—he had to try with all his power of will to keep from his mind the pictures of destruction these beastly things could bring about.

The chief of this strange council made a gesture of contempt with the grotesque hands that were so translucent yet ashy-pale against his scarlet robe, and the down-drawn thin lips reflected the thoughts that prompted it. The open opposition of Lieutenant McGuire failed to impress him, it seemed. At a word the one who had brought them sprang forward.

He addressed himself to the circle of men, and he harangued them mightily in harsh discordance. He pointed one lean hand at the two captives, then beat it upon his own chest. "They are mine," he was saying, as the men knew plainly. And they realized as if the weird talk came like words to their ears that this monster was demanding that the captives be given him.

An exchange of dismayed glances, and "Not so good!" said McGuire under his breath; "Simon Legree is asking for his slaves. Mean, ugly devil, that boy!"

The lean figures on the platform were bending forward, an expression of mirth—distorted, animal smiles—upon their flabby lips. They represented to the humans, so helpless before them, a race of thinking things in whom no last vestige of kindness or decency remained. But was there an exception? One of the circle was standing; the one beside them was sullenly silent as the other on the platform addressed their ruler.

He spoke at some length, not with the fire and vehemence of the one who had claimed them, but more quietly and dispassionately, and his cold eyes, when they rested on those of McGuire and Sykes, seemed more crafty than actively ablaze with malevolent ill-will. Plainly it was the councilor now, addressing his superior. His inhuman voice was silenced by a reply from the one on the throne.

He motioned—this gold-crowned figure of personified evil—toward the two men, and his hand swept on toward the one who had spoken. He intoned a command in harsh gutturals that ended in a sibilant shriek. And the two standing silent and hopeless exchanged looks of despair.

They were being delivered to this other—that much was plain—but that it boded anything but captivity and torment they could not believe. That last phrase was too eloquent of hissing hate.

The creature rose, tall and ungainly, from his throne; amid the salutations of his followers he turned and vanished through the arch. The others of his council followed, all but the one. He motioned to the two men to come with him, and the sullen one who had demanded the men for himself obeyed an order from this councilor who was his superior.

He snapped an order, and four of his men ranged themselves about the captives as a guard. Thin metal cords were whipped about the wrists of each; their hands were tied. The wire cut like a knife-edge if they strained against it.

The new director of their destinies was vanishing through an exit at one side of the great hall; their guard hustled them after. A corridor opened before them to end in a gold-lit portal; it was daylight out beyond where a street was filled with hurrying figures in many colors. With quavering shrieks they scattered like frightened fowls as an airship descended between the tall buildings that reflected its passing in opalescent hues.

It was a small craft compared with the one that had brought them, and it swept down to settle lightly upon the street with no least regard for those who might be crushed by its descent. Consideration for their fellows did not appear as a marked characteristic of this strange people, McGuire observed thoughtfully. They swarmed in endless droves, these multicolored beings who made of the thoroughfare an ever-changing kaleidoscope—and what was a life or two, more or less, among so many? He found no comfort for themselves in the thought.

Shoulder to shoulder, the two followed where the scarlet figure of the councilor moved toward the waiting ship. Only the professor paid further heed to their surroundings; he marveled aloud at the numbers of the people.

"Hundreds of them," he said; "thousands! They are swarming everywhere like rats!" His eyes passed on to the buildings in their glory of delicate hues, as he added, "And the contrast they make with their surroundings! It is all wrong some way; I wish I knew—"

They were in the ship when McGuire replied. "I hope we live long enough to satisfy your curiosity," he said grimly.

The ship was rising beneath them; the opal and quartz of the city's walls were flashing swiftly down.

CHAPTER NINE

THEY were in a cabin at the nose of the ship, seated on metal chairs, their hands unshackled and free. Their scarlet guardian reclined at ease somewhat to one side, but despite his apparent disregard his cold eyes seldom left the faces of the two men.

Windows closed them in; windows on each side, in front, above them, and even in the floor beneath. It was a room for observation whose metal-latticed walls served only as a framework for the glass. And there was much to be observed.

The golden radiance of sunlit clouds was warm above. They rose toward it, until, high over the buildings' tallest spires, there spread on every hand the bewildering beauty of that forest of minarets and sloping roofs and towers, whose many facets made glorious blendings of soft color. Aircraft at many levels swept in uniform directions throughout the sky. The ship they were in hung quiet for a time, then rose to a higher level to join the current of transportation that flowed into the south.

"We will call it south," said Professor Sykes. "The sun-glow, you will observe, is not directly overhead; the sun is sinking; it is past their noon. What is the length of their day? Ah, this interesting—interesting!" The certain fate they had foreseen was forgotten; it is not often given to an astronomer to check at first hand his own indefinite observations.

"Look!" McGuire exclaimed. "Open country! The city is ending!"

Ahead and below them the buildings were smaller and scattered. Their new master was watching with closest scrutiny the excitement of the men; he whispered an order into a nearby tube, and the ship slowly slanted toward the ground. He was studying these new specimens, as McGuire observed, but the lieutenant paid little attention; his eyes were too thoroughly occupied in resolving into recognizable units the picture that flowed past them so quickly. He was accustomed, this pilot of the army air service, to reading clearly the map that spreads beneath a plane, but now he was looking at an unfamiliar chart.

"Fields," he said, and pointed to squared areas of pale reds and blues; "though what it is, heaven knows. And the trees!—if that's what they are." The ship went downward where an area of tropical denseness made a tangled mass of color and shadow.

"Trees!" Lieutenant McGuire had exclaimed, but these forests were of tree-forms in weirdest shapes and hues. They grew to towering heights, and their branches and leaves that swayed and dipped in the slow-moving air were of delicate pastel shades.

"No sunlight," said the Professor excitedly; "they have no direct rays of the sun. The clouds act as a screen and filter out actinic rays."

McGuire did not reply. He was watching the countless dots of color that were people—people who swarmed here as they had in the city; people working at these great groves, crouching lower in the fields as the ship swept close; people everywhere in teeming thousands. And like the vegetation about them, they, too, were tall and thin, attenuated of form and with skin like blood-stained ash.

"They need the sun," Sykes was repeating; "both vegetable and animal life. The plants are deficient in chlorophyl—see the pale green of the leaves!—and the people need vitamines. Yet they evidently have electric power in abundance. I could tell them of lamps—"

His comments ceased as McGuire lurched heavily against him. The flyer had taken note of the tense, attentive attitude of the one in scarlet; the man was leaning forward, his eyes focused directly upon the scientist's face; he seemed absorbing both words and emotions.

How much could he comprehend? What power had he to vision the idea-pictures in the other's mind? McGuire could not know. But "Sorry!" he told Sykes; "that was clumsy of me." And he added in a whisper, "Keep your thoughts to yourself; I think this bird is getting them."

Buildings flashed under them, not massed solidly as in the city, yet spaced close to one another as if every foot of ground not devoted to their incredible agriculture were needed to house the inhabitants. The ground about them was alive with an equally incredible humanity that swarmed over all this world in appalling profusion.

Their horrid flesh! Their hideous features! And their number! McGuire had a sudden, sickening thought. They were larvae, these crawling hordes—vile worm-things that infested a beautiful world—that bred here in millions, their numbers limited only by the space for their bodies and the food for their stomachs. And he, McGuire, a *man*—he and this other man with his clear-thinking scientific brain were prisoners to this horde; captives, to be used or butchered by those vile, crawling things!

And again it was this world of contrast that drove home the conviction with its sickening certainty. A world of beauty, of delicate colors, of sweeping oceans and gleaming shores and towering cities with their grace and beauty and elfin splendor yet a world that shuddered beneath this devouring plague of grublike men.

THEY swept past cities and towns and over many miles of open land before their craft swung eastward toward the dark horizon. The master gave another order into the speaking tube and their ship shot forward, faster and yet faster, with a speed that pressed them heavily into their seats. Behind them was the glory of the sunlit clouds; ahead the gloomy gray-black masses that must make a stygian night sky over this lonely world—a world cut off by that vaporous shell from all communion with the stars.

They were over the water; before them a dark ocean reached out in forbidding emptiness to a darker horizon. Ahead, the only broken line in the vast level expanse was a mountain rising abruptly from the sea. It was a volcanic cone surmounting an island; the sunlight's glow reflected from behind them against the sombre mass that lifted toward the clouds. Their ship was high enough to clear it, but instead it swung, as McGuire watched, toward the south.

The island drifted past, and again they were on their course. But to the flyer there were significant facts that could not pass unobserved. Their own ship had swung in a great circle to avoid this mountain. And all through the skies were others that did the same. The air above and about the grim sentinel peak was devoid of flying shapes.

McGuire caught the eyes of the councilor, their keeper. "What is that?" he asked, though he knew the words were lost on the other. He nodded his head toward the distant peak, and his question was plainly in regard to the island. And for the first time since their coming to this wild world, he saw, flashing across the features of one of these men, a trace of emotion that could only be construed as fear.

The slitted cat eyes lost their look of complacent superiority. They widened involuntarily, and the face was drained of its blotched color. There was fear, terror unmistakable, though it showed for but an instant. He had control of his features almost at once, but the flyer had read their story.

Here was something that gave pause to this race of conquering vermin; a place in the expanse of this vast sea that brought panic to their hearts. And there came to him, as he stowed the remembrance away in his mind, the first glow of hope. These things could fear a mountain; it might be that they could be brought to fear a man.

THE sky was clearing rapidly of traffic and the mountain of his speculations was lost astern, when another island came slanting swiftly up to meet them as their ship swept down from the heights. It was a tiny speck in the ocean's expanse, a speck that resolved itself into the squared fields of colored growth, orchards whose brilliant, strange fruits glowed crimson in the last light of day, and enormous trees, beyond which appeared a house.

A palace, McGuire concluded, when he saw clearly the many-storied pile. Like the buildings they had seen, this also constructed of opalescent quartz. There were windows that glowed warmly in the dusk. A sudden wave of loneliness, almost unbearable, swept over the man.

Windows and gleaming lights, the good sounds of Earth; home…! And his ears, as he stepped out into the cool air, were assailed with the strange cackle and calling of weird folk; the air brought him scents, from the open ground beyond, of fruits and vegetation like none he had ever known; and the earth, the homeland of his vain imaginings, was millions of empty miles away…

The leader stopped, and McGuire looked dispiritedly at the unfamiliar landscape under dusky lowering skies. Trees towered high in the air—trees grotesque and weird by all Earth standards—whose limbs were pale green shadows in the last light of day. The foliage, too, seemed bleached and drained of color, but among the leaves were flashes of brilliance where night-blooming flowers burst open like star-shells to fill the air with heavy scents.

Between the men and the forest growth was a row of denser vegetation, great ferns twenty feet and more in height, and among them at regular intervals stood plants of another growth—each a tremendous pod held in air on a thick stalk. Tendrils coiled themselves like giant springs beside each pod, tendrils as thick as a man's wrist. The great pods were ranged in a line that extended as far as McGuire could see in the dim light.

His shoulders drooped as the guard herded him and his companion toward the building beyond. He must not be cast down—he would not! Who knew how much of such feeling was read by these keen-eyed observers? And the only thought with which he could fill his mind, the one forlorn ghost of a hope that he could cling to, was that of an island, a volcanic peak that rose from dark waters to point upward toward the heights.

The guard of four was clustered about; the figures were waiting now in the gathering dark—waiting, while the one in scarlet listened and spoke alternately into a jeweled instrument that hung by a slender chain about his neck. He raised one lean hand to motion the stirring guards to silence, listened again intently into the instrument, then pointed that hand toward the cloud-filled sky, while he craned his thin neck to look above him.

The men's eyes followed the pointing hand to see only the sullen black of unlit clouds. The last distant aircraft had vanished from the skies; not a ship was in the air—only the enveloping blanket of high-flung vapor that blocked out all traces of the heavens. And then!—

The cloud banks high in the skies flashed suddenly to dazzling, rolling flame. The ground under their feet was shaken as by a distant earthquake, while, above, the terrible fire spread, a swift, flashing conflagration that ate up the masses of clouds.

"What in thunder—" McGuire began; then stopped as he caught, in the light from above, the reflection of fierce exultation in the eyes of the scarlet one. The evil, gloating message of those eyes needed no words to explain its meaning. That this cataclysm was self-made by these beings, McGuire knew, and he knew that in some way it meant menace to him and his.

Yet he groped in thought for some definite meaning. No menace could this be to himself personally, for he and Sykes stood there safe in the company of the councilor himself. Then the threat of this flaming blast must be directed toward the earth!

The fire vanished, and once more, as Professor Sykes had seen on that night so long ago, the blanket of clouds was broken. McGuire followed the gaze of the scientist whose keen eyes were probing in these brief moments into the depths of star-lit space.

"There—there!" Sykes exclaimed in awe-struck tones. His hand was pointing outward through the space where flames had cleared the sky. A star was shining in the heavens with a glory that surpassed all others. It outshone all neighboring stars, and it sent its light down through the vast empty reaches of space, a silent message to two humans, despondent and heartsick, who stared with aching eyes.

Lieutenant McGuire did not hear his friend's whispered words. No need to name that distant world—it was Earth! Earth...! And it was calling to its own...

There was a flying-field—so plain before his mental eyes; men in khaki and leather who moved and talked and spoke of familiar things...and the thunder of motors...and roaring planes...

Some far recess within his deeper self responded strangely. What now of threats and these brute-things that threatened?—he was one with this picture he had visioned. He was himself; he was a man of that distant world of men; they would show these vile things how men could meet menace—or death... His shoulders were back and unconsciously he stood erect.

The scarlet figure was close beside them in the dusk, his voice vibrant with a quality which should have struck fear to his captives' hearts as he ordered them on. But the look in his crafty eyes changed to one of puzzled wonder at sight of the men.

Hands on each other's shoulders, they stood there in the gathering dark, where grotesque trees arched twistingly overhead. Their moment of depression had passed; Earth had called, and they had heard it, each after his own fashion. But to each the call had been one of clear courage. No longer cast off and forlorn, they were one with their own world.

"Down," said Professor Sykes with a whimsical smile; "down, but not out!" And the lieutenant responded in kind.

"Are we down-hearted?" he demanded loudly. And the two turned as one man to grin at the scarlet one as they thundered. "N-o-o!"

CHAPTER TEN

TWO men grinned in derision at the horrible, man-shaped thing that held their destinies in his lean, inhuman hands!—but they turned abruptly away to look again above them where that bright star still shone through an opening in the clouds.

"The earth! Home!" It seemed as if they could never tear their eyes away from the sight.

Their captor whistled an order, and the guard of four tugged vainly at the two, who resisted that they might gaze upon their own world until the closing clouds should blot it from sight. A cry from one of the red guards roused them.

The dark was closing in fast, and their surroundings were dim. Vaguely, McGuire felt more than saw one of the red figures whirled into the air. He sensed a movement in the jungle darkness where were groves of weird trees and the tangle of huge vegetable growths. What it was he could not say, but he felt the guard who clutched at him quiver in terror.

Their leader snatched at the instrument that hung about his neck and put it to his lips; he whistled an order, sharp and shrill. Blazing light that seemed to flame in the air was the response; the air was aglow with an all-pervading brilliance like that in the car that had whirled them from the landing field. The light was everywhere, and the building before them was surrounded by a dazzling envelope of luminosity.

Whatever of motion or menace there had been ceased abruptly. Their guard, three now in number instead of four, seized them roughly and hustled them toward an open door. No time, as they passed, for more than fleeting impressions; a hall of warm, glowing light—a passage that branched off—and, at the end, a room into which they were thrown, while a metal door clanged behind them.

These were no gentle hands that hurled the men staggering through the doorway, and Professor Sykes fell headlong upon the glassy floor. He sprang to his feet, his face aflame with anger. "The miserable beasts!" he shouted.

"Take it easy," admonished the flyer. "We're in the hoose-gow; no use of getting all fussed up if they don't behave like perfect gentlemen.

"There's a bunk in the corner," he said, and pointed to a woven hammock that was covered with soft cloths; "and here's another that I can sling. Twin beds! What more do you want?"

He opened a door and the splash of falling water came to them. A fountain cascaded to the ceiling to fall splashing upon a floor of inlaid, glassy tile. McGuire whistled.

"Room and bath," he said. "And you complained of the service!"

"I have an idea," he told the scientist, "that our scarlet friend who owns this place intends to treat us decently, even though his helpers are a bit rough. My hunch is that he wants to get some information out of us. That old bird back there in the council chamber told me as plain as day that they think they are going to conquer the earth. Maybe that's why we are here—as exhibits A and B, for them to study and learn how to lick us."

"You are talking what I would have termed nonsense a month ago," replied Sykes, "but now—well, I am afraid you are right. And," he said slowly, "I fear that they are equally correct. They have conquered space; they have ships propelled by some unknown power; they have gas weapons, as you and I have reason to know. And they have all the beastly ferocity to carry such a plan through to success. But I wonder what that sky-splitting blast meant."

"Bombardment," the flyer told him; "bombardment of the earth as sure as you're alive."

"More nonsense," said Sykes; "and probably correct... Well, what are we to do?—sit tight and give them as little information as we can? or—" His question ended unfinished; the alternative, it seemed, was not plain to him.

"There's only one answer," said McGuire. "We must get away; escape somehow."

Professor Sykes' eyes showed his appreciation of a spirit that could still dare to hope, but he asked dejectedly, "Escape? Good idea. But where to?"

"I have an idea," the flyer said slowly. "An idea about an island." He told the professor what he had observed—the fact that there was one spot of land on this globe from which the traffic of these monsters of Venus steered clear. This, he explained, must have some significance.

"Whatever is there, God only knows," he admitted, "but it is something these devils don't like a little bit. It might be interesting to learn more. We'll make a break for it; find a boat. No, we probably can't do it, but we can make a try. Now what is our first step, I wonder."

"Our first step," said Professor Sykes, measuring his words as if he might be working out some astronomical calculation, "is into the inverted shower-bath, if you feel as hot as I do. And our next step, when all is quiet for the night, is through the window I see beyond. I can see the branches of one of those undernourished trees from here."

"Last one in is a lop-eared Venusian!" said McGuire, throwing off his jacket. And in that strange room in a strange world, under the shadow of death and of tortures unknown, the two men stripped with all the care-free abandon of a couple of schoolboys racing to be first in the old swimming hole.

IT WAS some time later when the door opened and a long red hand pushed a tray of food into the room. The tray was of unbreakable crystal—he rattled it heedlessly upon the floor—and it held crystal dishes of unknown foods.

They were sampling them all when Sykes remarked plaintively, "I would like to know what under heaven I am eating."

"I've wished to know that in lots of restaurants," McGuire replied. "I remember a place down on—" He stopped abruptly, then chewed in silence upon a fruit like a striped pepper that stung his mouth and tongue while he scarcely felt it. References to Earth things plainly were to be avoided; the visions they brought before one's eyes were unnerving.

They made a pretence of sleeping in case they were being observed, and it was some hours later when the two stood quietly beside the open window. As Sykes had seen, there were branches of a pale, twisted tree-growth close outside. McGuire tried his weight upon them, then swung himself out, hand over hand, upon the branch that bent low beneath him. Sykes was close behind when he clambered to the ground to stand for some minutes, listening silently in the dark.

"Too easy!" the lieutenant whispered. "They are too foxy to leave a gateway like that—but here we are. The shore is off in this direction."

The dark of a night unrelieved by a single star was about them as they moved noiselessly away. They followed open ground at first. The building that had been their brief prison was upon their right; beyond and at the left was where the ship landed—it was gone now—and beyond that the wall of vegetation.

And again, in the dark, McGuire had an uncanny sense of motion. Soft bodies were slipping quietly one upon another; something that lived was there beyond them in the night. No sound or sign of life came from the house; no guard had been posted; and McGuire stopped again, before plunging into the tangled growth, to whisper, "Too easy, Sykes! There's something about this—"

He had pushed aside the fronds of a giant fern; a cautious step beyond his hands touched a slippery, pliant vine. And his whisper ended as he felt the thing turn and twist beneath his hand. It was alive!—writhing!—cold as the body of a monster snake, and just as vicious and savage in the way that it whipped down and about him in the gloom of the starless night.

The thing was alive! It threw its coils around his body in an embrace that left him breathless; a slender tendril was tightening about his neck; his hands and arms were bound.

His ankle was grasped as he was whirled aloft—a human hand that gripped him this time—and Sykes, forgetting discretion and the need for silence, was shouting in the darkness that gave no clue to their opponent. "Hang on!" he yelled. "I've got you, Mac!"

His shouts were cut short by another serpent shape that thrashed him and smashed the softer growing things to earth that it might wrap this man, too, in its deadly coils.

McGuire felt his companion's hold loosen as he was lifted from the ground; there were other arms flailing about him—living, coiling things that seemed to fight one with another for this prize. Abruptly, blindingly, the scene was vividly etched before him; the strange trees, the ferns, the writhing and darting serpent-arms! They were illumined in a dazzling, white light!

He was in the air, clutched strangely in constricting arms; an odor of rotted flesh was in his nostrils, sickening, suffocating! Beyond and almost beneath him a cauldron of green gaped open, and he saw within it a pool of thick liquid that eddied and steamed to give off the stench of putrescence.

All this in an instant of vision—and in that instant he knew the death they courted. It was a giant pod that held that pool—one of the growths he had seen ranged out like a line of sentinels. But the terrible tendrils that had been coiled and at rest were wrapped about him now, drawing him to that reeking pool of death and the waiting thick lips that would close above him. Sykes, too! The tendrils that had clutched him were whisking his helpless body where another gaping mouth was open—

AND THEN, in the blazing light that was more brilliant than any light of day in this world, the hold about McGuire relaxed. He saw, as he fell, the thick, green lips snap shut; and the arms that had held him pulled back into harmless, tight-wound coils.

Their bodies crashed to earth where a great fern bent beneath them to cushion their fall. And the men lay silent and gasping for great choking breaths, while from the building beyond came the cackle and shrieking of man-things in manifest enjoyment of the frustrated plans.

It was the laughter that determined McGuire.

"Damn the plants!" he said between hoarse breaths. "Man-eating plants—but they're—better—than—those devils! And there's only—one line of them; I saw them here before. Shall we go on?—make a break for it?"

Sykes rolled to the shelter of an arching frond and, without a word, went crawling away. McGuire was behind him, and the two, as they came to open ground, sprang to their feet and ran on through the weird orchard where tree trunks made dim, twisting lines. They ran blindly and helplessly toward the outer dark that promised temporary shelter.

A hopeless attempt—both men, knew the futility of it, while they stumbled onward through the dark. Behind them the night was hideous with noise as the great palace gave forth an eruption of shrieking, inhuman forms that scattered with whistling and wailing calls in all directions.

A mile or more of groping, hopeless flight, till a yellow gleam shone among the trees to guide them. A building, beyond a clearing, gave a bright illumination to the black night.

"We've run in a circle," choked McGuire, his voice weak and uncertain with exhaustion. "Like a couple of fools!"

He waited until the heavy breathing that shook his body might be controlled, then corrected himself. "No—this is another—a new one—see the towers! And listen—it's a radio station!"

The slender frameworks that towered high in air glowed like flame—a warning to the ships whose lights showed now and then far overhead. And, clear and distinct, there came to the listening men the steady, crackling hiss of an uninterrupted signal.

Against the lighted building moving figures showed momentarily, and McGuire pulled his friend into the safe concealment of a tangle of growth, while the group of yelling things sped past.

"Come on," he told Sykes; "we can't get away—not a chance! Let's have a look at this place, and perhaps—well, I have an idea!" He slipped silently, cautiously on, where a forest of jungle ferns gave promise of safe passage.

SOME warning had been sounded; the occupants of the building were scattered to aid in the man-hunt. Only one was left in the room where two Earth-men peeped in at the door.

The figure was seated upon an insulated platform, and his long hands manipulated keys and levers on a table before him. McGuire and Sykes stared amazedly at this broadcasting station whose air was filled with a pandemonium of crashing sound from some distant room, but McGuire was concerned mainly with the motion of a lean, blood-red hand that swung an object like a pointer in free-running sweeps above a dial on the table. And he detected a variation in the din from beyond as the pointer moved swiftly.

Here was the control board for those messages he had heard; this was the instrument that varied the sending mechanism to produce the wailing wireless cries that made words in some far-distant ears. McGuire, as he slipped into the room and crept within leaping distance of the grotesque thing so like yet unlike a man, was as silent as the nameless, writhing horror that had seized them in the dark. He sprang, and the two came crashing to the floor.

Lean arms came quickly about him to clutch and tear at his face, but the flyer had an arm free, and one blow ended the battle. The man of Venus relaxed to a huddle of purple and yellow cloth from which a ghastly face protruded. McGuire leaped to his feet and sprang to the place where the other had been.

"Hold them off as long as you can!" he shouted to Sykes, and his hand closed upon the pointer.

Did this station send where he was hoping? Was this the station that had communicated with the ship that had hovered above their flying field in that far-off land? He did not know, but it was a powerful station, and there was a chance—

He moved the pointer frantically here and there, swung it to one side and another; then found at last a point on the outside of the strange design beneath his hand where the pointer could rest while the crashing crackle of sound was stilled.

And now he swung the pointer—upon the plate—anywhere!— and the noise from beyond told instantly of the current's passage. He held it an instant, then pushed it back to the silent spot—a dash! A quick return that flashed back again to bring silence—a dot! More dashes and dots...and McGuire thanked a kindly heaven that had permitted him to learn the language of the air, while he cursed his slowness in sending.

Would it reach? Would there be anyone to hear? No certainty; he could only flash the wild Morse symbols out into the night. He must try to get word to them—warn them! And "Blake," he called, and spelled out the name of their field, "warning—Venus—"

"Hold them!" he yelled to Sykes at the sound of rushing feet. "Keep them off as long as you can!"

"...Prepare—for invasion. Blake, this is McGuire..." Over and over, he worked the swinging pointer into symbols that might in some way, by some fortunate chance, help that helpless people to resist the horror that lay ahead.

And while heavy bodies crashed against the door that Sykes was holding, there came from some deep-hidden well of memory an inspiration. There was a man he had once met—a man who had confided wondrous things; and now, with the knowledge of these others who had conquered space, he could believe wholly what he had laughed and joked about before. That man, too, had claimed to have travelled far from the earth; he had invented a machine; his name—

The pointer was swinging in frenzied haste to spell over and over the name of a man, and the name, too, of a forgotten place in the mountains of Nevada. It was repeating the message; then finished in one long crashing wail as a cloud of vapor shot about McGuire and his hand upon the pointer went suddenly limp.

CHAPTER ELEVEN

CAPTAIN Blake's game of solitaire had become an obsession. He drove himself to the utmost in the line of duty, and, through the day, the demands of the flying field filled his mind to forgetfulness. And for the rest, he forced his mind to concentrate upon the turn of the cards. He could not read—and he must not think!—so he sat through long evenings trying vainly to forget.

He looked up with an expressionless face as Colonel Boynton entered the room. The colonel saw the cards and nodded.

"Does that help?" he asked, and added without waiting for an answer, "I don't like cards, but I find my mathematics works well... My old problems—I can concentrate on them, and stop this eternal, damnable thinking, thinking—"

There was something of the same look forming about the eyes of both—that look that told of men who struggled gamely under the sentence of death, refusing to think or to fear, and waiting, waiting, impotently. Blake looked at the colonel with a carefully emotionless gaze. "It's hell in the big towns, I hear."

The Colonel nodded. "Can't blame them much, if that's what appeals to them. A year and a half!—and they've got to forget it. Why not crowd all the recklessness and excesses they can into the time that is left?—poor devils! But for the most part the world is wagging along, and people are going through the familiar motions."

"Well," said Blake, "I used to wonder at times how a man might feel if he were facing execution. Now we all know. Just going dumbly along, feeling as little as we can, thinking of anything, everything—except the one thing. They've turned to using dope, a lot of them, I hear. Maybe it helps; nobody cares much. Only a year and a half."

He raised his face from which all expression was consciously erased. "Any possible hope?" he asked. "Or do we take it when it comes and fight with what we've got as long as we can? There was some talk in the papers of an invention—Bureau of Standards cooperating with the big General Committee to investigate. Anything come of it?"

"A thousand of them," said the colonel, "all futile. No, we can't expect much from those things. Though there's a whisper that came to me from Washington. General Clinton—you may remember him; he was here when the thing first broke—says that some scientist, a real one, not another of these half-baked geniuses, has worked out a transformation of some kind. It was too deep for me, but it is based upon changing hydrogen into helium, I think. Liberates some perfectly tremendous amount of power. The general had it all down pat—"

He stopped speaking at the change in Captain Blake's face. The careful repression of all emotions was gone; the face was suddenly alive—

"I know," he said sharply; "I remember something of the theory. There is a difference in the atoms or their protons—the liberation of an electron from each atom—matter actually transformed into energy; theoretical, what I have read. But—but— Oh my God, Boynton, do you mean that they've got it?—that it will drive us through space?"

The colonel drove one fist into the palm of his other hand. "Fool! Idiot!" he exclaimed, and it was evident that the epithets were intended for himself.

"I had forgotten that you had been trained along that line. The general wants a man to work with them, somewhat as a liason officer to link the army requirements closely with their developments; we are hoping to work out a space ship, of course. You are just the man; I will radio him this minute. Be ready to leave—" The slamming of the door marked a hurried exit toward the radio room.

And abruptly, stifflingly, Captain Blake dared to hope. "Scientists will come through with something, some new method of propulsion. All the world is looking to them!" His thoughts were leaping from one possibility to another. "Some miracle of power that will drive a fleet through space as they have done, to battle with the enemy on his own ground—"

Could he help? Was there one little thing that he could do to apply their knowledge to practical ends? The thought thrilled him with overpowering emotion an hour later as he felt the lift of the plane beneath him.

"Report to General Clinton," the colonel's reply had said. "Captain Blake will be assigned to special duty." He opened the throttle to his ship's best cruising speed, but his spirit was soaring ahead to urge on the swift scout ship whose wings drove steadily into the gathering dusk.

And then, after long hours, Washington! Brief words with many men—and discouragement! The seat of government of the United States was a city of despondent men, weary, hopeless, but fighting. There was a look of strain on every face; the eyes told a story of sleepless nights and futile thinking and planning. Blake's elation was short lived.

He was sent to New York and on into the state, where the laboratories of a great electrical company had turned their equipment from commercial purposes to those of war. Here, surely, one might find fuel to feed the dying embers of hope; the new development must give greater promise than General Clinton had intimated.

"Nothing you can do as yet," he was told, when he had stated his mission. "It is still experimental, but we have worked out the transformation on a small scale, and harnessed the power."

Captain Blake was in no mood for temporizing; he was tired with being put off. He stared belligerently at the chief of this department.

"Power—hell!" he said. "We've got power now. How will you apply it? How will we use it for travelling through space?"

The great man of science was unmoved by the outburst. "That is poppycock," he replied; "the unscientific twaddle of the sensational press. We are practical men here; we are working to give you men who do the fighting better ships and better arms. But you will use them right here on Earth."

The calm assurance of this man who spoke with a voice of such confidence and authority left the flyer speechless. His brain sent a chaos of profane and violent expletives to the lips that dared not frame them. There was no adequate reply.

Blake jammed his hat upon his head and walked blindly from the room. Heedless of the protests of those he jostled on the street he went raging on, but some subconscious urge directed his steps. He found himself at the railway. There was a station, and a grilled window where he was asking for a ticket back to Washington. And on the following day—

"There is nothing I can do," he told General Clinton. "It is hopeless. I ask to be relieved."

"Why?" The general snapped the question at him. What kind of man was this that Boynton had sent him?

"They are fools," said Blake bluntly, "pompous, well-meaning fools! They are planning better motors, more power," He laughed harshly. "and they think that with them we can attack ships that are independent of the air."

"Still," asked General Clinton coldly, "for what purpose do you wish to be relieved? What do you intend to do?"

"Return to the field," said Captain Blake, "to work, and put my planes and personnel in the best possible condition; then, when the time comes, go up and fight like hell."

An unusual phrasing of a request when one is addressing one's commander; but the older man threw back his shoulders, that were bending under responsibilities too great for one man to bear, and took a long breath that relaxed his face and seemed to bring relief.

"You've got the right idea..." He spoke slowly and thoughtfully. "...the right philosophy. It is all we have left—to fight like hell when the time comes. Give my regards to Colonel Boynton; he sent me a good man after all."

ANOTHER long flight, westward this time, and, despite the failure of his hopes and of his errand, Blake was flying with a mind at peace. "It is all we have left," the general had said. Well, it was good to face facts, to admit them—and that was that! There was no use of thinking or worrying… He lifted the ship to a higher level and glanced at his compass. There were clouds up ahead, and he drove still higher into the night, until he was above them.

And again his peace of mind was not to last.

It was night when he swung the ship over his home port and signalled for a landing. A flood of light swept out across the field to guide him down. He went directly to the colonel's quarters but found him gone.

"In the radio room, I think," an orderly told him.

Colonel Boynton was listening intently in the silent room; he scowled with annoyance at the disturbance of Blake's coming; then, seeing who it was, he motioned quickly for the captain to listen in.

"Good Lord, Blake," he told the captain in an excited whisper; "I'm glad you're here. Another ship had been sighted; she's been all over the earth; just scouting and mapping, probably. And there have been signals the same as before—the same until just now. Listen!—it's talking Morse!—it's been calling for you!"

He thrust a head set into Blake's hands, then reached for some papers. "Poor reception, but there's what we've got," he said.

The paper held the merest fragments of messages that the operator had deciphered. Blake examined them curiously while he listened at the silent receiver.

"Maricopa"—the message, whatever it was, was meant for them, but there were only parts of words and disjointed phrases that the man had written down, "Venus attacking Earth…Captain Blake…Sykes and…"

At the name of Sykes, Blake dropped the paper.

"What does this mean?" he demanded. "Sykes!—why Sykes was the astronomer who was captured with McGuire!"

"Listen!" The colonel's voice was almost shrill with excitement.

The night was whispering faintly the merest echo of a signal from a station far away, but it resolved itself into broken fragments of sound that were long and short in duration, and the fragments joined to form letters in the Morse code.

"See Winslow," it told them, and repeated the message: "See Winslow at Sierra…" Some distant storm crashed and rattled for breathless minutes. "Blake see Winslow. This is McGuire, Blake. Winslow can help—"

The message ended abruptly. One long, wailing note; then again the night was voiceless...and in the radio room at Maricopa Flying Field two men stood speechless, unbreathing, to stare at each other with incredulous eyes, as might men who had seen a phantom—a ghost that spoke to them and called them by name.

"McGuire's alive!" stammered Blake. "They've taken him!"

Colonel Boynton was considering, weighing all the possibilities, and his voice, when he answered, had the ring of conviction.

"That was no hoax," he agreed; "that quavering tone could never be faked. That message was sent from the same station we heard before. Yes, McGuire is alive—or was up to the end of that sending... But, who the devil is Winslow?"

Blake shook his head despairingly. "I don't know," he said. "And it seems as if I should—"

It was hours later, far into the night, when he sprang from out of a half-conscious doze to find himself in the middle of the floor with the voice of McGuire ringing clearly in his ears. A buried memory had returned to the level of his conscious mind. He rushed over to the colonel's quarters.

"I've got it," he shouted to that officer whose head was projecting from an upper window. "I remember! McGuire told me about this Winslow—some hermit that he ran across. He has some invention—some machine—said he had been to the moon. I always thought Mac half believed him. We'll go over Mac's things and find the address."

"Do you think—do you suppose—?" began Colonel Boynton doubtfully.

"I don't dare to think," Blake responded. "God only knows if we dare hope; but Mac—Mac's got a level head; he wouldn't send us unless he knew! Good Lord, man!" he exclaimed, "Mac radioed us from Venus; is there anything impossible after that?"

"Wait there," said Colonel Boynton; "I'll be right down—"

CHAPTER TWELVE

LIEUTENANT McGuire awoke, as he had on other occasions, to the smell of sickly-sweet fumes and the stifling pressure of a mask held over his nose and mouth. He struggled to free himself, and the mask was removed. Another of the man-creatures whom McGuire had not seen before helped him to sit up.

A group of the attenuated figures, with their blood-and-ashes faces, regarded him curiously. The one who had helped him arise forced the others to stand back, and he gave McGuire a drink of yellow fluid from a crystal goblet. The dazed man gulped it down to feel a following surge of warmth and life that pulsed through his paralyzed body. The figures before him came sharply from the haze that had enveloped them. A window high above admitted a golden light that meant another day, but it brought no cheer or encouragement to the flyer. McGuire felt crushed and hopeless in the knowledge that his life must still go on.

If only that sleep could have continued—carried him out to the deeper sleep of death! What hope for them here? Not a chance! And then he remembered Sykes; he mustn't desert Sykes. He looked about him to see the same prison room from which he and Sykes had escaped. The body of the scientist was motionless on the hammock-bed across the room; an occasional deep-drawn breath showed that the man still lived.

No, he must not leave Sykes, even if he had the means of death. They would fight it through together, and perhaps—perhaps—they might yet be of service, might find some way to avert the catastrophe that threatened their world. Hopeless? Beyond doubt. But he must hope—and fight!

The leader had watched the light of understanding as it returned to the flyer's eyes. He motioned now to the others, and McGuire was picked up bodily by four of them and carried from the room.

McGuire's mind was alert once more; he was eager to learn what he could of this place that was to be their prison, but he saw little. A glory of blending colors beyond, where the golden light from without shone through opal walls—then he found himself upon a narrow table where straps of metal were thrown quickly about to bind him fast. He was tied hand and foot to the table that moved forward on smooth rollers to a waiting lift.

What next? he questioned. Not death, for they had been too careful to keep him alive, these repulsive things that stared at him with such cold malevolence. Then what? And McGuire found himself with unpleasant recollections of others he had seen strapped in similar fashion to an operating table.

The lift that he had thought would rise fell smoothly, instead, to stop at some point far below ground where the table with its helpless burden was rolled into a great room.

He could move his head, and McGuire turned and twisted to look at the maze of instruments that filled the room—a super-laboratory for experiments of which he dared not think.

"Whoever says I'm not scared to death is a liar," he whispered to himself, but he continued to look and wonder as he was wheeled before a gleaming machine of many coils and shining, metal parts. A smooth sheet of metal stood vertically beyond him; painted a grayish-white, he saw; but he could not imagine its use. A throng of people, seated in the room, turned blood-red faces toward the bound man and the metal sheet.

"Looks as if we were about to put on a show of some kind," he told himself, "and I am cast for a leading role." He watched as best he could from his bound position while a tall figure in robes of lustreless black appeared to stand beside him.

The newcomer regarded him with a face that was devoid of all emotion. McGuire felt the lack of the customary expression of hatred; there was not even that; and he knew he was nothing more than a strange animal, bound, and helpless, ready for this weird creature's experiments. The one in black held a pencil whose tip was a tiny, brilliant light.

Abruptly the room plunged to darkness, where the only visible thing was this one point of light. Ceaselessly it waved back and forth before his eyes; he followed it in a pattern of strange design; it approached and receded. Again and again the motion was repeated, until McGuire felt himself sinking—sinking—into a passive state of lethargy. His muscles relaxed; his mind was at rest; there seemed nothing in the entire universe of being but the single point of light that drew him on and on...till something whispered from the far reaches of black space...

It came to him, an insistent call. It was asking about the earth— his own world. *What of Earth's armies and their means of defense?* Vaguely he sensed the demand, and without conscious volition he responded. He pictured the world he had known; how plainly he saw the wide field at Maricopa, and the sweeping flight of a squadron of planes! *Yes—yes! How high could they ascend?* From one of the planes he saw the world below; the ships were near their ceiling; this was the limit of their climb. *And did they fight with gas? What of their deadliness?* And again he was seated in a plane, and he was firing tiny bullets from a tiny gun. No. They did not use gas. *But on the ground below—what fortifications? What means of defense?*

McGuire's mind was no longer his own; he could only respond to that invisible questioner, that insistent demand from out of the depths where he was floating. And yet there was something within him that protested, that clamored at his mind and brain.

Fortifications! They must know about fortifications—anti-aircraft guns—means for combatting aerial attack. Yes, he knew, and he must explain—and the thing within him pounded in the back of his brain to draw him back to himself.

He saw a battery of anti-aircraft guns in operation; the guns were firing; shells were bursting in little plumes of smoke high in the air. And that self within him was shouting now, hammering at him; "You are seeing it," it told him; "it is there before you on the screen. Stop! Stop!"

And for an instant McGuire had the strange experience of witnessing his own thoughts. Memories, mental records of past experience, were flashing through his mind; mock battles, and the batteries were firing! And, before him, on the metal screen, there glowed a vivid picture of the same thing. Men were serving the guns with sure swiftness; the bursts were high in the air—in a flash of understanding Lieutenant McGuire knew that he was giving his country's secrets to the enemy. And in that same instant he felt himself swept upward from the depths of that darkness where he had drifted. He was himself again, bound and helpless before an infernal contrivance of these devil-creatures. They had read his thoughts; the machine beside him had projected them upon the screen for all to see; a steady clicking might mean their reproduction in motion pictures for later study! He, Lieutenant McGuire, was a traitor against his will!

The screen was blank, and the lights of the room came on to show the thin lips that smiled complacently in a cruel and evil face.

McGuire glared back into that face, and he tried with all the mental force that he could concentrate to get across to the exultant one the fact that they had not wholly conquered him. This much they had got—but no more!

The thin-lipped one had an instrument in his hand, and McGuire felt the prick of a needle plunged into his arm. He tried to move his head and found himself powerless. And now, in the darkness of the room where all lights were again extinguished, the helpless man was fighting the most horrible of battles, and the battleground was within his own mind. He was two selves, and he fought and struggled with all his consciousness to keep those memories from flooding him.

With one part of himself he knew what it meant: a sure knowledge given these invaders of what they must prepare to meet; he was betraying his country; the whole of humanity! And that raging, raving self was powerless to check the flow of memory pictures that went endlessly through his mind and out upon the screen beyond...

He had no sense of time; he was limp and exhausted with his fruitless struggle when he felt himself released from the bondage of the metal straps and placed again in the hammock in his room. And he could only look wanly and hopelessly after the figure of Professor Sykes, carried by barbarous figures to the same ordeal.

SLEEP, through the long night, restored both McGuire and his companion to normal strength. The flyer was seated with his head bowed low in his cupped hands. His words seemed wrung from an agony of spirit. "So that's what they brought us here for," he said harshly; "that's why they're keeping us alive!"

Professor Sykes walked back and forth in their bare room while he shook his impotent fists in the air.

"I told them everything," he exploded; "everything!" Their astronomical knowledge must be limited; under this blanket of clouds they can see nothing, and from their ships they could make approximations only.

"And I have told them—the earth, and its days and seasons—its orbital velocity and motion—its relation to the orbit of this accursed planet. They had documents from the observatory and I explained them; I corrected their time of firing their big gun on its equatorial position. Oh, there is little I left untold—damn them!"

"I wish to heaven," said the flyer savagely, "that we had known; we would have jumped out of their beastly ship somehow ten thousand feet up, and we would have taken our information with us."

Sykes nodded agreement. "Well," he asked, "how about to-morrow, and the next day, and the next? They will want more facts; they will pump the last drop of information from us. Are we going to allow it?"

McGuire's tone was dry. "You know the answer to that as well as I do. We have just two alternatives; either we get out of here—find some place to hide in, then find some way to put a crimp in their plans; or we get out of here for good. It's twenty feet, not twenty thousand, from that window to the ground, but I think a head-first dive would do it."

Sykes did not reply at once; he seemed to be weighing some problem in his mind.

"I would prefer the water," he said at last. "If we *can* get away and reach the shore, and if there is not a possibility of escape—which I must admit I consider highly improbable—well, we can always swim out as far as we can go, and the result will be certain.

"This other is so messy." The man had stopped his ceaseless pacing, and he even managed a cheerful smile at the lieutenant. "And, remember, it might only cripple us and leave us helpless in their hands."

"Sounds all right to me," McGuire agreed, and there was a tone of finality in his voice as he added: "They've made us do that traitor act for the last time, anyway."

DAYLIGHT comes slowly through cloud-filled skies; the window of the room where the fountain sprayed ceaselessly was showing the first hint of gold in the eastern sky. Above was the utter darkness of the cloud-wrapped night as the two men swung noiselessly out into the grotesque branches of a tree to make their way into the gloom below. There, under the cover of great leaves, they crouched in silence, while the darkness about them faded and a sound of subdued whistling noises came to them from the night.

A wheel creaked, and in the dim light two figures appeared tugging at a cart upon which was a cage of woven wire. Beyond them, against the darker background of denser growth, tentacles coiled and twisted above the row of guardian plants that surrounded the house.

One of the ghostly forms reached within the cage and brought forth a struggling object that whimpered in fear. The low whine came distinctly to the hidden men. They saw a vague black thing tossed through the air and toward the deadly plants; they heard the swishing of pliant tentacles and the yelping cry of a frightened animal. And the cry rose to a shriek that ended with the gulping splash of thick liquid.

The giant pod next in line was open—they could see it dimly— and its tentacles were writhing convulsively, hungrily, across the ground. Another animal was taken from the cage and thrown to the waiting, serpent forms that closed about and whirled it high in air. Another—and another! The yelps of terror grew faint in the distance as the monsters passed on in their gruesome work. And the two men, palpitant with memories of their own experience, were limp and sick with horror.

In the growing light they saw more plainly the fleshy, pliant arms that whipped through the air or felt searchingly along the ground. No hope there for bird or beast that passed by in the night; nor for men, as they knew too well. But now, as the golden light increased, the arms drew back to form again the tight-wound coils that flattened themselves beside the monstrous pods whose lips were closing. Locked within them were the pools of liquid that could dissolve a living body into food for these vampires of the vegetable world.

"Damnable!" breathed Sykes in a savage whisper. "Utterly damnable! And this world is peopled with such monsters!"

The last deadly arm was tightly coiled when the men stole off through the lush growth that reached even above their heads. McGuire remembered the outlines he had seen from the air and led the way where, if no better concealment could be found, the ocean waited with promise of rest and release from their inhuman captors.

They counted on an hour's start—it would be that long before their jailer would come with their morning meal and give the alarm—and now they went swiftly and silently through the stillness of a strange world. The air that flicked misty-wet across their faces was heavy and heady with the perfume of night-blooming plants. Crimson blossoms flung wide their odorous petals, and the first golden light was filtered through tremendous tree-growths of pale lavenders and grays to show as unreal colors in the vegetation close about them.

They found no guards; the isolation of this island made the land itself their prison, and the men ran at full speed through every open space, knowing as they ran that there was no refuge for them—only the ocean waiting at the last. But their flight was not unobserved.

A great bird rose screaming from a tangle of vines; its heavy, flapping wings flashed red against the pale trees. A pandemonium of shrieking cries echoed its alarm as other birds took flight; the forest about them was in an uproar of harsh cries. And faintly, from far in the rear, came a babel of shrill calls—weird, inhuman!— the voices of the men-things of Venus.

"It's all off," said McGuire sharply; "they'll be on our trail now!" He plunged through where the trees were more open, and Sykes was beside him as they ran with a burst of speed toward a hilltop beyond.

They paused, panting, upon the crest. A wide expanse of foliage in delicate shadings swept out before them to wave gently in a sea of color under the morning breeze, and beyond was another sea that beckoned with white breakers on a rocky shore.

"The ocean!" gasped Sykes, and pointed a trembling hand toward their goal. "But—I had no idea—that suicide—was—such hard work!"

The tall figure of Lieutenant McGuire turned to the shorter, breathless man, and he gripped hard at one of his hands.

"Sykes," he said, "I'll never get another chance to say it—but you're one good scout...! Come on!"

McGuire fought to force his way through jungle growth, while screaming birds marked where they went. The sounds of their pursuers were close behind them when the two tore their way through the last snarled tangle of pale vine to stand on a sheer bluff, where, below, deep waters crashed against a rocky wall. They staggered with weariness and gulped sobbingly of the morning air.

McGuire could have sworn he was exhausted beyond any further effort, yet from somewhere he summoned energy to spring savagely upon a tall, blood-red figure whose purpling face rose suddenly to confront them.

One hand closed upon the metal tube that the other hand raised, and, with his final reserve of strength, the flyer wrapped an arm about the tall body and rushed it stumblingly toward the cliff. To be balked now!—to be brought back to that intolerable prison and the unthinkable role of traitor! The khaki-clad figure wrenched furiously at the deadly tube as they struggled and swayed on the edge of the cliff.

He freed his arm quickly, and, regardless of the clawing thing that tore at his face and eyes, he launched one long swing for the horrible face above him. He saw the awkward fall of a lean body, and he swayed helplessly out to follow when the grip of Sykes' hand pulled him back and up to momentary safety.

McGuire's mind held only the desire to kill, and he would have begun a staggering rush toward the shrieking mob that broke from the cover behind them, had not Sykes held him fast. At sight of the weapon, their own gas projector, still clutched in the flyer's hand, the pursuers halted. Their long arms pointed and their shrill calls joined in a chorus that quavered and fell uncertainly.

One, braver than the rest, dashed forward and discharged his weapon. The spurting gas failed to reach its intended victims; it blew gently back toward the others who fled quickly to either side. Above the trees a giant ship nosed swiftly down, and McGuire pointed to it grimly and in silence. The men before them were massed now for a rush.

"This is the end," said the flyer softly. "I wonder how this devilish thing works; there's a trigger here. I will give them a shot with the wind helping, then we'll jump for it."

The ship was above them as the slim figure of Lieutenant McGuire threw itself a score of paces toward the waiting group. From the metal tube there shot a stream of pale vapor that swept downward upon the others who ran in panic from its touch.

Then back—and a grip of a hand!—and two Earth-men who threw themselves out and downward from a sheer rock wall to the cool embrace of deep water.

They came to the top, battered from their fall, but able to dive under a wave and emerge again near one another.

"Swim!" urged Sykes. "Swim out! They may get us here—recover our bodies—resuscitate us. And that wouldn't do!"

Another wave, and the two men were swimming beyond it; swimming feebly but steadily out from shore, while above them a great cylinder of shining metal swept past in a circling flight. They kept on while their eyes, from the wave tops, saw it turn and come slowly back in a long smooth descent.

It was a hundred feet above the water a short way out at sea, and the two men made feeble motions with arms and legs, while their eyes exchanged glances of dismay.

A door had opened in the round under-surface, and a figure, whose gas-suit made it a bloated caricature of a man, was lowered from beneath in a sling. From the stern of the ship gaseous vapor belched downward to spread upon the surface of the water. The wind was bringing the misty cloud toward them. "The gas!" said McGuire despairingly. "It will knock us out, and then that devil will get us! They'll take us back! Our last chance—gone!"

"God help us!" said Sykes weakly. "We can't—even—die—" His feeble strokes stopped, and he sank beneath the water. McGuire's last picture as he too sank and the waters closed over his head, was the shining ship hovering beyond.

He wondered only vaguely at the sudden whirling of water around him. A solid something was rising beneath his dragging feet; a firm, solid support that raised him again to the surface. He realized dimly the air about him, the sodden form of Professor Sykes some few feet distant. His numbed brain was trying to comprehend what else the eyes beheld.

A metal surface beneath them rose higher, shining wet, above the water; a metal tube raised suddenly from its shield, to swing in quick aim upon the enemy ship approaching from above.

His eyes moved to the ship, and to the man-thing below in the sling. Its clothes were a mass of flame, and the figure itself was falling headlong through the air. Above the blazing body was the metal of the ship itself, and it sagged and melted to a liquid fire that poured, splashing and hissing, to the waters beneath. In the wild panic the great shape threw itself into the air; it swept out and up in curving flight to plunge headlong into the depths...

The gas was drifting close, as McGuire saw an opening in the structure beside him. The voice of a man, human, kindly, befriending, said something of "hurry" and "gas," and "lift them carefully but make haste." The white faces of men were blurred and indistinct as McGuire felt himself lowered into a cool room and laid, with the unconscious form of Sykes, upon a floor.

He tried to remember. He had gone down in the water—Sykes had drowned, and he himself—he was tired—tired. "And this..." The thought seemed a certainty in his mind. "...this is death. How—very—peculiar—" He was trying to twist his lips to a weak laugh as the lighted ports in the wall beside him changed from gold to green, then black—and a rushing of torn waters was in his ears...

CHAPTER THIRTEEN

LIEUTENANT McGuire had tried to die. He and Professor Sykes had welcomed death with open arms, and death had been thwarted by their enemies who wanted them alive—wanted to draw their knowledge from them as a vampire bat might seek to feast. And, when even death was denied them, help had come.

The enemy ship had gone crashing to destruction where its melting metal made hissing clouds of steam as it buried itself in the ocean. And this craft that had saved them—Lieutenant McGuire had never been on a submarine, but he knew it could be only that that held him now and carried him somewhere at tremendous speed.

This was miracle enough! But to see, with eyes which could not be deceiving him, a vision of men, human, white of face—men like himself—bending and working over Sykes' unconscious body—that could not be immediately grasped.

Their faces, unlike the bleached-blood horrors he had seen, were aglow with the flush of health. They were tall, slenderly built, graceful in their quick motions as they worked to revive the unconscious man. One stopped, as he passed, to lay a cool hand on McGuire's forehead, and the eyes that looked down seemed filled with the blessed quality of kindness.

They were human—his own kind!—and McGuire was unable to take in at first the full wonder of it.

Did the tall man speak? His lips did not move, yet McGuire heard the words as in some inner ear.

"We were awaiting you, friend Mack Guire." The voice was musical, thrilling, and yet the listening man could not have sworn that he heard a voice at all. It was as if a thought were placed within his mind by the one beside him.

The one who had paused hurried on to aid the others, and McGuire let his gaze wander.

The porthole beside him showed dimly a pale green light; they were submerged, and the hissing rush of water told him that they were travelling fast. There was a door in the farther wall; beyond was a room of gleaming lights that reflected from myriads of shining levers and dials. A control room. A figure moved as McGuire watched, to press on a lever where a red light was steadily increasing in brightness. He consulted strange instruments before him, touched a metal button here and there, then opened a switch, and the rippling hiss of waters outside their craft softened to a gentler note.

The tall one was beside him again.

"Your friend will live," he told him in that wordless tongue, "and we are almost arrived. The invisible arms of our anchorage have us now and will draw us safely to rest."

The kindly tone was music in McGuire's ears, and he smiled in reply. "Friends!" he thought. "We are among friends."

"You are most welcome," the other assured him, "and, yes, you are truly among friends." But the lieutenant glanced upward in wonder, for he knew that he had uttered no spoken word.

Their ship turned and changed its course beneath them, then came finally to rest with a slight rocking motion as if cushioned on powerful springs. Sykes was being assisted to his feet as the tall man reached for McGuire's hand and helped him to rise.

The two men of Earth stood for a long minute while they stared unbelievingly into each other's eyes. Their wonder and amazement found no words for expression but must have been apparent to the one beside them.

"You will understand," he told them. "Do not question this reality even to yourselves. You are safe!... Come." And he led the way through an opening doorway to a wet deck outside. Beyond this was a wharf of carved stone, and the men followed where steps were inset to allow them to ascend.

Again McGuire could not know if he heard a tumult of sound or sensed it in some deeper way. The air about them was aglow with soft light, and it echoed in his ears with music unmistakably real—beautiful music!—exhilarating! But the clamor of welcoming voices, like the words from their tall companion, came soundlessly to him.

THERE were people, throngs of them, waiting. Tall like the others, garbed, like those horrible beings of a past that seemed distant and remote, in loose garments of radiant colors. And everywhere were welcoming smiles and warm and friendly glances.

McGuire let his dazed eyes roam around to find the sculptured walls of a huge room like a tremendous cave. The soft glow of light was everywhere, and it brought out the beauty of flowing lines and delicate colors in statuary and bas-relief that adorned the walls. Behind him the water made a dark pool, and from it projected the upper works of their strange craft.

His eyes were hungry for these new sights, but he turned with Sykes to follow their guide through the colorful crowd that parted to let them through. They passed under a carved archway and found themselves in another and greater room.

But was it a room? McGuire marveled at its tremendous size. His eyes took in the smooth green of a grassy lawn, the flowers and plants, and then they followed where the hand of Sykes was pointing. The astronomer gripped McGuire's arm in a numbing clutch; his other hand was raised above.

"The stars," he said. "The clouds are gone; it is night!"

And where he pointed was a vault of black velvet. Deep hues of blue seemed blended with it, and far in its depths were the old familiar star-groups of the skies. "Ah!" the scientist breathed, "the beautiful, friendly stars!"

Their guide waited; then, "Come," he urged gently, and led them toward a lake whose unruffled glassy surface mirrored the stars above. Beside it a man was waiting to receive them.

McGuire had to force his eyes away from the unreal beauty of opal walls like the fairy structures they had seen. There was color everywhere that blended and fused to make glorious harmony that was pure joy to the eyes.

The man who waited was young. He stood erect, his face like that of a Grecian statue, and his robe was blazing with the flash of jewels. Beside him was a girl, tall and slender, and sweetly serious of face. Like the man, her garments were lovely with jeweled iridescence, and now McGuire saw that the throng within the vast space was similarly apparelled.

The tall man raised his hand.

"Welcome!" he said, and McGuire realized with a start that the words were spoken aloud. "You are most welcome, my friends, among the people of that world you call Venus."

Professor Sykes was still weak from his ordeal; he wavered perceptibly where he stood, and the man before them them turned to give an order. There were chairs that came like magic; bright robes covered them; and the men were seated while the man and girl also took seats beside them as those who prepare for an intimate talk with friends.

Lieutenant McGuire found his voice at last. "Who are you?" he asked in wondering tones. "What does it mean? We were lost— and you saved us. But you—you are not like the others." And he repeated, "What does it mean?"

"No," said the other with a slight smile, "we truly are not like those others. They are not men such as you and I. They are something less than human—animals, vermin—from whom God, in His wisdom, has seen fit to withhold the virtues that raise men higher than the beasts."

His face hardened as he spoke and for a moment the eyes were stern, but he smiled again as he continued.

"And we," he said, "you ask who we are. We are the people of Venus. I am Djorn, ruler, in name, of all. 'In name' I say, for we rule here by common reason; I am only selected to serve. And this is my sister, Althora. The name, with us, means 'radiant light.'" He turned to exchange smiles with the girl at his side. "We think her well named," he said.

"The others..." He waved toward the throng that clustered about. "...you will learn to know in time."

Professor Sykes felt the need of introductions.

"This is Lieutenant—" he began, but the other interrupted with an upraised hand.

"Mack Guire," he supplied; "and you are Professor Sykes.... Oh, we know you!" he laughed; "we have been watching you since your arrival; we have been waiting to help you."

The professor was open-mouthed.

"Your thoughts," explained the other, "are as a printed page. We have been with you by mental contact at all times. We could hear, but, at that distance, and—pardon me!—with your limited receptivity, we could not communicate.

"Do not resent our intrusion," he added; "we listened only for our own good, and we shall show you how to insulate your thoughts. We do not pry."

Lieutenant McGuire waved all that aside. "You saved us from them," he said; "that's the answer. But—what does it mean? Those others are in control; they are attacking our Earth, the world where we lived. Why do you permit—?"

Again the other's face was set in sterner lines.

"Yes," he said, and his voice was full of unspoken regret, "they do rule this world; they *have* attacked your Earth; they intend much more, and I fear they must be successful. Listen. Your wonderment is natural, and I shall explain.

"We are the people of Venus. Some centuries ago we ruled this world. Now you find us a handful only, living like moles in this underworld."

"Underworld?" protested Professor Sykes. He pointed above to the familiar constellations. "Where are the clouds?" he asked.

The girl, Althora, leaned forward now. "It will please my brother," she said in a soft voice, "that you thought it real. He has had pleasure in creating that—a replica of the skies we used to know before the coming of the clouds."

Professor Sykes was bewildered. "That sky—the stars—they are not real?" he asked incredulously. "But the grass—the flowers—"

Her laugh rippled like music. "Oh, they are real," she told him, and her brother gave added explanation.

"The lights," he said, "we supply the actinic rays that the clouds cut off above. We have sunlight here, made by our own hands; that is why we are as we are and not like the red ones with their bleached skins. We had our lights everywhere through the world when we lived above, but those red beasts are ignorant; they do not know how to operate them; they do not know that they live in darkness even in the light."

"Then we are below ground?" asked the flyer. "You live here?"

"It is all we have now. At that time of which I tell, it was the red ones who lived out of sight; they were a race of rodents in human form. They lived in the subterranean caves with which this planet is pierced. We could have exterminated them at any time, but, in our ignorance, we permitted them to live, for we, of Venus—I use your name for the planet—do not willingly take life."

"They have no such compunctions!" Professor Sykes' voice was harsh; he was remembering the sacrifice to the hungry plants.

A flash as of pain crossed the sensitive features of the girl, and the man beside her seemed speaking to her in soundless words.

"Your mind-picture was not pleasant," he told the scientist; then continued:

"Remember, we were upon the world, and these others were within it. There came a comet. Oh, our astronomers plotted its course; they told us we were safe. But at the last some unknown influence diverted it; its gaseous projection swept our world with flame. Only an instant; but when it had passed there was left only death...."

He was lost in recollection for a time; the girl beside him reached over to touch his hand.

"Those within—the red ones—escaped," he went on. "They poured forth when they found that catastrophe had overwhelmed us. And we, the handful that were left, were forced to take shelter here. We have lived here since, waiting for the day when the Master of Destinies shall give us freedom and a world in which to live."

"You speak," suggested the scientist, "as if this had happened to you. Surely you refer to your ancestors; you are the descendants of those who were saved."

"We are the people," said the other. "We lived then; we live now; we shall live for a future of endless years.

"Have you not searched for the means to control the life principle—you people of Earth?" he asked. "We have it here. You see." And he waved a hand toward the standing throng, We are young to your eyes and the others who greeted you were the same."

McGuire and the scientist exchanged glances of corroboration.

"But your age," asked Sykes, "measured in years?"

"We hardly measure life in years."

Professor Sykes nodded slowly; his mind found difficulty in accepting so astounding a fact. "But our language?" he queried. "How is it that you can speak our tongue?"

The tall man smiled and leaned forward to place a hand on a knee of each of the men beside him. "Why not," he asked, "when there doubtless is relationship between us.

"You called the continent Atlantis. Perhaps its very existence is but a fable now; it has been many centuries since we have had instruments to record thought force from Earth, and we have lost touch. But, my friends, even then we of Venus had conquered space, and it was we who visited Atlantis to find a race more nearly like ourselves than were the barbarians who held the other parts of Earth.

"I was there, but I returned. There were some who stayed and they were lost with the others in the terrible cataclysm that sank a whole continent beneath the waters. But some, we have believed, escaped."

"Why have you not been back?" the flyer asked. "You could have helped us so much."

"It was then that our own destruction came upon us. The same comet, perhaps, may have caused a change of stresses in your Earth and sunk the lost Atlantis. Ah! That was a beautiful land, but we have never seen it since. We have been—here.

"But you will understand, now," he added, "that, with our insight into your minds, we have little difficulty in mastering your language."

This talk of science and incredible history left Lieutenant McGuire cold. His mind could not wander long from its greatest concern.

"But the earth!" he exclaimed. "What about the earth? This attack! Those devils mean real mischief!"

"More than you know; more than you can realize, friend Mack Guire!"

"Why?" demanded the flyer. "Why?"

"Have your countries not reached out for other countries when land was needed?" asked the man, Djorn. "Land—land! Space in which to breed—that is the reason for the invasion.

"This world has no such continents as yours. Here the globe is covered by the oceans; we have perhaps one hundredth of the land areas of your Earth And the red ones breed like flies. Life means nothing to them; they die like flies, too. But they need more room; they intend to find it on your world."

"A strange race," mused Professor Sykes. "They puzzled me. But—'less than human,' I think you said. Then how about their ships? How could they invent them?"

"Ours—all ours! They found a world ready and waiting for them. Through the centuries they have learned to master some few of our inventions. The ships!—the ethereal vibrations! Oh, they have been cleverer than we dreamed possible."

"Well, how can we stop them?" demanded McGuire. "We must. You have the submarines—"

"One only," the other interrupted. "We saved that, and we brought some machinery. We have made this place habitable; we have not been idle. But there are limitations."

"But your ray that you projected—it brought down their ship!"

"We were protecting you, and we protect ourselves; that is enough. There is One will deliver us in His own good time; we may not go forth and slaughter."

There was a note of resignation and patience in the voice that filled McGuire with hopeless forebodings. Plainly this was not an aggressive race. They had evolved beyond the stage of wanton slaughter, and, even now, they waited patiently for the day when some greater force should come to their aid.

The man beside them spoke quickly. "One moment—you will pardon me—someone is calling—" He listened intently to some soundless call, and he sent a silent message in reply.

"I have instructed them," he said. "Come and you shall see how impregnable is our position. The red ones have resented our destruction of their ship."

The face of the girl, Althora, was perturbed. "More killings?" she asked.

"Only as they force themselves to their own death," her brother told her. "Be not disturbed."

THE throng in the vast space drew apart as the figure of their leader strode quickly through with the two men following close. There were many rooms and passages; the men had glimpses of living quarters, of places where machinery made soft whirring sounds; more sights than their eyes could see or their minds comprehend. They came at last to an open chamber.

The men looked up to see a tremendous inverted-cone above, and there was the gold of cloudland glowing through an opening at the top. It was the inside of a volcano where they stood, and McGuire remembered the island and its volcanic peak where the ship had swerved aside. He felt that he knew now where they were.

Above them, a flash of light marked the passage of a ship over the crater's mouth, and he realized that the ships of the reds were not avoiding the island now. Did it mean an attack? And how could these new friends meet it?

Before them on the level volcanic floor were great machines that came suddenly to life, and their roar rose to a thunder of violence, while, in the center, a cluster of electric sparks like whirling stars formed a cloud of blue fire. It grew, and its hissing, crackling length reached upward to a fine-drawn point that touched the opening above.

"Follow!" commanded their leader and went rapidly before them where a passage wound and twisted to bring them at last to the light of day.

The flame of the golden clouds was above them in the midday sky, and beneath it were scores of ships that swept in formations through the air.

"Attacking?" asked the lieutenant with ill-concealed excitement.

"I fear so. They tried to gas us some centuries ago; it may be they have forgotten what we taught them then."

One squadron came downward and swept with inconceivable speed over a portion of the island that stretched below. The men were a short distance up on the mountain's side, and the scene that lay before them was crystal clear. There were billowing clouds of gas that spread over the land where the ships had passed. Other ships followed; they would blanket the island in gas.

The man beside them gave a sigh of regret. "They have struck the first blow," he said. He stood silent with half-closed eyes; then said, "I have ordered resistance." And there was genuine sorrow and regret in his eyes as he looked toward the mountain top.

McGuire's eyes followed the other's gaze to find nothing at first save the volcanic peak in hard outline upon the background of gold; then only a shimmer as of heat about the lofty cone. The air above him quivered, formed to ripples that spread in great circles where the enemy ships were flashing away.

Swifter than swift aircraft, with a speed that shattered space, they reached out and touched—and the ships, at that touch, fell helplessly down from the heights. They turned awkwardly as they fell or dropped like huge pointed projectiles. And the waters below took them silently and buried in their depths all trace of what an instant sooner had been an argosy of the air.

The ripples ceased, again the air was clear and untroubled, but beneath the golden clouds was no single sign of life.

The flyer's breathless suspense ended in an explosive gasp. "What a washout!" he exclaimed, and again he thought only of this as a weapon to be used for his own ends. "Can we use that on their fleets?" he asked. "Why, man—they will never conquer the earth; they will never even make a start."

The tall figure of Djorn turned and looked at him. "The lust to kill!" he said sadly. "You still have it—though you are fighting for your own, which is some excuse.

"No, this will not destroy their fleets, for their fleets will not come here to be destroyed. It will be many centuries before ever again the aircraft of the reds dare venture near."

"We will build another one and take it where they are—" The voice of the fighting man was vibrant with sudden hope.

"We were two hundred years building and perfecting this," the other told him. "Can you wait that long?"

And Lieutenant McGuire, as he followed dejectedly behind the leader, heard nothing of Professor Sykes' eager questions as to how this miracle was done.

"Can you wait that long?" this man, Djorn, had asked. And the flyer saw plainly the answer that spelled death and destruction to the world.

CHAPTER FOURTEEN

THE mountains of Nevada are not noted for their safe and easy landing places. But the motor of the plane that Captain Blake was piloting roared smoothly in the cool air while the man's eyes went searching, searching, for something, and he hardly knew what that something might be.

He went over again, as he had done a score of times, the remarks of Lieutenant McGuire. Mac had laughed that day when he told Blake of his experience.

"I was flying that transport," he had said, "and, boy! when one motor began to throw oil I knew I was out of luck. Nothing but rocky peaks and valleys full of trees as thick and as pointed as a porcupine's quills. Flying pretty high to maintain altitude with one motor out, so I just naturally *had* to find a place to set her down. I found it, too, though it seemed too good to be true off in that wilderness.

"A fine level spot, all smooth rock, except for a few clumps of grass, and just bumpy enough to make the landing interesting. But, say, Captain! I almost cracked up at that, I was so darn busy staring at something else.

"Off in some trees was a dirigible—Sure; go ahead and laugh; I didn't believe it either, and I was looking at it. But there had been a whale of a storm through there the day before, and it had knocked over some trees that had been screening the thing, and there it was!

"Well, I came to in time to pull up her nose and miss a rock or two, and then I started pronto for that valley of trees and the thing that was buried among them."

Captain Blake recalled the conversation word for word, though he had treated it jokingly at the time. McGuire had found the ship and a man—a half-crazed nut, so it seemed—living there all alone.

And he wasn't a bit keen about Mac's learning of the ship. But leave it to Mac to get the facts—or what the old bird claimed were facts.

There was the body of a youngster there, a man of about Mac's age. He had fallen and been killed the day before, and the old man was half crazy with grief. Mac had dug a grave and helped bury the body, and after that the old fellow's story had come out.

He had been to the moon, he said. And this was a space ship. Wouldn't tell how it operated, and shut up like a clam when Mac asked if he had gone alone. The young chap had gone with him, it seemed, and the man wouldn't talk—just sat and stared out at the yellow mound where the youngster was buried.

Mac had told Blake how he argued with the man to prove up on his claims and make a fortune for himself. But no—fortunes didn't interest him. And there were some this-and-that and be-damned-to-'em people who would never get *this* invention—the dirty, thieving rats!

And Mac, while he laughed, had seemed half to believe it. Said the old cuss was so sincere, and he had nothing to sell. And—there was the ship! It never got there without being flown in, that was a cinch. And there wasn't a propellor on it nor a place for one—just open ports where a blast came out, or so the inventor said.

Captain Blake swung his ship on another slanting line and continued to comb the country for such marks as McGuire had seen. And one moment he told himself he was a fool to be on any such hunt, while the next thought would remind him that Mac had believed. And Mac had a level head, and he had radioed from Venus!

There was the thing that made anything seem possible. Mac had got a message through, across that space, and the enemy had ships that could do it. Why not this one?

And always his eyes were searching, searching, for a level rocky expanse and a tree-filled valley beyond, with something, it might be, shining there, unless the inventor had camouflaged it more carefully now.

IT WAS later on the same day when Captain Blake's blocky figure climbed over the side of the cockpit. Tired? Yes! But who could think of cramped limbs and weary muscles when his plane was resting on a broad, level expanse of rock in the high Sierras and a sharp-cut valley showed thick with pines beyond. He could see the corner only of a rough log shack that protruded.

Blake scrambled over a natural rampart of broken stone and went swiftly toward the cabin. But he stopped abruptly at the sound of a harsh voice.

"Stop where you are," the voice ordered, "and stick up your hands! Then turn around and get back as fast as you can to that plane of yours." There was a glint of sunlight on a rifle barrel in the window of the cabin.

Captain Blake stopped, but he did not turn. "Are you Mr. Winslow?" he asked.

"That's nothing to you! Get out! Quick!"

Blake was thinking fast. Here was the man, without doubt—and he was hostile as an Apache; the man behind that harsh voice meant business. How could he reach him? The inspiration came at once. McGuire was the key.

"If you're Winslow," he called in a steady voice, "you don't want me to go away; you want to talk with me. There's a young friend of yours in a bad jam. You are the only one who can help."

"I haven't any friends," said the rasping voice, "I don't want any! Get out!"

"You had one," said the captain, "whether you wanted him or not. He believed in you—like the other young chap who went with you to the moon."

There was an audible gasp of dismay from the window beyond, and the barrel of the rifle made trembling flickerings in the sun.

"You mean the flyer?" asked the voice, and it seemed to have lost its harsher note. "The pleasant young fellow?"

"I mean McGuire, who helped give decent burial to your friend. And now he has been carried off—out into space—and you can help him. If you've a spark of decency in you, you will hear what I have to say."

The rifle vanished within the cabin; a door opened to frame a picture of a tall man. He was stooped; the years, or solitude, perhaps, had borne heavily upon him; his face was a mat of gray beard that was a continuation of the unkempt hair above. The rifle was still in his hand.

But he motioned to the waiting man, and "Come in!" he commanded. "I'll soon know if you're telling the truth. God help you if you're not.... Come in."

An hour was needed while the bearded man learned the truth. And Blake, too, picked up some facts. He learned to his great surprise that he was talking with an educated man, one who had spent a lifetime in scientific pursuits. And now, as the figure before him seemed more the scientist and less the crazed fabricator of wild fancies, the truth of his claims seemed not so remote.

Half demented now, beyond a doubt! A lifetime of disappointments and one invention after another stolen from him by those who knew more of law than of science. And now he held fortune in the secret of his ship—a secret which he swore should never be given to the world.

"Damn the world!" he snarled. "Did the world ever give anything to me? And what would they do with this? They would prostitute it to their own selfish ends; it would be just one more means to conquer and kill; and the capitalists would have it in their own dirty hands so that new lines of transportation beyond anything they dared dream would be theirs to exploit."

Blake, remembering the history of a commercial age, found no ready reply to that. But he told the man of McGuire and the things that had made him captive; he related what he, himself, had seen in the dark night on Mount Lawson, and he told of the fragmentary message that showed McGuire was still alive.

"There's only one way to save him," he urged. "If your ship is what you claim it is—and I believe you one hundred per cent—it is all that can save him from what will undoubtedly be a horrible death. Those things were monsters—inhuman!—and they have bombarded the earth. They will come back in less than a year and a half to destroy us."

Captain Blake would have said he was no debater, but the argument and persuasion that he used that night would have done credit to a Socrates. His opponent was difficult to convince, and not till the next day did the inventor show Blake his ship.

"Small," he said as he led the flyer toward it. "Designed just for the moon trip, and I had meant to go alone. But it served; it took us there and back again."

He threw open a door in the side of the metal cylinder. Blake stood back for only a moment to size up the machine, to observe its smooth duralumin shell and the rounded ends where portholes opened for the expelling of its driving blast. The door opening showed a thick wall that gave insulation. Blake followed the inventor to the interior of the ship.

The man had seen Winslow examining the thick walls. "It's cold out there, you know," he said, and smiled in recollection, "but the generator kept us warm." He pointed to a simple cylindrical casting aft of the ship's center part. It was massive, and braced to the framework of the ship to distribute a thrust that Blake knew must be tremendous. Heavy conduits took the blast that it produced and poured it from ports at bow and stern. There were other outlets, too, above and below and on the sides, and electric controls that were manipulated from a central board.

"You've got a ship," Blake admitted, "and it's a beauty. I know construction, and you've got it here. But what is the power? How do you drive it? What throws it out through space?"

"Aside from one other, you will be the only man ever to know." The bearded man was quiet now and earnest. The wild light had faded from his eyes, and he pondered gravely in making the last and final decision.

"Yes, you shall have it. It may be I have been mistaken. I have known people—some few—who were kindly and decent; I have let the others prejudice me. But there was one who was my companion—and there was McGuire, who was kind and who believed. And now you, who will give your life for a friend and to save humanity!... You shall have it. You shall have the ship! But I will not go with you. I want nothing of glory or fame, and I am too old to fight. My remaining years I choose to spend out here." He pointed where a window of heavy glass showed the outer world and a grave on a sloping hill.

"But you shall have full instructions. And, for the present, you may know that it is a continuous explosion that drives the ship. I have learned to decompose water into its components and split them into subatomic form. They reunite to give something other than matter. It is a liquid—liquid energy, though the term is inaccurate—that separates out in two forms, and a fluid ounce of each is the product of thousands of tons of water. The potential energy is all there. A current releases it; the energy components reunite to give matter again—hydrogen and oxygen gas. Combustion adds to their volume through heat.

"It is like firing a cannon in there..." He pointed now to the massive generator. "...a super-cannon of tremendous force and a cannon that fires continuously. The endless pressure of expansion gives the thrust that means a constant acceleration of motion out there where gravity is lost.

"You will note," he added, "that I said 'constant acceleration.' It means building up to speeds that are enormous."

Blake nodded in half-understanding.

"We will want bigger ships," he mused. "They must mount guns and be heavy enough to take the recoil. This is only a sample; we must design, experiment, build them! Can it be done? ... It *must* be done!" he concluded and turned to the inventor.

"We don't know much about those devils of the stars, and they may have means of attack beyond anything we can conceive, but there is just one way to learn: go up there and find out, and take a licking if we have to. Now, how about taking me up a mile or so in the air?"

The other smiled in self-deprecation. "I like a good fighter," he said; "I was never one myself. If I had been I would have accomplished more. Yes, you shall go up a mile or so in the air— and a thousand miles beyond." He turned to close the door and seal it fast.

Beside the instrument board he seated himself, and at his touch the generator of the ship came startlingly to life. It grumbled softly at first, then the hoarse sound swelled to a thunderous roar, while the metal grating surged up irresistibly beneath the captain's feet. His weight was intolerable. He sank helplessly to the floor....

Blake was white and shaken when he alighted from the ship an hour later, but his eyes were ablaze with excitement. He stopped to seize the tall man by the shoulders.

"I am only a poor devil of a flying man," he said, "but I am speaking for the whole world right now. You have saved us; you've furnished the means. It is up to us now. You've given us the right to hope that humanity can save itself, if humanity will do it. That's my next job—to convince them. We have less than a year and a half...."

THERE was one precious week wasted while Captain Blake chafed and waited for a conference to be arranged at Washington. A spirit of hopelessness had swept over the world—hopelessness and a mental sloth that killed every hope with the unanswerable argument: "What is the use? It is the end." But a meeting was arranged at Colonel Boynton's insistence, though his superiors scoffed at what he dared suggest.

Blake appeared before the meeting, and he told them what he knew—told it to the last detail, while he saw the looks of amusement or commiseration that passed from man to man.

There were scientists there who asked him coldly a question or two and shrugged a supercilious shoulder; ranking officers of both army and navy who openly excoriated Colonel Boynton for bringing them to hear the wild tale of a half-demented man. It was this that drove Blake to a cold frenzy.

The weeks of hopeless despair had worn his nerves to the breaking point, and now, with so much to be done, and so little time in which to do it, all requirements of official etiquette were swept aside as he leaped to his feet to face the unbelieving men.

"Damn it!" he shouted, "will you sit here now and quibble over what you think in your wisdom is possible or not. Get outside those doors—there's an open park beyond—and I'll knock your technicalities all to hell!"

The door slammed behind him before the words could be spoken to place him under arrest, and he tore across a velvet lawn to leap into a taxi.

There was a rising storm of indignant protest within the room that he had left. There were admirals, purple of face, who made heated remarks about the lack of discipline in the army, and generals who turned accusingly where the big figure of Colonel Boynton was still seated.

It was the Secretary of War who stilled the tumult and claimed the privilege of administering the rebuke which was so plainly needed. "Colonel Boynton," he said, and there was no effort to soften the cutting edge of sarcasm in his voice, "it was at your request and suggestion that this outrageous meeting was held. Have you any more requests or suggestions?"

The colonel rose slowly to his feet.

"Yes, Mr. Secretary," he said coldly, "I have. I know Captain Blake. He seldom makes promises; when he does he makes good. My suggestion is that you do what the gentleman said—step outside and see your technicalities knocked to hell." He moved unhurriedly toward the door.

It was a half-hour's wait, and one or two of the more openly skeptical had left when the first roar came faintly from above. Colonel Boynton led the others to the open ground before the building. "I have always found Blake a man of his word," he said quietly, and pointed upward where a tiny speck was falling from a cloud-flecked sky.

Captain Blake had had little training in the operation of the ship, but he had flown it across the land and had concealed it where fellow officers were sworn to secrecy. And he felt that he knew how to handle the controls.

But the drop from those terrible heights was a fearful thing, and it ended only a hundred feet above the heads of the cowering, shouting humans who crouched under the thunderous blast, where a great shell checked its vertical flight and rebounded to the skies.

Again and again the gleaming cylinder drove at them like a projectile from the mortars of the gods, and it roared and thundered through the air or turned to vanish with incredible speed straight up into the heights, to return and fall again ... until finally it hung motionless a foot above the grass from which the uniformed figures had fled. Only Colonel Boynton was there to greet the flyer as he laid his strange craft gently down.

"Nice little show, Captain," he said, while his broad face broke into the widest of grins. "A damn nice little show! But take that look off of your face. They'll listen to you now; they'll eat right out of your hand."

CHAPTER FIFTEEN

IF LIEUTENANT McGuire could have erased from his mind the thought of the threat that hung over the earth he would have found nothing but intensest pleasure in the experiences that were his.

But night after night they had heard the reverberating echoes of the giant gun speeding its messenger of death toward the earth, and he saw as plainly as if he were there the terrible destruction that must come where the missiles struck. Gas, of course; that seemed the chief and only weapon of these monsters, and Djorn, the elected leader of the Venus folk, confirmed him in this surmise.

"We had many gases," he told McGuire, "but we used them for good ends. You people of Earth—or these invaders, if they conquer Earth—must some day engage in a war more terrible than wars between men. The insects are your greatest foe. With a developing civilization goes the multiplication of insect and bacterial life. We used the gases for that war, and we made this world a heaven." He sighed regretfully for his lost world.

"These red ones found them, and our factories for making them. But they have no gift for working out or mastering the other means we had for our defense—the electronic projectors, the creation of tremendous magnetic fields; you saw one when we destroyed the attacking ships. Our scientists had gone far—"

"I wish to Heaven you had some of them to use now," said the lieutenant savagely, and the girl, Althora, standing near, smiled in sympathy for the flyer's distress. But her brother, Djorn, only murmured, "The lust to kill; that is something to be overcome."

The fatalistic resignation of these folk was disturbing to a man of action like McGuire. His eyes narrowed, and his lips were set for an abrupt retort when Althora intervened.

"Come," she said, and took the flyer's hand. "It is time for food."

She took him to the living quarters occupied by her brother and herself, where opal walls and jewelled inlays were made lovely by the soft light that flooded the rooms.

"Just one tablet," she said, and brought him a thin white disc, "then plenty of water. You must take this compressed food often and in small quantities till your system is accustomed."

"You make this?" he asked.

"But certainly. Our chemists are learned men. We should lack for food, otherwise, here in our underground home."

He let the tablet dissolve in his mouth. Althora leaned forward to touch his hand gently.

"I am sorry," she said, "that you and Djorn fail to understand one another. He is good—so good! But you—you, too, are good, and you fear for the safety of your own people."

"They will be killed to the last woman and child," he replied, "or they will be captured, which will be worse."

"I understand," she told him, and pressed his hand; "and if I can help, Lieutenant Mack Guire, I shall be so glad."

He smiled at her stilted pronunciation of his name. He had had the girl for an almost constant companion since his arrival; the sexes, he found, were on a level of mutual freedom, and the girl's companionship was offered and her friendship expressed as openly as might have been that of a youth. Of Sykes he saw little; Professor Sykes was deep in astronomical discussions with the scientists of this world.

But she was charming, this girl of a strange race so like his own. A skin from the velvet heart of a rose and eyes that looked deep into his and into his mind when he permitted; eyes, too, that could crinkle to ready laughter or grow misty when she sang those weird melodies of such thrilling sweetness.

Only for the remembrance of Earth and the horrible feeling of impotent fury, Lieutenant McGuire would have found much to occupy his thoughts in this loveliest of companions.

He laughed now at the sounding of his name, and the girl laughed with him.

"But it *is* your name, is it not?" she asked.

"Lieutenant Thomas McGuire," he repeated, "and those who like me call me 'Mac.'"

"Mac," she repeated. "But that is so short and hard sounding. And what do those who love you say?"

The flyer grinned cheerfully. "There aren't many who could qualify in that respect, but if there were they would call me Tommy."

"That is better," said Althora with engaging directness; "that is much better—Tommy." Then she sprang to her feet and hurried him out where some further wonders must be seen and exclaimed over without delay. But Lieutenant McGuire saw the pink flush that crept into her face, and his own heart responded to the telltale betrayal of her feeling for him. For never in his young and eventful life had the man found anyone who seemed so entirely one with himself as did this lovely girl from a distant star.

He followed where she went dancing on her way, but not for long could his mind be led away from the menace he could not forget. And on this day, as on many days to come, he struggled and racked his brain to find some way in which he could thwart the enemy and avert or delay their stroke.

IT WAS another day, and they were some months on their long journey away from the earth when an inspiration came. Althora had offered to help, and he knew well how gladly she would aid him; the feeling between them had flowered into open, if unspoken, love. Not that he would subject her to any danger—he himself would take all of that when it came—but meanwhile—

"Althora," he asked her, "can you project your mind into that of one of the reds?"

"I could, easily," she replied, "but it would not be pleasant. Their minds are horrible; they reek of evil things." She shuddered at the thought, but the man persisted.

"But if you could help, would you be willing? I can do so little; I can never stop them; but I may save my people from some suffering at least. Here is my idea:

"Djorn tells me that I had it figured right. They plan an invasion of the earth when next the two planets approach. He has told me of their armies and their fleets of ships that will set off into space. I can't prevent it; I am helpless! But if I knew what their leader was thinking—"

"Torg!" she exclaimed. "You want to know the mind of that beast of beasts!"

"Yes," said the man. "It might be of value. Particularly if I could know something of their great gun—where it is and what it is—well, I might do something about that."

The girl averted her eyes from the savage determination on his face. "No—no!" she exclaimed; "I could not. Not Torg!"

McGuire's own face fell at the realization of the enormity of this favor he had demanded. "That's all right," he said and held her soft hand in his; "just forget it. I shouldn't have asked."

But she whispered as she turned to walk away, "I must think, I must think. You ask much of me, Tommy; but oh, Tommy, I would do much for you!" She was sobbing softly as she ran swiftly away.

And the man in khaki—this flyer of a distant air-service—strode blindly off to rage and fume at his helplessness and his inability to strike one blow at those beings who lived in that world above.

There were countless rooms and passages where the work of the world below went on. There were men and women whose artistic ability found outlet in carvings and sculpture, chemists and others whose work was the making of foods and endless experimentation, some thousand of men and women in the strength of their endless youth, who worked for the love of the doing and lived contentedly and happily while they waited for the day of their liberation. But of fighters there were none, and for this Lieutenant McGuire grieved wholeheartedly.

He was striding swiftly along where a corridor ended in blackness ahead. There was a gleaming machine on the floor beside him when a hand clutched at his arm and a warning voice exclaimed, "No further, Lieutenant McGuire; you must not go!"

"Why?" questioned the lieutenant. "I've got to walk—do something to keep from this damnable futile thinking."

"But not there," said the other; "it is a place of death. Ten paces more and you would have vanished in a flicker of flame. The projector," He touched the mechanism beside them, "is always on. Our caves extend in an endless succession; they join with the labyrinth where the red ones used to live. They could attack us but for this. Nothing can live in its invisible ray; they are placed at all such entrances."

"Yet Djorn," McGuire told himself slowly, "said they had no weapons. He knows nothing of war. But, great heavens! what wouldn't I give for a regiment of scrappers—good husky boys with their faces tanned and a spark in their eyes and their gas masks on their chests. With a regiment, and equipment like this—"

And again he realized the futility of armament with none to serve and direct it.

It was a month or more before Althora consented to the tests. Djorn advised against it and made his protest emphatic, but here, as in all things, Althora was a free agent. It was her right to do as she saw fit, and there was none to prevent in this small world where individual liberty was unquestioned.

And it was still longer before she could get anything of importance. The experiments were racking to her nerves, and McGuire, seeing the terrible strain upon her, begged her to stop. But Althora had gained the vision that was always before her loved one's eyes—a world of death and disaster—and he, here where the bolt would be launched, and powerless to prevent. She could not be dissuaded now.

It was a proud day for Althora when she sent for McGuire, and he found her lying at rest, eyes closed in her young face that was lined and tortured with the mental horror she was contacting. She silenced his protests with a word.

"The gun," she whispered; "they are talking about the gun ... and the bombardment ... planning...."

More silent concentration. Then:

"The island of Bergo," she said, "—remember that! The gun is there ... a great bore in the earth ... solid rock ... but the casing of titanite must be reinforced ... and bands shrunk about the muzzle that projects ... heavy bands ... it shows signs of distortion—the heat!..."

She was listening to the thoughts, and selecting those that bore upon gun.

"... Only fifty days ... the bombardment must begin ... Tahnor has provided a hundred shells; two thousand tals of the green gas-powder in each one ... the explosive charges ready ... yes—yes!..."

"Oh!" she exclaimed and opened her troubled eyes. "The beast is so complacent, so sure! And the bombardment will begin in fifty days! Will it really cause them anguish on your Earth, Tommy?"

"Just plain hell; that's all!"

McGuire's voice was low; his mind was reaching out to find and reject one plan after another. The gun!... He must disable it; he could do that much at least. For himself—well, what of it?—he would die, of course.

The guard he had been taught to place about his own thoughts must have relaxed, for Althora cried out in distress.

"No—no!" she protested; "you shall not! I have tried to help you, Tommy dear—say that I have helped you!—but, oh, my beloved, do not go. Do not risk your life to silence this one weapon. They would still have their ships. Remember what Djorn has told of their mighty fleets, their thousands of fighting men. You cannot stop them; you can hardly hinder them. And you would throw away your life! Oh, please do not go!"

McGuire was seated beside her. His face was hidden in one hand while the other was held tight between the white palms of Althora's tense hands. He said nothing, and he shielded his eyes and locked his mind against her thought force.

"Tommy," said Althora, and now her voice was all love and softness, "Tommy, my dear one! You will not go, for what can you do? And if you stay—oh, my dear!—you can have what you will—the secret of life shall be yours—to live forever in perpetual youth. You may have that. And me, Tommy.... Would you throw your life away in a hopeless attempt, when life might hold so much? Am I offering so little, Tommy?"

And still the silence and the hand that kept the eyes from meeting hers; then a long-drawn breath and a slim figure in khaki that stood unconsciously erect to look, not at the girl, but out beyond the solid walls, through millions of miles of space, to the helpless speck called Earth.

"You offer me heaven, my dear," he spoke softly. "But sometimes..." And his lips twisted into a ghost of a smile. "...sometimes, to earn our heaven, we have to fight like hell. And, if we fail to make the fight, what heaven worth having is left?

"And the people," he said softly; "the homes in the cities and towns and villages. My dear, that's part of loving a soldier; you can never own him altogether; his allegiance is divided. And if I failed my own folk what right would I have to you?"

He dared to look at the girl who lay before him. That other vision was gone but he had seen a clear course charted, and now, with his mind at rest, he could smile happily at the girl who was looking up at him through her tears.

She rose slowly to her feet and stood before him to lay firm hands upon his shoulders. She was almost as tall as he, and her eyes, that had shaken off their tears but for a dewy fringe, looked deep and straight into his.

"We have thought," she said slowly, "we people of this world, that we were superior to you and yours; we have accepted you as someone a shade below our plane of advancement. Yes, we have dared to believe that. But I know better. We have gone far, Tommy, we people of this star; we have lived long. Yet I am wondering if we have lost some virtues that are the heritage of a sterner race.

"But I am learning, Tommy; I am so thankful that I can learn and that I have had you to teach me. We will go together, you and I. We will fight our fight, and, the Great One willing, we will earn our heaven or find it elsewhere—together."

She leaned forward to kiss the tall man squarely upon the lips with her own soft rose-petal lips that clung and clung ... and the reply of Lieutenant McGuire, while it was entirely wordless, seemed eminently satisfactory.

ALTHORA, the beautiful daughter of Venus, had the charm and allure of her planet's fabled namesake. But she thought like a man and she planned like a man. And there was no dissuading her from her course. She was to fight beside McGuire—that was her intention—and beyond that there was no value in argument. McGuire was forced to accept the insistent aid, and he needed help.

Sykes dropped his delving into astronomical lore and answered to the call, but there was no other assistance. Only the three, McGuire, Althora and Sykes. There were some who would agree to pilot the submarine that was being outfitted, but they would have no part in the venture beyond transporting the participants.

More than once McGuire paused to curse silently at the complaisance of this people. What could he not do if they would help. Ten companies of trained men, armed with their deadly electronic projectors that disintegrated any living thing they reached—and he would clutch at his tousled hair and realize that they were only three, and go grimly back to work.

"I don't know what we can do till we get there," he told Sykes. "Here we are, and there is the gun; that is all we know, except that the thing must be tremendous and our only hope is that there is some firing mechanism that we can destroy. The gun itself is a great drilling in the solid rock, lined with one of their steel alloys, and with a big barrel extending up into the air; Althora has learned that.

"They went deep into the rock and set the firing chamber there; it's heavy enough to stand the stress. They use a gas-powder, as Althora calls it, for the charge, and the same stuff but deadlier is in the shell. But they must have underground workings for loading and firing. Is there a chance for us to get in there, I wonder! There's the big barrel that projects. We might … but no!—that's too big for us to tackle, I'm afraid."

"How about that electronic projector on the submarine?" Sykes suggested. "Remember how it melted out the heart of that big ship? We could do a lot with that."

"Not a chance! Djorn and the others have strictly forbidden the men to turn it on the enemy since they have given no offense.

"No offense!" he repeated, and added a few explosive remarks.

"No, it looks like a case of get there and do what dirty work we can to their mechanism before they pot us—and that's that!"

But Sykes was directing his thoughts along another path.

"I wonder…" he mused. "…it might be done. They have laboratories."

"What are you talking about? For the love of heaven, man, if you're got an idea, let's have it. I'm desperate."

"Nitrators!" said the scientist. "I have been getting on pretty good terms with the scientific crowd here, and I've seen some mighty pretty manufacturing laboratories. And they have equipment that was never meant for the manufacture of nitro-explosives, but, with a few modifications—yes, I think it could be done."

"You mean nitro-glycerine? TNT?"

"Something like that. Depends upon what materials we can get to start with."

The lieutenant was pounding his companion upon the back and shouting his joy at this faintest echo of encouragement.

"We'll plant it alongside the gun—No, we'll get into their working underground. We'll blow their equipment into scrap-iron, and perhaps we can even damage the gun itself!" He was almost beside himself with excitement at thought of a weapon being placed in his straining helpless hands.

It was the earth-shaking thunder of the big gun that hastened their final preparations and made McGuire tremble with suppressed excitement where he helped Sykes to draw off a syrupy liquid into heavy crystal flasks.

There were many of these, and the two men would allow no others to touch them, but stored them themselves and nested each one in a soft bed within the submarine. Then one last repetition of their half-formed plans to Djorn and his followers and a rush toward the wharf where the submarine was waiting.

Althora was waiting, too, and McGuire wasted minutes in a petition that he knew was futile.

"Wait here, Althora," he begged. "I will come back; this is no venture for you to undertake. I can take my chances with them, but you—! It is no place for you," he concluded lamely.

"There is no other place for me," she said; "only where you are." And she led the way while the others followed into the lighted control room of the big under-water craft.

McGuire's eyes were misty with a blurring of tears that were partly from excitement, but more from a feeling of helpless remonstrance that was mingled with pure pride. And his lips were set in a straight line.

The magnetic pull that held them to their anchorage was reversed; the ship beneath them was slipping smoothly beneath the surface and out to sea, guided through its tortuous windings of water-worn caves and rocky chambers under the sea by the invisible electric cords that drew it where they would.

And ahead on some mysterious island was a gun, a thing of size and power beyond anything of Earth. He was going to spike that gun if it was the last act of his life; and Althora was going with him. He drew her slim body to him, while his eyes stared blindly, hopefully, toward what the future held.

CHAPTER SIXTEEN

THROUGHOUT the night they drove hour after hour at terrific speed. The ship was running submerged, for McGuire was taking no slightest chance of their being observed from the air. He and the others slept at times, for the crew that handled the craft very evidently knew the exact course, and there were mechanical devices that insured their safety. A ray was projected continuously ahead of them; it would reflect back and give on an indicator instant warning of any derelict or obstruction. Another row of quivering needles gave by the same method the soundings from far ahead.

But the uncertainty of what their tomorrow might hold and the worry and dread lest he find himself unable to damage the big gun made real rest impossible for McGuire.

But he was happy and buoyant with hope when, at last, the green light from the ports showed that the sun was shining up above, and the slackening drive of the submarine's powerful motors told that their objective was in sight.

They lay quietly at last while a periscope of super-sensitiveness was thrust cautiously above the water. It brought in a panoramic view of the shoreline ahead, amplified it and projected the picture in clear-cut detail upon a screen. If Lieutenant McGuire had stood on the wet deck above and looked directly at the island the sight could have been no clearer. The colors of torn and blasted tree-growths showed in all their pale shades, and there was stereoscopic depth to the picture that gave no misleading illusions as to distance.

The shore was there with the white spray of breakers on a rocky shoal, and a beach beyond. And beyond that, in hard outline against a golden sky, was a gigantic tube that stood vertically in air to reach beyond the upper limits of the periscope's vision.

McGuire tingled at the sight. To be within reach of this weapon that had sent those blasting, devastating missiles upon the earth! He paced back and forth in the small room to stop and stare again, and resume his pacing that helped to while away the hours they must wait. For there were man-shapes swarming over the land, and the dull, blood-red of their loose uniforms marked them as members of the fighting force spawned by this prolific breed.

"Not a chance until they're out of the picture," said the impatient man; "they would snow us under. It's just as I thought, we must wait until the gun is ready to fire; then they will beat it. They won't want to be around when that big boy cuts loose."

"And then?" asked Althora.

"Then Sykes and I will take our collection of gallon flasks ashore, and I sure hope we don't stumble." He grinned cheerfully at the girl.

"That reinforced concrete dome seems to be where they get down into the ground; it is close to the base of the gun. We will go there—blow it open if we have to—but manage in some way to get down below. Then a time-fuse on the charge, and the boat will take me off, and we will leave as fast as these motors can drive us."

He omitted to mention any possible danger to Sykes and himself in the handling of their own explosive, and he added casually, "You will stay here and see that there is no slip-up on the getaway."

He had to translate the last remark into language the girl could understand. But Althora shook her head.

"You do try so hard to get rid of me, Tommy," the laughed, "but it is no use. I am going with you—do not argue—and I will help you with the attack. Three will work faster than two—and I am going."

McGuire was silent, then nodded his assent. He was learning, this Earth-man, what individual freedom really meant.

ONLY the western sky showed golden masses on the shining screen when McGuire spoke softly to the captain:

"Your men will put us ashore; you may ask them to stand by now." And to Professor Sykes, "Better get that 'soup' of yours ready to load."

The red-clad figures were growing dim on the screen, and the blotches of colors that showed where they were grouped were few. Some there were who left such groups to flee precipitately toward a waiting airship.

This was something the lieutenant had not foreseen. He had expected that the force that served the gun would have some shock-proof shelter; he had not anticipated a fighting ship to take them away.

"That's good," he exulted; "that is a lucky break. If they just get out of sight we will have the place to ourselves."

There were no red patches on the screen now, and the picture thrown before them showed the big ship, its markings of red and white distinct even in the shadow-light of late afternoon, rising slowly into the air. It gathered speed marvelously and vanished to a speck beyond the land.

"We're getting the breaks," said McGuire crisply. "All right—let's go!"

The submarine rose smoothly, and the sealed doors in the superstructure were opened while yet there was water to come trickling in. Men came with a roll of cloth that spread open to the shape of a small boat, while a metal frame expanded within it to hold it taut.

McGuire gasped with dismay as a seaman launched it and leaped heavily into the frail shell to attach a motor to one end.

"Metal!" the captain reassured him; "woven metal, and water-tight! You could not pierce it with anything less than a projector."

Sykes was ready with one of the crystal flasks as the boat was brought alongside, and McGuire followed with another. They took ten of the harmless-looking containers, and both men held their breaths as the boat grounded roughly on the boulder-strewn shore.

They lifted them out and bedded them in the sand, then returned to the submarine. This time Althora, too, stepped into the boat. They loaded in the balance of the containers; the motor purred. Another landing, and they stood at last on the island, where a mammoth tube towered into the sky and the means for its destruction was at their feet.

But there was little time; already the light was dimming, and the time for the firing of the big weapon was drawing near. The men worked like mad to carry the flasks to the base of the gun, where a dome of concrete marked the entrance to the rooms below.

Each man held a flask of the deadly fluid when Althora led the way where stairs went deep down into the earth under the domed roof. This part of the work had been foreseen, and the girl held a slender cylinder that threw a beam of light, intensely bright.

They found a surprising simplicity in the arrangements underground. Two rooms only had been carved from the solid rock, and one of these ended in a wall of gray metal that could be only the great base of the gun. But nowhere was a complication of mechanism that might be damaged or destroyed, nor any wiring or firing device.

A round door showed sharp edges in the gray metal, but only the strength of many men could have removed its huge bolts, and these two knew there must be other doors to seal in the mighty charge.

"Not a wire!" the scientist exclaimed. "How do they fire it?" The answer came to him with the question.

"Radio, of course; and the receiving set is in the charge itself; the barrel of the gun is its own antenna. They must fire it from a distance—back on the island where we were, perhaps. It would need to be accurately timed."

"Come on!" shouted McGuire, and raised the flask of explosive to his shoulder.

Each one knew the need for haste; each waited every moment for the terrible blast of gun-fire that would jar their bodies to a lifeless pulp or, by detonating their own explosive, destroy them utterly. But they carried the flasks again to the top, and the three of them worked breathlessly to place their whole supply where McGuire directed.

The massive barrel of the gun was beside them; it was held in tremendous castings of metal that bolted to anchorage in the ground. One great brace had an overhanging flange; the explosive was placed beneath it.

Professor Sykes had come prepared. He attached a detonator to one of the flasks, and while the other two were placing the explosive in position he fastened two wires to the apparatus with steady but hurrying fingers; then at full speed he ran with the spool from which the wires unwound.

McGuire and Althora were behind him, running for the questionable safety of the sand-hills. Sykes stopped in the shelter of a tiny valley where winds had heaped the sand.

"Down!" he shouted. "Get down—behind that sand dune, there!"

He dropped beside them, the bared ends of the wires in his hands. There was a battery, too, a case no larger than his hands. Professor Sykes, it appeared, had gained some few concessions from his friends, who had learned to respect him in the field of science.

One breathless moment he waited; then—

"Now!" he whispered, and touched the battery's terminals with the bare wires.

To McGuire it seemed, in that instant of shattering chaos, that the great gun itself must have fired. He had known the jar of heavy artillery at close range; he had had experience with explosives. He had even been near when a government arsenal had thrown the countryside into a hell of jarring, ear-splitting pandemonium. But the concussion that shook the earth under him now was like nothing he had known.

The hill of sand that sheltered them vanished to sweep in a sheet above their heads. And the air struck down with terrific weight, then left them in an airless void that seemed to make their bodies swell and explode. It rushed back in a whirling gale to sweep showers of sand and pebbles over the helpless forms of the three who lay battered and stunned.

An instant that was like an age; then the scientist pointed with a weak and trembling hand where a towering spire of metallic gray leaned slowly in the air. So slowly it moved, to the eyes of the watchers—a great arc of gathering force and speed that shattered the ground where it struck.

"The gun!" was all that the still-dazed lieutenant could say. "The—the gun!" And he fell to shivering uncontrollably, while tears of pure happiness streamed down his face.

The mammoth siege gun—the only weapon for bombardment of the helpless Earth—was a mass of useless metal, a futile thing that lay twisted and battered on the sands of the sea.

THE submarine now showed at a distance; it had withdrawn, by prearrangement, to the shelter of the deeper water. McGuire looked carefully at the watch on his wrist, and listened to make certain that the explosion had not stopped it. Sykes had told him the length of the Venusian day—twenty hours and nineteen minutes of Earth time, and he had made his calculations from the day of the Venusians. And, morning and night, McGuire had set his watch back and had learned to make a rough approximation of the time of that world.

The watch now said five-thirteen, and the sun was almost gone; a line of gold in the western sky; and McGuire knew that it was a matter only of minutes till the blast of the big gun would rock the island. One heavy section of the great barrel was resting upon the shattered base, and McGuire realized that this blocking of the monster's throat must mean it would tear itself and the island around it to fragments when it fired. He ran toward the beach and waved his arms wildly in air to urge on the speeding craft that showed dim and vague across the heaving sea.

It drove swiftly toward them and stopped for the launching of the little boat. There was a delay, and McGuire stood quivering with impatience where the others, too, watched the huddle of figures on the submarine's deck.

It was Althora who first sensed their danger. Her voice was shrill with terror as she seized McGuire's arm and pointed landward.

"Tommy—Tommy!" she said. "They are coming! I saw them!"

A Swarming of red figures over the nearby dunes gave quick confirmation of her words. McGuire looked about him for a weapon—anything to add efficiency to his bare hands—and the swarm was upon them as he looked.

He leaped quickly between Althora and the nearest figures that stretched out grasping hands, and a red face went white under the smashing impact of the flyer's fist.

They poured over the sand-hills now—-scores of leaping man-shapes—and McGuire knew in an instant of self-accusation that there had been a shelter after all, where a portion of the enemy force had stayed. The explosion had brought them, and now—

He struck in a raging frenzy at the grotesque things that came racing upon them. He knew Sykes was fighting too. He tore wildly at the lean arms that bound him and kept him from those a step or two away who were throwing the figure of a girl across the shoulders of one of their men, while her eyes turned hopelessly toward McGuire.

They threw the two men upon the sand and crowded to kneel on the prostrate bodies and strike and tear with their long hands, then tied them at ankles and wrists with metal cords, and raised them helpless and bound in the air.

One of the red creatures pointed a long arm toward the demolished gun and shrieked something in a terror-filled tone. The others, at the sound, raced off through the sand, while those with the burden of the three captives followed as best they could.

"The gun!" said Professor Sykes in a thick voice. The words were jolted out of him as the two who carried him staggered and ran. "They know—that it—hasn't—gone off—"

The straggling troop that strung out across the dim-lit dunes was approaching another domed shelter of heavy concrete. They crowded inside, and the bodies of the three were thrown roughly to the floor, while the red creatures made desperate haste to close the heavy door. Then down they went into the deeper safety of a subterranean room, where the massive walls about them quivered to a nerve-deadening jar. It shook those standing to the floor, and the silence that followed was changed to a bedlam by the inhuman shrieking of the creatures who were gloating over their safety and the capture they had achieved. They leaped and capered in a maniacal outburst and ceased only at the shrill order of one who was in command.

At his direction the three were carried out of doors and thrown upon the ground. McGuire turned his head to see the face of Althora. There was blood trickling from a cut on her temple, and her eyes were dazed and blurred, but she managed a trembling smile for the anxious eyes of the man who could only struggle hopelessly against the thin wires that held him.

Althora hurt! Bound with those cutting metal cords! Althora— in such beastly hands! He groaned aloud at the thought.

"You should never have come; I should never have let you. I have got you into this!" He groaned again in an agony of self-reproach, then lay silent and waited for what must come. And the answer to his speculations came from the night above, where the lights of a ship marked the approach of an enemy craft.

THE ships of the red race could travel fast, as McGuire knew, but the air monster whose shining, pointed beak hung above them where they lay helpless in the torturing bonds of fine wire, was to give him a new conception of speed.

It shot to the five thousand-foot level, when the captives were safe aboard, and the dark air shrieked like a tortured animal where the steel shell tore it to tatters. And the radio, in an adjoining room, never ceased in its sputtering, changing song.

The destruction of the Earth-bombarding gun! The capture of the two Earth-men who had dared to fight back! And a captive woman of the dreaded race of true Venusians! There was excitement and news enough for one world. And the discordant singing of the radio was sounding in the ears of the leaders of that world.

They were waiting on the platform in the great hall where Sykes and McGuire had stood, and their basilisk eyes glared unwinkingly down at the three who were thrown at their feet.

The leader of them all, Torg himself, arose from his ornate throne and strode forward for a closer view of the trophies his huntsmen had brought in. A whistled word from him and the wires that had bound Althora's slim ankles were cut, while a red-robed warrior dragged her roughly to her feet to stand trembling and swaying as the blood shot cruelly through her cramped limbs.

Torg's eyes to McGuire were those of a devil feasting on human flesh, as he stared appraisingly and gloatingly at the girl who tried vainly to return the look without flinching. He spoke for a moment in a harsh tone, and the seated councilors echoed his weird notes approvingly.

"What does he say?" McGuire implored, though he knew there could be nothing of good in that abominable voice. "What does he say, Althora?"

The face that turned slowly to him was drained of the last vestige of color. "I—do not—know," she said in a whisper scarcely audible; "but he thinks—terrible things!"

She seemed speaking of some nightmare vision as she added haltingly, "There is a fleet of many ships, and Torg is in command. He has thousands of men, and he goes forth to conquer your Earth. He goes there to rule." She had to struggle to bring the words to her lips now. "And—he takes me—with—him!"

"No—no!" the flyer protested, and he struggled insanely to free his hands from the wires that cut the deeper into his flesh. The voice of Althora, clear and strong now, brought him back.

"I shall never go, Tommy; never! The gift of eternal life is mine, but it is mine to keep only if I will. But, for you and your friend—" She tried to raise her hands to her trembling lips.

"Yes," said Lieutenant McGuire quietly, "for us—?"

But there were some things the soft lips of Althora refused to say. Again she tried vainly to raise her hands, then turned her white, stricken face that a loved one might not see the tears that were mingling with the blood-stains on her cheeks, nor read in her eyes the horror they beheld.

But she found one crumb of comfort for the two doomed men.

"You will live till the sailing of the ships, Tommy," she choked, "and then—we will go together, Tommy—you and I."

Her head was bowed and her shoulders shaking, but she raised her head proudly erect as she was seized by a guard whose blood-red hands forced her from the room.

And the dry, straining eyes of Lieutenant McGuire, that watched her going, saw the passing to an unknown fate of all he held dear, and the end of his unspoken dreams.

He scarcely felt the grip of the hands that seized him, nor knew when he and Sykes were carried from the room where Torg, the Emperor, held his savage court. The stone walls of the room where they were thrown could not hold his eyes; they looked through and beyond to see only the white and piteous face of a girl whose lips were whispering, "We will go together, Tommy—you and I."

CHAPTER SEVENTEEN

THE little ship that Captain Blake had thrown with reckless speed through the skies over Washington, D. C., made history that day in the records of the earth. None, now, could doubt that here, at last, was the answer that the world had hoped for until hope had died. Unbelievable in its field of action, incredible in its wild speed, but real, nevertheless!—the countries of the earth were frantic in their acclaim. Only the men who formed the International Board of Defense failed to join in the enthusiasm. They sat by day and night in earnest conference on ways and means.

From Earth and sub-Venus converge a titanic offensive of justice on the unspeakable man-things of Torg.

This little ship—so wonderful, and so inadequate! It was only a promise of what might come. There must be new designs made; men must learn to dream in new terms and set down their dreams in cold lines and figures on drafting boards. A cruiser of space must be designed, to mount heavy guns, carry great loads, absorb the stresses that must come to such a structure in flight and in battle. And above all, it must take the thrust of this driving force—new and tremendous—of which men knew so little as yet. And then many like it must be built.

The fuel must be prepared, and this, alone, meant new and different machinery, which itself must be designed before the manufacturing process could begin.

There was work to be done—a world of work!—and so few months in which to do it. The attack from the distant gun had long since ceased and the instruments of the astronomers showed the enemy planet shrinking far off in space. But it would return; there was only a year for preparation.

CAPTAIN BLAKE was assigned to the direction of design. An entire office building in Washington was vacated for his use, and in a few hours he rallied a staff of assistants who demanded the entire use of a telephone system that spread countrywide. And the call went out that would bring the best brains of the land to the task before them.

The windows of the building shone brightly throughout the nights when the call was answered, and engineers and draftsmen worked at fever heat on thrusts and stresses and involved mathematical calculations. And, while owners of great manufacturing plants waited with unaccustomed patience for a moment's talk with Blake, the white sheets on the drafting boards showed growing pictures of braces and struts and curved plates, of castings for gun mounts, and ammunition hoists. And the manufacturers were told in no uncertain terms exactly what part of this experimental ship they would produce, and when it must be delivered.

"If only we dared go into production," said Blake; "but it is out of the question. This first ship must demonstrate its efficiency; we must get the 'bugs' out of our design; correct our errors and be ready with a production schedule that will work with precision."

Only one phase of this proposed production troubled him; the manufacture must be handled all over the world. He talked with men from England and France, from Germany and Italy and a host of other lands, and he raged inwardly while he tried to drive home to them the necessity for handling the work in just one way—his way—if results were to be achieved.

The men of business he could convince, but his chief disquiet came from those whose thoughts were of what they termed "statesmanship," and who seemed more apprehensive of the power that this new weapon would give the United States of America than they were of the threat from distant worlds.

From his friends in high quarters came hints of the same friction, but he knew that the one demand Winslow had laid down was being observed—the secret of the mysterious fuel would remain with us. Winslow had shown little confidence in the countries of the old world, and he had sworn Blake to an agreement that his strange liquids—that new form of matter and substance— should remain with this country.

And swiftly the paper ship grew. The parts were in manufacture, and arriving at the assembly plant in Ohio. Blake's time was spent there now, and he caught only snatches of sleep on a cot in his office, while he worked with the forces of men who succeeded each other to keep the assembly room going night and day.

There was a huge hangar that was designed for the assembling of a giant dirigible; it housed another ship now. Hardly a ship, yet it began to take form where great girders held the keel that was laid, and duralumin plates and strong castings were bolted home.

A thousand new problems, and innumerable vexing errors—the "bugs" that inhere with a new, mechanical job—yet the day came when the ship was a thing of sleek beauty, and her thousand feet of length enclosed a maze of latticed struts where ammunition rooms and sleeping quarters, a chart room and control stations were cleverly interspaced. And above, where the great shape towered high in the big hangar, were the lean snouts of cannon, and recesses that held rapid-fire guns and whole batteries of machine guns for close range.

Rows of great storage batteries were installed, to furnish the first current for the starting of the ship, till her dynamos that were driven by the exhaust blast itself could go into action and carry on. And then—

An armored truck that ground slowly up under heavy guard to deliver two small flasks of liquid whose tremendous weight must be held in containers of thick steel, and be hoisted with cranes to their resting place within the ship. And Captain Blake, with his heart in his throat through fear of some failure, some slip in their plans— Captain Blake, of the gaunt, worn frame, and face haggard from sleepless nights—stood quietly at a control board while the great doors of the hangar swung open.

At the closing of a switch the current from the batteries flowed through the two liquids, to go on in conductors of heavy copper to a generator that was heavy and squat and devoid of moving parts. Within it were electrodes that were castings of copper, and between them the miracle of regenerated matter was taking place.

What came to them as energy from the cables was transformed to a tangible, vast bulk of gas, of hydrogen and oxygen that had once been water, and the pressure of the gas made a roaring inferno of the exhausts. A spark plug ignited it, and the heat of combustion added pressure to pressure, while the quivering, invisible live steam poured forth to change to vaporous clouds that filled the hangar.

The man at the control board stood trembling with knowledge of the power he had unleashed. He moved a lever to crack open a valve, and the clouds poured now from beneath the ship, that raised slowly and smoothly in the air. It hung quietly poised, while the hands that directed it sent a roaring blast from the great stern exhaust, and the creation of many minds became a thing of life that moved slowly, gliding out into the sunlight of the world.

The cheers of crowding men, insane with emotion at sight of their work's fulfillment, were lost in the ship's thunder. The blunt bow lifted where the sun made dazzling brilliance of her sweeping curves, and with a blast that thundered from her stern the first unit of the space forces of the Earth swept upward in an arc of speed that ended in invisibility. No enveloping air could hold her now; she was launched in the ocean of space that would be her home.

CAPTAIN Blake, the following day, sat in Washington before a desk piled high with telegrams of congratulation. His tired face was smiling as he replaced a telephone receiver that had spoken words of confidence and commendation from the President of the United States. But he pushed the mass of yellow papers aside to resume his examination of a well-thumbed folder marked: "Production Schedule." The real work was yet to be done.

It was only two short months later that he sat before the same desk, with a face that showed no mark of smiles in its haggard lines.

His ship was a success, and was flying continuously, while men of the air service were trained in its manipulation and gunners received practice in three-dimensioned range finding and cruiser practice in the air. Above, in the airless space, they learned to operate the guns that were controlled from within the air-tight rooms. They were learning, and the ship performed the miracles that were now taken as matters of fact.

But production!

Blake rose wearily to attend a conference at the War Department. He had asked that it be called, and the entire service was represented when he reached there. He went without preamble or explanation to the point.

"Mr. Secretary," he said, and faced the Secretary of War, "I have to report, sir, that we have failed. It is utterly impossible, under present conditions, to produce a fleet of completed ships.

"You know the reason; I have conferred with you often. It was a mistake to depend on foreign aid; they have failed us. I do not criticize them. Their ways are their own, and their own problems loom large to them. The English production of parts has come through, or is proceeding satisfactorily, but the rest is in hopeless confusion. The Red menace from Russia is the prime reason, of course. With the Reds mobilizing their forces, we cannot blame her neighbors for preparing to defend themselves. But our program!—and the sure invasion that will come in six short months!—to be fighting among ourselves—it is damnable!"

He paused to stare in wordless misery at the silent gathering before him. Then—

"I have failed," he blurted out. "I have fallen down on the job. It was my responsibility to get the cooperation that insured success. Let me step aside. Is there anyone now who can take up the work and bring order and results from this chaos of futility?"

He waited long for a reply. It was the Secretary of War who answered in a quiet voice.

"We must not be too harsh," he said, "in our criticism of our foreign friends, but neither should we be unfair to Captain Blake. You do yourself an injustice; there is no one who could have done more than you. The reason is here." He struck at a paper that he held in his hand. "Europe is at war. Russia has struck without warning; her troops are moving and her air force is engaged this minute in an attack upon Paris. It is a traitor country at home that has defeated us in our war with another world."

"I think," he added slowly, "there is nothing more that could have been done. You have made a brave effort. Let us thank you, Captain Blake, while we can. We will fight, when the time comes, as best we can; that goes without saying."

A blue and gold figure arose slowly to speak a word for the navy. "It is evident by Captain Blake's own admission, that the proposed venture must fail. It has been evident to some of us from the start." It was a fighter of the old school who was speaking; his voice was that of one whose vision has dimmed, who sees but the dreams of impractical visionaries in the newer inventions, and whose reliance for safety is placed only in the weapons he knows.

"The naval forces of the United States will be ready," he told them, "and I would ask you to remember that we can still place dependence upon the ships that float in the water, and the forces who have manned them since the history of this country began."

Blake, on his feet, again addressed the Secretary for War.

"Mr. Secretary," he said, a fighting glint in his eyes, "I make no reply to this gentleman. His arm of the service will speak for itself as it has always done. But your own words have given me new hope and new energy. I ask you, Mr. Secretary, for another chance. The industrial forces of the United States are behind us to the last man and the last machine. I have talked with them. I know!

"We have only six months left for a prodigious effort. Shall we make it? For the safety of our country and the whole world let us attempt the impossible: go ahead on our own; turn the energy and the mind of this whole country to the problem.

"The great fleet of the world can never be. Shall we build and launch the Great Fleet of the United States, and take upon our own shoulders the burden and responsibility of defense?

"It cannot be done by reasonable standards, but the time is past for reason. Possible or otherwise, we must do it. We will—if you will back me in the effort!"

There was a rising discord of excited voices in the room. Men were leaping to their feet to shake vehement fists in the faces of those who wagged their heads in protest. The Secretary of War arose to still the storm. He turned to walk toward the waiting figure of Captain Blake.

"You can't do it," he said, and gripped the Captain by the hand; "you can't do it—but you may. This country has seen others who have done the impossible when the impossible had to be done. It's your job; the President will confirm my orders. Go to it, Blake!"

CHAPTER EIGHTEEN

THE wires that bound the men were removed, and McGuire and Sykes worked in agony to bring life back to the hands and feet that were swollen and blue. Then—red guards who forced them to stumble on their numbed legs, where darting pains made them set their lips tight—a car that went swiftly through the darkness of a tube to stop finally in another building—a room with metal walls, one window with a balcony beyond, high above the ground—a door that clanged behind them; and the two men, looking one at the other with dismayed and swollen eyes, knew in their hearts that here, beyond a doubt, was their last earthly habitation.

They said nothing—there was nothing of hope or comfort to be said—and they dropped soddenly upon the hard floor, where finally the heavy breathing and nervous starts of Professor Sykes showed that to him at least had come the blessed oblivion of exhausted sleep. But there was no sleep for Lieutenant McGuire.

There was a face that shone too clearly in the dark, and his thoughts revolved endlessly in words of reproach for his folly in allowing Althora's love to lead her to share his risk. From the night outside their window came a ceaseless clatter and hubbub, but to this he was oblivious.

Only with the coming of morning's soft golden light did McGuire know the reason for the din and activity that echoed from outside—and the reason, too, for their being placed in this room.

Their lives should end with the sailing of the fleet, and there, outside their window, were the ships themselves. Ships everywhere, as far as he could see across the broad level expanse, and an army of men who scurried like ants—red ones, who worked or directed the others, and countless blues and yellows who were loading the craft with enormous cargoes.

"Squawk, damn you!" said Lieutenant McGuire to the distant shrieking throng; "and I hope they're ready for you when you reach the earth." But his savage voice carried no conviction. What was there that Earth could do to meet this overwhelming assault?

"What is it?" asked Sykes. He roused from his sleep to work his aching muscles gingerly, then came and stood beside McGuire.

"They have put us here as a final taunt," McGuire told him. "There is the fleet that is going to make our world into a nice little hell, and Torg, the beast! has put us here to see it leave. Then we get ours, and they don't know that we know that."

"Your first way was the best," the scientist observed; "we should have done it then. We still can."

"What do you mean?" The flyer's voice was dull and lifeless.

Sykes pointed to the little balcony and the hard pavement below.

"Althora," he said, and McGuire winced at the name, "seemed to think that we were in for some exquisite torture. Here is the way out. It is a hundred-foot drop; they think we are safe; but they have been unintentionally kind."

"Yes," his companion agreed, "they don't know that we know of the torture. We will wait…and when I am sure that—Althora— is—gone…when there is nothing I can do to help—"

"Help?" queried the professor gently. "There is nothing now of help, nor anyone who can help us. We must face it, my boy; *c'est fini.* Our little journey is approaching its end."

There was no reply, and McGuire stood throughout the day to stare with eyes of smouldering hatred where the scurrying swarms of living things made ready to invade and infest the earth.

Food and water was pushed through the doorway, but he ate little of the odd-colored fruits; the only thing that could hold his thoughts from the hopeless repetition of unanswerable "whys" was the sight of the fleet. And every bale and huge drum was tallied mentally as it passed by his eyes. The ships were being loaded, and with their sailing—But, no! He must not let himself think of that!

Throughout the day ships came and departed, and one leviathan, ablaze in scarlet; sailed in to settle where great steel arms enfolded it, not far from the watching men. Scarlet creatures in authority directed operations, and workmen swarmed about the great ship. Once McGuire swore softly and viciously under his breath, for he'd seen a figure that could be only that of Torg, and the crowd saluted with upraised arms as the scarlet figure passed into the scarlet ship. This, McGuire knew, was the flagship that should carry Torg himself. Torg and—. He paled at the thought of the other name.

The only break in the long day came with the arrival of a squad of guards, who hustled the two men out into a passage and drove them to another room, where certain measurements were taken. The brawn of the two were different from these red ones, but it was a moment before McGuire realized the sinister significance of the proceedings. Their breadth of shoulders, the thickness of their chests—what had these figures to do with their captivity? And then the flyer saw the measures compared with the dimensions of a steel cage. Its latticed shape could be endlessly compressed, and within, he saw, were lancet points that lined the ghastly thing throughout.

Long enough to torture, but not to kill; a thousand delicate blades to pierce the flesh; and the instrument, it seemed, was of a size that could enclose the writhing, helpless body of a man.

Other unnameable contrivances about the room took on new significance with the knowledge that here was the chamber of horrors whose workings had been seen by Althora in the mind of their captor—horrors of which she could not speak.

McGuire was sick and giddy as the guards led him roughly back to their prison room. And Professor Sykes, too, required no explanation of what they had seen.

The guards were many, and resistance was useless, but each man looked silently at the other's desperate eyes when the metal cords were twisted again about their wrists, and their hands were tied securely to metal rings anchored in the wall beside the window.

"And there," said the flyer, "goes our last chance of escape. They were not as dumb as we thought; they knew how good a leap to the pavement would look after we had been in there."

"Less than human!" Sykes was quoting the comment of Althora's brother. "I think Djorn was quite conservative in his statement."

McGuire examined carefully the cords that tied his hands to the wall beside him. The knots were secure, and the metal ring was smooth and round. "I didn't know," he said, as he worked and twisted, "but there might be a cutting edge, but we haven't a chance. No getting rid of these without a wire cutter or an acetylene torch— and we seem to be just out of both."

Professor Sykes tried to adopt the other's nonchalant tone. "Careless of us," he began—then stopped breathless to press his body against the wall.

"It's there!" he said. "Oh, my God, if I could only get it, it might work—it might!"

"The battery," he explained to the man beside him, whose assumed indifference vanished at this suggestion of hope; "—the little battery that I used on the gun, to fire the explosive. It has an astounding amperage, and a voltage around three hundred. It's in my pocket—and I can't reach it!"

"You can't keep a good man licked!" McGuire exulted. "You mean that the current might melt the wire?"

"Soften it, perhaps, depending upon the resistance." Sykes refused to share the other's excitement. "But we can't get at it."

"We've got to," was the answer. "Move over this way." The man in khaki twisted his arms awkwardly to permit him to bend his body to one side, and beads of sweat stood out on his forehead as the strain forced the thin bonds into his wrists. But he brought his agonized face against the other's body, and gripped the fabric of Sykes' coat between his teeth.

The twisting of his head raised the cloth an inch at a time, and despite Sykes' efforts to hold the garment with his elbow, it slipped back time and again. McGuire straightened at intervals to draw a choking breath and ease the strain upon his tortured wrists; then back again in his desperate contortions to worry at the cloth and pull and hold—and try again to raise the heavy pocket where a battery made sagging folds.

He was gasping when finally the cloth was brought where the scientist's straining fingers could grasp it to writhe and twist in clumsy efforts that would force the battery's terminals within reach.

"I'll try it on mine," said Sykes. "It may be hot—and you've had your share." He was holding the flat black thing to bring the copper tips against the metal about his wrists. McGuire saw the man's lips go white as a wisp of smoke brought to his nostrils the sickening odor of burned flesh.

The metal glowed, and the man was writhing in silent self-torture when at last he threw his weight upon the strands and fell backward to the floor. He lay for a moment, trembling and quivering—but free. And the knowledge of that freedom and of the greater torture they would both escape, gave him strength to rise and work with crippled hands at his companion's bonds, till McGuire, too, was free—free to forget his own swollen, bleeding wrists in compassionate regard for the other.

Like an injured animal, Professor Sykes had licked with his tongue at his wrists, where hot wire had burned deep and white, and he was trying for forgetfulness an hour later, in examination of the door to their room.

"What is the idea?" McGuire inquired, when he turned from his ceaseless contemplation of the fleet. "Not trying to get out, are you?"

"I am trying to stay in," said Sykes, and looked again at the object that interested him. "These long bolts," he explained, "top and bottom; operated from outside, but exposed in here. They come together when unlocked; five inches apart now. If I had something to hold them apart—

"You haven't a piece of steel about five inches long, have you?—or anything to substitute for it? If you have, I can lock this door so the devils won't come in and surprise us before we can make the jump."

"The battery?" suggested McGuire.

Sykes shook his head. "I tried it. Too long, and besides it would crumble. They operate these with a lever; I saw it outside." He went on silently with his study of the door and the little gap between heavy bolts, which, if closed, would mean security from invasion.

"They're about through," McGuire spoke from his post at the window after some time. "The rush seems to be about over. I imagine they'll pull out in the morning."

He pointed as Sykes stood beside him. "Those big ones over beyond have not been touched all day; only some of the crew, I judge, working around them. And way over you see forty or fifty whaling big ones. They must have been ready before we came. They have finished on these nearer by. It looks like a big day for the brutes."

And Professor Sykes led him on to talk more of the preparations he had seen, and his deductions as to the morrow. It was all too evident what was really on the lieutenant's mind. It was not the thought of their own immediate death, but the terrible dread and horror of Althora's fate, that hammered and hammered in his brain. To speak of anything else meant a moment's relief.

Sykes pointed to a tall mast that was set in the plaza pavement, some hundred feet away. Wires swung from it to several points, one of them ending above their window and entering the building. "What is that?" he asked, "—some radio device? That ball of metal on the top might be an aerial." But McGuire had fallen silent again, and stared stonily at the deadly fighting ships he was powerless to combat.

IN THE morning that followed, there was no uncertainty. This was the day! And from a balconied window up high in the side of a tall stone building, two men stood wordless and waiting while they watched the preparations below.

The open space was a sea of motion like flowing blood, where thousands of figures in dull red marched in rank after rank to be swallowed in the mammoth ships that McGuire had noted in the distance. Then other colors, and swarms of what they took to be women-folk of this wild race—a medley of color that flowed on and on as if it would never cease, to fill one after another of the great ships.

"Transports, that's what they are," said McGuire. "I can see now why they have no steel beaks like the others. They don't need any rams, nor ports for firing that beastly gas. They are gray, too, while the fighting ships are striped with red, all except the scarlet one of Torg's. Those are colonists we are watching, and soldiers to conquer the Earth where the damned swarm settles."

He stopped to stare at a body of red-clad soldiers, drawn up at attention. They made a lane, and their arms were raised in the salute that seemed only for Torg. They stood rigid and motionless; then, from below the watching men, came one in the full splendor of his scarlet regalia. The air echoed with the din of his shouted name, but the bedlam of noise fell on deaf ears for McGuire. He could hear nothing, and in all the vast kaleidoscope of color he could see only one object—the white face of a girl who was half led and half carried by a guard of the red ones, where their Emperor led the way.

It was a strangled cry that was torn from the flyer's throat—the name of this girl who was going to the doom she had failed to avoid. Her life, she had said, was hers to keep only if she willed, but her plans had failed, and she went faltering and stumbling after a scarlet man beast.

"Althora!" called the flyer, and the figure of the girl was struggling with her guards in a frenzy that tore their hands free. She turned to look toward the sound of the voice, and her face was like that of one dead as her eyes found the man she loved.

"Tommy," she called, "oh, Tommy, my dear! Goodbye!" The words were ended by the clutch of the scarlet Emperor who turned to seize her.

A clatter came from the door behind them, but Lieutenant McGuire gave no heed. Only Professor Sykes sprang back from the balcony to seize and struggle with the moving bolts.

The man on the balcony was hardly less than a maniac as he glared wildly about, but he was not too unreasoning to see the folly of a wild leap into the throng below. He could never reach her—never. And then his eyes fell upon the wire that led from above him to the great pole in the open plaza. There was shouting from behind where the executioners were wrestling with the bolts.

"Hold them," the flyer shouted, "just for a minute! For God's sake, Sykes, keep them back! There's a chance!"

He sprang to the balustrade of the balcony, but he saw as he leaped where Professor Sykes had raised his leg to force the thickness of his knee between the bolts whose levers outside were bringing them closer together.

"Go to it," was the answer. "I can hold them..." A stifled groan. "...for a minute!" Professor Sykes had found his substitute for five inches of steel, and the living flesh yielded but slowly to the pressure of the bolts.

McGuire was working frantically at the wire, then held himself in check while he carefully unwound it from its fastening. There was a splice, and he worked with bleeding fingers to unfasten the tight coils. And then the end was free and in his hands. He dropped to the balcony to pull in the slack, and he wrapped the end about beneath his arms and twisted it tight, then leaped out into space. No thought of himself nor of Sykes in this one wild moment, only of Althora in the grip of those beastly hands.

He was struggling to turn himself in the air as the colored masses of people seemed sweeping toward him, and he shot as a living pendulum, feet first, into the waiting heads.

He was on his feet in an instant and tearing at the twisted wire that held him. About him was clamor and confusion, but beyond the nearer figures he saw the one who waited, and beside her a thing in scarlet that shrieked orders to his men.

He flung off one who leaped toward him, and ducked another to dash through and reach his man. And he neither saw nor felt the creature's ripping talons as he drove a succession of rights and lefts to the blood-red face.

The scarlet one went backward under the fusillade of blows; he was down, a huddle of color upon the pavement, and a horde of paralyzed soldiers had recovered from their stupefaction and were rushing upon the flyer. He turned to meet them, but their rush ended as quickly as it began—only a step or two they came, then stopped, to add their wild voices to the confusion of ear-splitting shrieks that rose from all sides.

McGuire crouched rigid, tense and waiting, nor did he sense for an instant that the assault was checked and that the faces of all about him were turned to the sky. It was the voice of Althora that aroused him:

"Tommy! Tommy!" she was calling, and now she was at his side, her arms about him. "What is it, Tommy? Look! Look!" And she too was gazing aloft. And then, above all other sounds McGuire heard the roar—

The clouds were golden above with the brilliance of midday—and against them, hard and sharp of outline, was a shining shape. A cloud of vapor streamed behind it as it shot down from the clouds, and the thunder of its coming was like the roar of many cannon.

A ship of the red ones was in the air—a fighting ship, whose stripes showed red—and it drove at the roaring menace with its steel beak and a swirling cloud of gas. It seemed that they must crash, when to McGuire's eyes came the stabbing flash of heavy guns from the shining shape. A crashing explosion came down to them as the great beak parted and fell, and the body of the red-striped monster opened in bursting smoke and flame, tore slowly into fragments and fell swiftly to the earth.

It struck with a shattering crash some distance away, but one pair of eyes failed to follow it in its fall. For in the clear air above, with the golden light of distant clouds upon it, a roaring monster of silvery sheen had rolled and swept upward to the heights. And it showed, as it turned, a painted emblem on its bow, a design of clear-cut color, unbelievably familiar—a circle of blue, and within it a white star and a bull's eye of red—the mark of the flying service of the United States!

McGuire never knew how he got Althora and himself back to the building whence he had come. Nor did he see the struggling figures on a balcony, or the leap and fall of a maimed body, where

Professor Sykes, when the door had yielded, found surcease and oblivion on the pavement below.

He was to learn that later, but now he had eyes only for a sight that could be but a dream, an unreal vision of a disordered brain. He held the slim form of Althora to him in a crushing grip, while he stared, dry-eyed, above, and his own voice seemed to shout from afar off: "They're ours!" that voice was screaming in a frenzy of exultation. "They're our ships! They've come across!"

The fighting fleet of the red man-things of Venus was taking to the air! The ships rose in a swarm of speeding, darting shapes, and the great one of Torg was in the lead, climbing in fury toward the heights.

Far above them the clouds of gold silhouetted a strange sight, and the air was shaking with the thunder from on high, where, straight and true, a line of silver ships in the sharp V of battle formation drove downward in a deadly, swift descent.

And even afar off, the straining eyes of a half-crazed man could see the markings on their bow—a circle and a star—and the colors of his own lost fighters of the air.

CHAPTER NINETEEN

THE Earth-fleet was a slanting line of swiftness that swept downward from the clouds. A swarm of craft was rising from below. The red-striped fighters met the attack first with a cloud of gas.

The scarlet monster—the flagship of Torg, the Emperor—was in the lead, and they shot with terrific speed across the bows of the oncoming fleet to leave a whirlwind of deadly vapor as they passed. McGuire held his breath in an agony of fear as the cloud enveloped the line of ships, but their bow guns roared staccato crashes in the thunder of their exhausts as they entered the cloud. And they were firing from the stern as they emerged, while two falling cylinders of red and white proved the effectiveness of their fire.

The formation held true as it swept upward and back where the swarming enemy was waiting. They were outnumbered three to one, McGuire saw, and his heart sang within him as he watched the sharp, speeding V that climbed upward to the enemy's level then swung to throw itself like a lance of light at the massed ships that awaited the attack.

Another cloud of gas!—and a shattered ship!—and again the line emerged to correct its broken formation and drive once more toward the circling swarm.

They came to meet them now, the clusters of red-striped fighting ships, and they tore in from all sides upon the American line, their hooked beaks gleaming in the sun.

And now, at an unseen signal, the formation broke. Each ship fought for its life, and the stabbing flashes of their guns made ceaseless jets of light against the smoke and gas clouds that were darkening the sky.

"A dog-fight!" breathed Lieutenant McGuire; "and what a dog-fight!" His words were lost in the terrific thunder from above; the roar of the ships and the dull thuds of the guns engulfed them in a maelstrom of noise that battered like physical blows on the watchers below. He swore unconsciously and called down curses upon the enemy as he saw two fighters meet while the shining beak of a ship of the reds crashed through the body of an opposing craft.

The red ship dipped at the bow; it backed off with terrific force; and from the curved beak a ship with the insignia of the red, white and blue slid downward in a swift fall to the death that waited.

They had fought themselves clear, and the Americans, by what must have been arrangement or wireless order, went roaring to the heights. There were some who followed, but the guns of the speeding ships drove them off. Red-and-white shapes fell swiftly from the clouds where the fighting had been, and McGuire knew that his fellows had given an account of themselves in the fighting at close range.

Again the thundering line was sharp and true, and another unswerving attack was launching itself from above. And again the deadly formation, with ever-increasing speed, drove into the enemy with flashing guns, then parted to close with the ones that drove crushingly upon them, while the sharper clatter of rapid-firing guns came to shatter the air.

The fighting craft had been rising from their level field in a succession that seemed endless. They were all in the air now, and only the great transports remained on the paved field.

A red-striped fighter swept downward in retreat, and, from the smoke clouds, a silvery shape followed in pursuit. It reached the red and white one with its shells, and the great mass crashed with terrific impact on the field. Its pursuer must have seen the monsters still on the ground, and it swung to rake them with a shower of small-caliber shells.

There were machine-guns rattling as it passed above the thronged reds—the troops who were huddled in terror in the open court. It tore on past them—past a figure in khaki who raced forward with the golden form of a girl within his arms, then released her to wave frantically as the silver ship shot by.

Unobserved, McGuire and Althora had been, where they stood beside the buildings; the eyes of their enemies, like their own, were on the monstrous battle above. But now they had called themselves to the attention of the reds, and there were some who rushed upon them with faces livid with rage.

McGuire reached for a weapon from a victim of the machine-gun fire and prepared to defend himself, but the weapon was never used. He saw the silvery shape reverse itself in the air; it turned sharply to throw itself back toward the solitary figure in uniform of their service and the golden-clad girl beside him.

The flyer raised his weapon, but the jostling swarm that rushed upon him melted; the ripping fire of machine guns was deafening in his ears. Their deadly tattoo continued while the great ship sank slowly to touch and rest its huge bulk upon the pavement. A door in the ship's curved side opened that the blocky figure of a man might leap forth.

He was grimy of face, and his uniform was streaked with the smoke and sweat of battle, but the face beneath the grime, and the hands that reached to embrace and pound the flyer upon the back, could be only those of one he had known as his captain—Captain Blake.

"You son-of-a-gun!" the shouting figure was repeating. "You damned Irish son-of-a-gun! AWOL—but you can't get away with it! Come on—get in here! I'm needed up above!"

McGuire was struggling to speak from a throat that was suddenly tight and voiceless. Then—

"Althora," he gasped; "take Althora!" and he motioned toward the girl. And then he remembered the companion he had left in the room above. The battle that had flashed so suddenly had blasted from his mind all other thoughts.

"My God!" he said. "—Sykes! I—must get Sykes!"

He turned to run back to the building, only to stop in consternation where a huddle of clothing lay beneath the balcony of their prison room.

It was Sykes—Sykes who had sacrificed himself to make possible the escape of his friend—and McGuire dropped to his knees to touch the body that he knew was shattered beyond any hope of life. He raised the limp burden in his arms and staggered back where more khaki-clad figures had gathered. Two came quickly out to meet him, and he let them take the body of his friend.

"*C'est fini!*"—he repeated the words that Sykes had said; "the end of our little journey!" The arms of Althora were about him as Blake hurried them into the waiting ship, and the roar of enormous power marked the rising of this space ship to throw itself again into the fray.

A SMALL room with a dome of shatter-proof glass; a pilot who sat there to look in all directions, a control-board beneath his hands. Beside him on his elevated station was room for Captain Blake, and McGuire and Althora, too. The ship was climbing swiftly. McGuire saw where flashing shapes circled and roared in a swelling cloud of smoke and gas.

Blake spoke sharply to an aide, "General orders! All ships climb to resume formation!"

An enemy ship was before them; it flashed from nowhere to bear down with terrific speed. The floor beneath them shook with the jarring of heavy guns, and McGuire saw the advancing shape bursting with puffs of smoke, while their own ship shot upward with a sickening twist. A silver ship was falling!—and another!

"Two more of ours gone," said Captain Blake through set teeth. "How many of them are there, Mac? Tell me what you know We've got a hell of a fight on our hands."

"They're all here," McGuire told him, in jerky, breathless speech. "These are transports on the ground. Their weapons are gas and speed, and the rams on their beaked ships. There are other weapons—deadlier ones!—but they haven't got them; they belong to another race. I'll tell you all that later!"

"Keep them at a distance, Blake," he said. "Make them come to you—then nail them as they come."

"Right!" was the answer; "that's good dope. We didn't know what they had; expected some devilish things that could down us before we got within effective range; had to mix it with them to find out what they could do, and get in a few solid cracks before they did it.

"How high are we?" He glanced quickly at an instrument. "Ten thousand. Order all ships to withdraw," he instructed his aide. "Rendezvous at fifty thousand feet for echelon formation."

Another brush with an enemy craft that slipped quickly to one side—then the smoke clouds were behind them, and a score, of silvery shapes were climbing in vertical flight for the level at fifty thousand.

They were fewer now than they had been, and the line that formed behind the flagship of Blake was shorter than the one that had made the V which shot down so bravely to engage with an unknown foe.

The enemy was below; an arrangement of mirrors showed this from the commander's station. They were emerging from the clouds of smoke to swarm in circling flight through the sky. And now the bow of their own craft was depressed at an order from Blake, and the others were behind them as they drove to renew the attack.

"They're ganging up on us again," said Blake. "We'll fool them this time; we'll just kid them a little."

The flagship swerved before reaching the enemy, and the others followed in what looked like frightened retreat. Again they were in the heights, and some few of the enemy were following. Blake led in another descent.

No waiting swarm to greet them now! Blake gave a quick order. The roaring column shifted position as it fell; the flagship was the apex of a great V whose arms flung out and backward on either side—a V formation that curved and twisted through space and thundered upon the smaller formations that scattered before the blasting guns.

"Our bow guns are the effective weapons," Blake observed; his casual tone was a sedative to McGuire's tense nerves. "We can use a broadside only of lighter weight; the kick of the big 'sights' has to be taken straight back. But we're working, back home, on recoil-absorbing guns. We'll make fighting ships of these things yet."

He spoke quietly to the pilot to direct their course toward a group that came sweeping upon them, and the massed fire of the squadron was squarely into the oncoming beaks that fell beneath them where the mirrors showed them crashing to the earth.

They were scattered now; the enemy was in wild disorder; and Blake spoke sharply to his aide.

"Break formation," he ordered; "every ship for itself. Engage the enemy where they find them; shoot down anything they see; prevent the enemy reforming!" He was taking quick advantage of the other's scattered forces, and he scattered his own that he knew could take care of themselves while they engaged the enemy only by ones or twos or threes.

"Clear the air of them!" he ordered. "Not one of them must escape!"

The skies were a maze of darting shapes that crossed and recrossed to make a spider's web of light. Ship drove at ship, to swerve off at the last, while the air quivered and beat upon them with the explosion of shells and guns.

"There's our meat!" Blake directed the pilot, and pointed ahead where a monster in scarlet was swelling into view.

It came swiftly upon them, darting down from above, and McGuire clutched at the arm of the man beside him to shout: "It's the leader; the flagship! It's the Emperor—Torg, himself! Give him hell, Blake, but look out—he's fast!"

The ship was upon them like a flash of fire; no time for anything but dodging, and the pilot threw his craft wildly aside with a swerve that sent the men sprawling against a stanchion. Then up and back, where the other had turned to come up from below.

"Fast!" McGuire had said, but the word was inadequate to describe the speed of the fiery shape.

Another leap in the air, as their pilot swung his controls, and the red shape brushed past them in a cloud of gas, while the quick-firers ripped futilely into space where the great ship had been.

"Get your bow guns on him!" Blake roared. The ship beneath them strained and shuddered with the incredible thunder of the generator that threw them bodily in the air. The pilot had opened in full force the ports that blasted their bows aside.

No time to gather new speed; they were motionless as the scarlet monster came upon them, but they were in position to receive him. The eight-inch rifles of the forward turret thundered again and again, to be answered by flashes of flame from the scarlet ship.

McGuire crouched over the bent form of the pilot, whose steady fingers held the ship's bow straight upon the flashing death that bore down upon them. Another salvo!—and another!—hits all of them... Smoke bursting from ripping plates, and flaming fire more vivid than the scarlet shape itself!—and the floor beneath McGuire's feet drove crushingly upward as their pilot pulled a lever to the full.

The great beak flashed beneath—and the mirrors, where McGuire's eyes were fastened, showed the terrific drive continue down and down, where a brilliant cylinder that marked the power of Venus tore shriekingly on to carry an Emperor to his crashing death.

THE skies were clear of the red-striped ships. Only the survivors of the attacking force showed their silvery shapes as they gathered near their flagship. There were two that pursued a small group of the enemy, but they were being outdistanced in the race.

"We have won," said Blake in a tone of wonder that showed how only now had come a realization of what the victory meant. "We have won, and the earth—is saved!"

And the voice of McGuire echoed his fervent "Thank God!" while he gripped the soft hand that clung tightly to his, as if Althora, this radiant creature of Venus, were timid and abashed among the joyful, shouting men-folk from another world.

"And now what, Captain?" asked McGuire of his command. "Will you land? There is an army of reds down there asking for punishment."

Blake had turned away; his hand made grimy smears across his face where he wiped away the tears that marked a brave man's utter thankfulness. He covered his emotion with an affectation of disapproval as he swung back toward McGuire.

"Captain?" he inquired. "Captain? Where do you get that captain stuff?"

He pointed to an emblem on his uniform, a design that was unfamiliar to the eyes of McGuire.

"You're talking to an admiral now!—the first admiral of the newest branch of your country's fighting service—commanding the first fleet of the Space ships of the United States of America!" He threw one arm about the other's shoulders. "We'll have to get busy, Mac," he added, "and think up a new rank for you.

"And, yes, we are going to land," he continued in his customary tones; "there may be survivors of our own crashes. But we'll have to count on you, Mac, to show us around this little new world of yours."

THERE was an army waiting, as McGuire had warned, but it was waiting to give punishment and not to take it. The vast expanse of the landing field was swarming with them, and the open country beyond showed columns of marching troops.

They had learned, too, to take shelter; barricades had been hastily erected, and the men had shields to protect them from the fire of small arms.

Their bodies were enclosed in their gas-tight uniforms whose ugly head-pieces served only to conceal the greater ugliness beneath. They met the ships as they landed with a showering rain of gas that was fired from huge projectors.

"Not so good!" Blake was speaking in the safety of his ship. "We have masks, but great heavens, Mac!—there must be a million of those brutes. We can spray them with machine-gun fire, but we haven't ammunition enough to make a dent in them. And we've got to get out and get to our crashed ships."

He waited for McGuire's suggestions, but it was Althora who replied.

"Wait!" she said imperatively. She seemed to be listening to some distant word. Then:

"Djorn is coming," she exclaimed, and her eyes were brilliantly alight. "He says to you…" She pointed to McGuire. "…that you were right, that we must fight like hell sometimes to deserve our heaven—oh, I told him what you said—and now he is coming with all his men!"

"What!" asked Blake in amazement. "How does she know?"

"Telepathy," McGuire explained, "she is talking with her brother, the leader of the real inhabitants of Venus."

He told the wondering man briefly of his experience and of the people themselves, the real owners of this world.

"But what can they do?" Blake demanded.

And McGuire assured him: "Plenty!"

He turned to Althora to ask, "How are they coming? How will they get here?"

"They are marching underground; they have been coming for two days. They knew of our being captured, but the people have been slow in deciding to fight. Djorn dared not tell me of their coming; he feared he might be too late.

"They will come out of that building," she said, and indicated the towering structure that had been their prison. "It has the old connection with the underground world."

"Well, they'd better be good!" said Blake incredulously.

He was still less optimistic when the building before them showed the coming of a file of men. They poured forth, in orderly fashion and ranged themselves in single file along the walls.

There must be a thousand, McGuire estimated, and he wondered if the women, too, were fighting for their own. Then, remembering Althora's brave insistence, he knew his surmise was correct.

Each one was masked against the gas; their faces were concealed; and each one held before him a tube of shining metal with a larger bulbous end that rested in their hands.

"Electronic projectors," the lieutenant whispered. "Keep your eye on the enemy; you are going to learn something about war."

The thin line was advancing now and the gas billowed about them as they came. There were some few who dropped, where masks were defective, but the line came on, and the slim tubes were before them in glittering menace.

At a distance of a hundred feet from the first of the entrenched enemy there was a movement along the line, as if the holders of the tubes had each set a mechanism in operation. And before the eyes of the Earth-men was a spectacle of horror like nothing in wars they had known.

The barricades were instantly a roaring furnace; the figures that leaped from behind them only added to the flames. From the steady rank of the attackers poured an invisible something before which the hosts of the enemy fell in huddles of flame. Those nearest were blasted from sight in a holocaust of horror, and where they had been was a scattering of embers that smoked and glowed; even the figures of distant ones stumbled and fell.

The myriad fighters of the army of the red ones, when the attackers shut off their invisible rays, was a screaming mob that raced wildly over the open lands beyond.

Althora's hands were covering her eyes, but McGuire and Blake, and the crowding men about them, stared in awe and utter astonishment at the devastation that was sweeping this world. An army annihilated before their eyes! Scores of thousands, there must be, of the dead!

The voice of Blake was husky with horror. "What a choice little bit out of hell!" he exclaimed. "Mac, did you say they were our friends? God help us if they're not!"

"They are," said McGuire grimly. "Those are Althora's people who had forgotten how to fight; they are recapturing something that they lost some centuries ago. But can they ever destroy the rest of that swarm? I don't think they have the heart to do it."

"They do not need." It was Althora speaking. "My people are sickened with the slaughter. But the red ones will go back into the earth, and we will seal them in!—it is Djorn who tells me—and the world will be ours forevermore."

A MATTER of two short days, crammed with the realization of the astounding turn of events—and McGuire and Althora stood with Blake and Djorn, the ruler, undisputed, of the beautiful world of Venus. A fleet of great ships was roaring high in air. One only, the flagship, was waiting where their little group stood.

The bodies of the fallen had been recovered; they were at rest now in the ships that waited above. McGuire looked about in final wonder at the sparkling city bathed in a flood of gold. A kindly city now—beautiful; the terrors it had held were fading from his mind. He turned to Althora.

"We are going home," he said softly, "you and I."

"Home?" Althora's voice was vibrant with dismay.

"We need you here, friend Mack Guire," the voice of Djorn broke in, in protest. "You have something that we lack—a force and vision—something we have lost."

"We will be back," the flyer assured him. "You befriended me. Anything I can do in return—" The grip of his hand completed the sentence.

"But there is a grave to be made on the summit of Mount Lawson," he added quietly. "I think he would have preferred to lie there—at the end of his journey—and I must return to the service where I have not yet been mustered out."

"But you said—you were going home," faltered Althora. "Will that always be home to you, Tommy?"

"Home, my dear," he whispered in words that reached her only, "is just where you are." His arm went about her to draw her toward the waiting ship. "There or here—what matter? We will be content."

Her eyes were misty as they smiled an answer. Within the ship that was lifting them, they turned to watch a city of opal light grow faintly luminous in the distance...an L-shaped continent shrunk to tiny size...and the nebulous vapors of the cloudland that enclosed this world folded softly about.

"We will lead," the voice of Blake was saying to an aide, "same formation that we used coming over. Give the necessary orders. But," he added slowly to himself, "the line will be shorter; there are fewer of us now."

An astronomical officer laid a chart before the commander. "We are on the course, sir," he reported.

"Full speed," Blake ordered, the thundering generator answering from the stern. The Space Fleet of America was going home.

THE END